THIN ICE

CAPITAL CRIME SERIES

THIN
ICE

NICK WILKSHIRE

DUNDURN
TORONTO

All characters in this work are fictitious. Any resemblance to real persons, living or dead, is purely coincidental.

Editor: Allison Hirst
Design: Jesse Hooper
Cover design by Carmen Giraudy
Cover image: © ChristopheLedent/iStockphoto
Printer: Webcom

Library and Archives Canada Cataloguing in Publication

Wilkshire, Nick, 1968-, author
    Thin ice / Nick Wilkshire.

(Capital crime series)
Issued in print and electronic formats.
ISBN 978-1-4597-1552-3 (pbk.).--ISBN 978-1-4597-1553-0 (pdf)

    I. Title.

PS8645.I44T55 2014   C813'.6   C2014-901012-5
                                             C2014-901013-3

1 2 3 4 5   18 17 16 15 14

 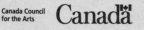

Conseil des Arts du Canada Canada Council for the Arts Canada ONTARIO ARTS COUNCIL CONSEIL DES ARTS DE L'ONTARIO an Ontario government agency un organisme du gouvernement de l'Ontario

We acknowledge the support of the **Canada Council for the Arts** and the **Ontario Arts Council** for our publishing program. We also acknowledge the financial support of the **Government of Canada** through the **Canada Book Fund** and **Livres Canada Books**, and the **Government of Ontario** through the **Ontario Book Publishing Tax Credit** and the **Ontario Media Development Corporation**.

Care has been taken to trace the ownership of copyright material used in this book. The author and the publisher welcome any information enabling them to rectify any references or credits in subsequent editions.

                                             J. Kirk Howard, President

The publisher is not responsible for websites or their content unless they are owned by the publisher.

Printed and bound in Canada.

VISIT US AT
Dundurn.com | *@dundurnpress* | *Facebook.com/dundurnpress* | *Pinterest.com/dundurnpress*

Dundurn
3 Church Street, Suite 500
Toronto, Ontario, Canada
M5E 1M2

For Matt, as you open a new chapter …

PROLOGUE

He hadn't run a step but was already sweating in the cool morning air, his heart racing as he stood on the Somerset footbridge and scanned the jogging path on the other side of the canal. To the north, the bridge was barely visible through the mist that obscured the copper rooftops of the Château Laurier beyond. To the south, he could make out the deserted path to where it snaked right, following the bend in the canal. The chirping of the birds and the distant sound of traffic were all that punctuated the silence.

Maybe he's not coming....

He fought the creeping desperation as he leaned on the railing and watched a dislodged pebble fall into the water below, momentarily absorbed by the echo of the splash and the simple perfection of the circles floating outward from the entry point. Looking up toward the dogleg in the path, he spotted a form rounding the corner, five hundred metres off and heading toward him. He set off over the bridge, and as he reached the other side, the figure came into focus. It was definitely a man, of average height, wearing a running jacket and baseball cap.

It's him!

His heart rate kicked up a notch as he hurried down to the lower path and headed south, glancing across the water at the empty walking path on the other side of the canal and the deserted roadway above. Looking back down the path in front of him, he noted the other jogger was closing fast. The sound of the approaching footfalls were muffled by the shroud of mist, but he felt each one shudder through his spine as they grew closer and he reached into the pouch of his hoodie for the knife. When he looked back at the oncoming runner, he knew something was wrong — the gait and the proportions were all off. He released the knife and slid his hand back out as he passed within a few feet of a man in his forties who flipped him a wave. He lowered his head and kept going until the next bench, looking back over the ground he had just covered, and the other runner's progress past the pedestrian bridge. Glancing at his watch again, he noted the time — six fifteen. Pretty soon, the path would begin to fill with the morning crowd.

If he's not here in the next five minutes …

He headed back toward the bridge at a trot, with the occasional glance over his shoulder to scan the deserted trail. He had only seen two cars on Colonel By Drive in the past ten minutes, but he knew that would soon change. He could feel the air growing warmer as the sun threatened to burn off the morning haze and light the still-murky path.

He was crossing back over the bridge when he spotted another runner at the curve down by Waverly Street.

Even from this distance it was clear the guy was *moving*, and would cover the half-kilometre to the bridge in seconds. He turned and set back off down to the path. As he began to jog, he adjusted his hood over the peak of his hat and glanced toward the oncoming form, noticing the purposeful, athletic stride and the wraparound sunglasses, despite the morning mist. He increased his pace as they neared each other, and at about fifty feet he made out the training camp logo that removed any doubt as to the other man's identity. He took a firm grip on the concealed knife and edged closer to the centre of the path as they both entered a shadow cast by one of the larger overhanging maples. As the other jogger wiped some sweat from his brow, he lunged.

The knife plunged deep between the ribs over the upper left chest, the force of the collision thrusting the blade sideways as it tore through flesh and cartilage until it stuck fast in solid bone. Apart from the sickening tearing sound, there was only a muffled groan as the victim reeled off balance and clutched at his chest, disoriented by the sudden attack and unable to counter the powerful momentum that propelled him backwards until the top rung of the iron railing hit the small of his back, gravity suspending him for an instant before toppling him over. Leaning over the rail, the breathless attacker watched the futile attempt to dislodge the knife as the slap of water shattered the silence on the deserted path. He watched with relief as the brownish-green waters of the canal enveloped his wide-eyed victim, with only a succession of ugly, irregular ripples to disturb the calm of the surface and suggest that he had ever existed.

CHAPTER 1

Jack Smith sat on his balcony in the warm morning air, sipping his coffee and trying to ignore the little voice telling him to head down to the corner store for a pack of cigarettes. It had been over two weeks since he last smoked, and he had been telling himself he was over the worst, but the same thought had been occurring each morning lately, with increasing intensity.

Why not just have one?

He was almost out of his chair before he recognized his addictive mind's familiar ruse and, knowing he would never stop at one, decided to focus instead on the Saturday paper. He scanned the front page and started reading a story on the Ottawa mayoral race, but soon lost interest. It was a humid morning, with summer lingering into late September with what was likely the final heat wave of the year, an occasion he planned to celebrate in his own way. He was on call for a few more hours, after which he was headed to Toronto, where he would meet up with a bunch of his university buddies to relive the excesses of more carefree times. He smiled as he considered extending his trip by a day or two. He had worked a lot of extra hours over the summer and this would be the first time he had really cut loose in months. He was overdue.

Smith traded the front section of the paper for the sports page, and the latest on Ottawa's off-season coup — the signing of the number one overall pick in the spring draft, Curtis Ritchie. Ever since the announcement of the blockbuster acquisition on draft day, the whole city had buzzed with the possibilities; from a significant boost to the score sheet, to a guaranteed playoff berth, maybe even a shot at the Stanley Cup. At the very least, the deal had ruled out the possibility that the young superstar might end up in Toronto, playing for Ottawa's archrival down Highway 401. As the summer passed and training camp approached, rumours started flying that Ritchie wasn't ready for the big leagues yet, and would be better off developing for a year with the farm team. But whether it was this year or next, there was no doubt he was going to have a major impact.

So he should, thought Smith, *given the proven players and future draft picks Ottawa had sacrificed to land him*. Ritchie's rookie salary was capped by the league just shy of seven figures, but despite the threatened phasing out of signing bonuses in the next collective agreement between the league and players, Ritchie had gotten a substantial one — rumoured to be several million. That was peanuts though, compared to the long-term, multi-million-dollar contract predicted by the pundits once his first couple of seasons were out of the way — and he was only eighteen years old. No wonder the press had tagged him "Ritchie Rich."

Smith had always loved hockey, and though his skills on the ice got him considerable respect at the frequent police tournaments, Junior B in St. John's was the highest level he had ever achieved. He had been invited to a couple of feeder camps as a teenager and been given a look by some scouts, but nothing concrete had ever developed. Part of the problem was that his size and ability to handle himself with the gloves off made him more attractive as an enforcer than the type of player he had aspired to be. But even with any dream of turning pro long gone, Smith still followed the game with interest. He was reading the latest training camp gossip when the ring tone of his cell shattered his peace. At seven thirty on a Saturday morning, it could only be one person.

"Three hours," he said, after reaching in and plucking his cell phone off the kitchen counter. "That's how long I've got before I hit the road, you hear me?"

"Relax, Smitty, I'm sure your little boozefest won't be affected, but we do have a call."

"What is it?"

"Body in the canal."

"Really? Some homeless guy?" Smith knew it wouldn't be the first.

"I'm headed there now, about five minutes away from your place."

Smith looked out at the grey clouds forming in the distance, threatening to spoil an otherwise perfect day. It was unlike his partner not to have more information, which could only mean they would be first on the scene.

"See you downstairs."

12

❆ ❆ ❆

"So what have we got?" Smith said, sliding into the passenger seat as David Marshall pulled the car away from the curb. Although the two had only been partners for a few years, they enjoyed a familiarity that suggested a much longer connection. As the most senior investigator in the Major Crimes Unit, Marshall had seen more than his fair share of murder and mayhem in his years with both the Toronto and Ottawa police forces. Jaded by office politics and plagued by a long-standing back injury, he had been considering early retirement around the time Smith arrived in Ottawa, just over three years ago. He had watched the troubled integration of the Unit's newest arrival with interest, as Smith had fought for acceptance among his peers — a process made more difficult by the quirky Irish brogue that had followed him all the way from Torbay, Newfoundland. He had been impressed by Smith's abilities as an investigator, but mostly with his pluck; especially when the outsider had put a decisive end to a series of Newfie jokes in a brawl that had netted his tormentor a busted lip and a bloody nose. Smith may have made an enemy or two that day, but the jokes had stopped, and everybody stuck to "Smitty" within his earshot, which seemed to suit him just fine. Whether it was because he felt a duty to mentor the new kid, or just because of the vicarious energy Marshall seemed to derive from the arrangement, he hadn't resisted being partnered with Smith and had decided to stick around. Most days, he seemed glad he had.

"I was in Mechanicsville when I heard the traffic and called in myself. I figured maybe we can rule ourselves out early if it's some boozer who took his last dip."

"And save my trip — good thinking." Smith offered a package of gum. "What were you doing down there, anyway?"

"Hockey, what else?" Marshall snapped out a piece and popped it in his mouth. "Bobby's got sort-outs all weekend at Tom Brown Arena."

"I guess it's that time of year." It seemed odd to Smith to be playing hockey when the mercury was still hitting the thirties.

They made their way quickly through the light weekend traffic to the west side of the Rideau Canal and parked at the end of Somerset, where the path was cordoned off and a uniform stood guard.

"What have we got?"

"Just pulling him out now," the young constable replied, escorting them through a thin crowd clad mostly in running gear. "A jogger noticed a body floating upside down, twenty feet from shore, and called it in."

"He's here?" Marshall asked, as they made their way down to the lower path, to where the divers were pulling the body toward the iron railing that lined the canal.

"Waiting for you up there, when you're done."

"There goes my homeless theory," Smith said, as they approached the railing and the victim's lower half came into view.

"What do you mean?"

"Look at those shoes. They're the new Nikes. They're, like, two hundred bucks."

"Could still be an accident," Marshall said. "Maybe he was stretching by the rail and …"

"Holy Shit," the uniform blurted, as the divers turned the body over to pull it up over the rail, and the knife handle came into view, buried to the hilt in the victim's chest, above a large stain in the light grey T-shirt.

"You might want to rethink your trip to T.O., Smitty," Marshall said, as Smith moved closer, staring open-mouthed as the diver pulled back sodden strands of hair from the victim's face.

Marshall was intrigued by his partner's reaction, given that they had both seen enough bodies over the years to have developed a healthy detachment.

"What's the matter?"

"Mother of Christ," Smith gasped, as he looked from the victim's face to the official training camp T-shirt, half of the logo stained in blood. "It's him."

"Who?"

"It's Ritchie Ri —" he stammered. "It's Curtis Ritchie."

CHAPTER 2

"Let's get him covered up," Marshall said, as they all stood around, staring in disbelief at the NHL's poster boy, a bone-handled knife sticking out of his chest.

"We need the crime scene guys out here, right away." Smith gestured to the uniform, adding, as the young man started toward the bridge: "And make sure no civilians get down here." He turned to Marshall, who was still staring at Ritchie's body, as one of the divers covered his head and torso with a plastic tarp.

"Wait a sec." Marshall knelt by the body and took a closer look at the protruding knife. The sodden cotton of the T-shirt was pulled back and the entry point was clearly visible, at least four inches below the blade. "That's a hell of a gash, if that blade's as long as I think it is." He straightened up and motioned to the diver to replace the tarp. "I think we can rule out an accident."

"Eighteen years old, and the world by the balls." Smith was shaking his head. "What a fucking waste."

"Amen to that," Marshall said, as his phone went off. As he took the call, Smith looked down the path to the south. For half a kilometre, it ran in a straightaway, parallel to the Rideau Canal until it curved to the right near Waverly Street. Even in full morning sunlight, the thick foliage from the overhanging trees cast the path in shade, obscuring it completely from the road and the residential areas beyond, and from the other trail twenty feet above at the top of the bank. He had to admit, this was a pretty good location to take someone out discreetly. They would have to wait for the time of death, but Smith was assuming it had happened early this morning. He glanced back down the trail, imagining it in the morning mist as a shiver ran down his spine.

Looking across the canal, and beyond the rolling slope up to Colonel By Drive, Smith's gaze settled on a trendy-looking condo building and noticed some of the units had balconies. He turned to look for one of the uniforms just as Marshall ended his call.

"We should get someone over to canvass those condos."

Marshall nodded. "That was Beaudoin." He didn't say anything else. He didn't need to.

"I know, Marshy."

"You can go to Toronto and get shit-faced anytime, right?"

"Right," he said, gesturing toward the bridge, where the crime scene crew had reached the path, headed their way.

❄ ❄ ❄

Smith stood on the balcony of the condo, looking across the canal toward the still-cordoned crime scene. He could see the technicians working away, and noticed that the crowd on the upper trail near the Somerset bridge had grown considerably.

"This is quite a view you have here, Ms. Emond," Marshall said, as an attractive woman set down a tray with a coffee carafe, a pewter creamer and sugar bowl set and three matching, oversized mugs.

"Help yourselves, please."

"That's very kind of you. Thanks." Marshall picked up a mug and they all sat around the wicker table.

"I still feel awful that I didn't do something right away," she said. Though she had described seeing a man leaning over the iron railing, above rippling water, Jane Emond hadn't witnessed the actual attack, nor seen Curtis Ritchie's fall into the canal. She hadn't thought what she had seen was worth reporting at all, until she noticed the police cordon a couple of hours later.

"I don't think there's anything you could have done to save him," Smith said, as Emond ran her manicured fingers over the top of her mug. He put her in her mid-thirties and he couldn't help notice the absence of a wedding band. From the condo and its contents though — all notably high-end — she seemed to be doing just fine on her own. What the hell would she want with marriage?

"Do you have any idea what happened?" she asked, interrupting his thoughts. "I guess I shouldn't ask. I know you can't …"

"I'm afraid we don't know much yet, but we'll find out," Marshall said. "Can we go back to the man you saw by the rail? You said he was big. Can you be any more specific about his appearance?"

"He looked … imposing, even from over here. He was wearing what looked like a hoodie, and maybe sunglasses."

"Did you get a sense of his height?"

"Hard to say, and he was leaning on the rail when I saw him, maybe bent over a bit. He certainly wasn't short."

Smith watched as she tucked a strand of hair behind her ear. "Are you sure about the sunglasses, Ms. Emond?"

"Jane, please. And yes, he was definitely wearing dark sunglasses. It seemed odd, since it wasn't sunny at all, at that time."

"And do you know exactly what time it was that you saw him?"

"Between six thirty-five and six-forty. I'm fairly certain because I had just listened to the local news, and it's usually about five minutes long. I poured myself a coffee and went straight over to the railing. That's when I saw the ripples in the water, and then I noticed the man."

"Are you usually out here at that hour of the morning?" Marshall asked, as he sipped his coffee.

Emond smiled, revealing pearly-white teeth. "No, not on a Saturday. I was actually thinking of going for a run myself. I try to get out a few times a week, never on the lower path though, it creeps me out a bit. But I never thought …" She shook her head. "Anyway, I decided I was content to drink coffee and enjoy the warm morning air instead."

"Can't blame you," Marshall smiled back. "So you see the rippled water, then this big guy leaning over the rail. What then?"

"I watched him as he looked around for a few seconds. I wasn't sure if he was thinking of going in himself, like maybe he dropped something in there by mistake. But he didn't. He just moved away from the rail and started jogging off toward the bridge."

"Did you see whether he left the path at the bridge?"

"Yes, he definitely went up toward Queen Elizabeth Drive. I lost sight of him in the trees."

"Was he running fast, or just jogging?"

"Just jogging. That's kind of why I didn't think much of what I saw down by the water. He didn't look like someone who had done anything wrong. For all I know, he tossed a downed tree branch into the water, you know?"

Smith sensed her guilt at not calling it in right away and gave her an exculpatory nod, which she acknowledged with a brief smile, before lowering her mouth to the rim of her mug.

"And just to be clear," Marshall continued. "The man you saw was wearing a hoodie and sunglasses and had a large build. Would you say he was fat?"

"No, he didn't seem fat, though with the hoodie, and the distance, it's hard to say. He didn't carry himself like he was overweight."

"He had an athletic stride, then?"

"Yeah, I guess."

"Do you recall if he was wearing shorts, or pants?"

"Pants; I think they were dark."

"And the shoes?"

She shook her head. "I really can't recall. They may have been obscured by the railing."

"Fair enough." Smith scribbled some final notes, then flipped his notebook shut. "We'll need you to come down to the Elgin Street station and give a formal statement, if you don't mind."

"That's not a problem," Emond said, as Smith glanced at Marshall, who seemed to be enjoying a last sip of the gourmet coffee.

Marshall reluctantly set the coffee cup down. "Yes, thank you. And if there's anything else that you think might be useful, please give us a call," he added, handing her his card, as Smith did the same.

"I will." She escorted them inside and across the immaculate living room to the entrance area, stopping to retrieve something from a desk drawer on the way.

"I should give you my card. You're more likely to reach me at the office if you have any follow-up questions. "But I've only got one." She hesitated, looking at them each in turn before handing the card to Smith. He wasn't surprised to see the multiple names embossed on the card.

"What kind of law do you practice?"

"Not criminal, unfortunately," she said, stopping in front of the door. "I might have been more useful to you if I did, but I practice mostly family law."

Smith extended his hand.

"You've been very helpful, Ms. Emond."

"Jane." She gave a playful sigh as she opened the door for him.

"And thanks for the coffee," Marshall added, stepping out into the hall. They stood in silence as they waited for the elevator.

"What are you smilin' at?" Marshall asked as Smith fingered the card and tucked it in his pocket.

❊   ❊   ❊

Ellen Ritchie sat on the sofa, with Smith and Marshall arranged in the two facing club chairs. James Cormier, the Ottawa Raftsmen's owner, had personally arranged to send a car for her as soon as he learned the news, and booked her a spacious suite at a downtown hotel. Smith glanced toward the large windows, partially obscured by drapes and wondered if the Raftsmen's management realized that Mrs. Ritchie's view included her son's murder scene. She blew her nose and moved along the sofa as her boyfriend handed her a glass of water and sat down. Ritchie's eyes were red-rimmed and her features drawn, and something about the oversized sweatshirt she was wearing, bearing her dead son's team logo, made her seem even more forlorn.

"You sure you're up for this, Ellen?" the man at her side asked, eliciting a determined nod. "'Cause you don't have to do it right now."

"No, I want to do it now, before it sinks in," she said, looking down at her feet. "Besides, I told these detectives here that I'd see them, so that's that."

"We appreciate that, Mrs. Ritchie," Marshall said. "Timing is important in these matters," he added, with a glance at the other man. Smith could tell his partner didn't care for Tom Saunders, and he had to admit he felt the same. There was something off-putting about him, but they would get to that.

"First of all, let me say how sorry we both are for your loss," Marshall began. "I didn't know Curtis, but I get the sense that the whole city lost something today. Can I ask you when you last saw him?"

"A couple of weeks ago," she said, taking a sip of the water. "Just before training camp started. He was so happy. His dreams were finally coming true." She smiled as a tear ran down her face and splashed onto the coffee table. "It was such a whirlwind summer for him, what with the draft, and the contract, then finding a place to live here in Ottawa. He was so excited about coming to camp and playing for the Raftsmen. I just can't believe this is happening. It's so cruel."

"And you, Mr. Saunders?"

"I saw him last week. Wednesday, I think. I've been in town the past few days, visiting with my sister."

"How did he seem on Wednesday?"

Saunders shrugged. "Top of the world. We had a couple of steaks and shot the breeze. He was telling me about training camp, and the way the team was shaping up. Excited, you know?"

"How long have you known Curtis, Mr. Saunders?"

"Ellen and I have been seein' each other for, what's it, five years now?"

Ritchie nodded, as Marshall returned his focus to Ellen Ritchie.

"Did Curtis buy a house here in Ottawa?"

She plucked a tissue from the box and blew her nose. "No. He wanted to build, and he wanted to take his time picking out the perfect location. He was renting a condo over by the big hotel."

"The Château Laurier?"

Ritchie nodded, dabbing at her eyes. The adjacent condo building was the most exclusive in town, with the smallest units going for a million or more. "One of the reasons he liked it so much was running along the canal. He just loved it."

"He ran a lot, I guess?"

"Oh yes, and more than ever this summer. He wanted to be in top shape for camp. I think he was running every day."

"Do you know if he always ran the same route?"

"I don't really know, but he always liked to go early, at first light, usually."

"Did he run alone?" Smith asked.

"He always did back in Peterborough, but I don't know about here."

Marshall asked some routine questions about Curtis Ritchie's habits and his whereabouts in the past few weeks, before looking to Smith.

"Did your son have a girlfriend?" Smith asked, as Ritchie and Saunders turned to him.

"Not that I know of." Ellen Ritchie shook her head. "I mean, there were girls — I'm sure there were lots of 'em — but nothing steady. Curtis always said he didn't want to get tied down. He didn't want to risk anything getting in the way of his goal."

"I'm sure he was pretty popular," Smith prompted. He had read about a woman in Peterborough who had claimed Ritchie had fathered her child, but as far as he knew it had never gone anywhere. He wondered whether Ritchie's prospects for a multi-million contract in the near future had spawned more, similar claims. "I mean, a good-looking kid like that, hockey star and the future he had …" He trailed off and sensed the unspoken dialogue going on between Ritchie and Saunders. It was Saunders who broke the silence.

"There was no shortage of gold diggers trying to get their hooks into him, if that's what you mean," he sneered.

"Wasn't there a woman in Peterbor —" Smith began, before Ritchie interrupted.

"That little slut tried her best, but everyone knew Curtis had nothin' to do with her."

"Who was this, and what did she try, Mrs. Ritchie?"

"Nancy Ridgeway, a waitress at a greasy spoon in Peterborough. She tried to get Curtis to pay her to shut her up, but he refused." She shook her head. "He knew what she was up to, and he wasn't afraid to stand up to her. That was back in the spring. She hired a lawyer and threatened to sue, but it never went anywhere. Then she tried to get the cops involved — you can check it out for yourselves — but nothin' ever came of that, either. Everyone knew exactly what she was."

Smith nodded, making a note to follow up with the OPP in Peterborough, before continuing. "I'm sure his career prospects attracted all sorts of attention, both good and bad. Did Curtis ever mention any threats, or enemies, or anything like that?"

She shook her head. "No. There was lots of media, and people hounding him all the time for autographs or pictures, but mostly they just wanted to be near him. He was such a good kid. Everybody loved him," she added, snuffling into a tissue. "He was building me a new house in Peterborough, and next year he was going to build me a cottage. He already had the land scoped out, up on Belmont Lake, near Havelock ..." She broke down and started sobbing, her shoulders jerking up and down as the tears ran down her cheeks. "We were as close as any mother and son could be."

As Ritchie blew her nose, Smith exchanged a glance with Marshall and leaned forward in his chair.

"What do you mean, Mrs. Ritchie?"

She stopped crying for a moment and looked up at Marshall, then Smith. "I wasn't Curtis's biological mother. He was adopted."

"We weren't aware of that," Smith said, seeing her puzzlement.

"I figured everyone knew, ever since that article in *Sports Illustrated*."

"When did you adopt him?" Marshall asked, as Smith scribbled notes.

"I didn't." She sighed and dabbed at her eyes. "Bob — my first husband — adopted him when Curtis was two."

"That would be Bob ... Ritchie?"

"Yes, he was married at the time, and his first wife died of breast cancer when Curtis was young — six or seven. I met Bob a few years later. I guess you could say he and Curtis adopted me."

Smith was scribbling furiously, trying to keep track of the Ritchies' complicated lineage. Marshall seemed just as perplexed.

"And Bob?" he said, not sure what to expect in the silence that followed.

"He died of a heart attack when Curtis was twelve. About six years ago. I thought I'd never get over it, until I met Tom." She gave him a grim smile. "So you see, detectives, this family's had more than its share of tragedy. But this …" She trailed off, looking down and blowing her nose.

"I really am sorry, Mrs. Ritchie," Marshall said, as he glanced toward Smith and saw a look that confirmed the interview was over for now.

"Do you guys know how this all works?" Saunders asked suddenly, as he handed Ritchie another tissue. "With the insurance and all?" He seemed to recognize the bewilderment his question had caused and continued with his thought. "I mean, how're we gonna finish the house now? It's half built."

Smith glanced at Marshall before answering, the same surprise mirrored in his partner's normally inscrutable features. "Did Curtis have a lawyer, or a business manager?"

"He had an agent, in Toronto," Ritchie said, perking up as Saunders frowned.

"You should probably take it up with him, then."

"Well, those are all of our questions for now," Marshall said, as they got up to leave. We can see ourselves out. We appreciate your time, and again, we're very sorry for your loss."

Ritchie nodded and sniffled, and Saunders got up and followed them to the door to the suite.

"You guys are gonna catch this motherfucker, right?" he whispered as they stood in the doorway.

"We're going to give it everything we've got, Mr.

Saunders," Marshall assured him as Smith took a step back, not from the sour whiff of liquor on Saunders' breath, but the feral heat at the core of his red-tinged eyes that continued to burn after the door had closed.

CHAPTER 3

Smith stood at the floor-to-ceiling window, looking out over the locks below leading down to the Ottawa River. The view across to Gatineau, and the rolling hills of Chelsea beyond, was spectacular enough and would only improve as the leaves completed their transition through every shade of brown, red, and gold as fall gave way to winter. He looked back at the sound of Marshall's voice from the far end of the hall that led to the bedrooms. It echoed across the vast hardwood, furnished only with a leather sectional and a massive projection screen television, connected to what looked like a state of the art sound system and a sleek gaming console.

"You gotta see this."

Marshall had appeared at the end of the hallway, beckoning him over.

"What?"

"Look at the size of the friggin' bed," he said, as they arrived in the doorway of the master bedroom. "And that's a 3D flat screen. It's gotta be a sixty-inch."

"Looks like a cellphone screen next to the one in the living room," Smith remarked, noticing a different gaming system connected to the enormous television and a wireless controller sitting on the bedside table. He glanced at the open case sitting on the floor in front of the television. "Hey, that's the newest hockey game. I've seen the commercials for it. It looks awesome."

"This is the life, all right," Marshall said, looking out at the same view Smith had been admiring from the living room.

"You sure you wanna trade places with him, Marshy?" Smith said, stepping through a door and switching on a light, finding himself in the largest walk-in closet he had ever seen. He whistled and ran a gloved hand through a long rack of clothes. Apart from a few suits and dress shoes, it was mostly casual stuff, but it was all high-end, far beyond the means of the average investigator. The assortment of sport shoes alone, piled in a corner of the closet, was worth a fortune. Marshall seemed more interested in the oversized swimsuit calendar that hung next to a massive mirror at the far end of the dressing area.

"September was always my favourite month," he said, walking through to the en suite, with its marble Jacuzzi tub, double sinks, and pewter hardware. "How many girls you figure he could fit in there at once?"

"Get your mind out of the gutter," Smith said, as a member of the identification team appeared at the door behind them.

"You might be interested in these."

Marshall took the key ring she held out, as Smith looked on, recognizing the familiar Porsche logo.

"It just gets better and better."

❄ ❄ ❄

Smith picked at the last of his fries before giving up and sitting back in the booth as Marshall wrapped up his call. He had eaten too fast, and the greasy burger platter was already swinging its way through his stomach like a wrecking ball. It was only mid-afternoon, but he felt exhausted. They were only seven hours into the investigation, and there was no obvious resolution in sight. But an attack like the one that had killed Curtis Ritchie, especially in broad daylight, always left clues. Smith remained confident that they would have a meaningful lead before much longer.

"That was Sauvé," Marshall said, tucking his phone into his pocket and nodding to the waitress for more coffee. "They just finished interviewing a jogger who was on the lower path around six fifteen. Says he passed someone in the area of the scene — a big guy in a hoodie wearing a hat and sunglasses. He says he remembers because it wasn't sunny." Marshall paused to take a sip of coffee before continuing. "He also says he first noticed the big guy on the other side of the Somerset Bridge, where he was stretching. The guy crossed the footbridge and got on the lower path and started heading toward the witness."

"But he didn't attack?"

"No, but he did say the other guy seemed to move toward the middle of the path as they got closer, not like he was going to block the way or anything, but it was noticeable. Then at the last minute, he backed off and they passed each other. Witness says he gave him a nod and got nothing back."

"Anything else?"

"The guy's hands were in the pouch of his hoodie, in front there." Marshall pointed to his belly.

"Concealing the knife."

"Could be."

"And how does this witness compare to Curtis Ritchie, in terms of height, build, hair colour, or whatever?"

"I don't know, but we're definitely going to want to re-interview him."

Smith nodded, then plucked a fresh napkin from the holder and began sketching as Marshall looked on.

"So, the perp's waiting here," he said, pointing to his rendition of the bridge, on the opposite side of the canal from the path where Ritchie was murdered. "He's pretending to stretch or whatever, but really he's watching the lower path on the other side. The path from the south is, what, half a click dead straight?"

"About that, yeah."

"He sees the witness coming down the path. Let's assume he's close to Ritchie's height and weight, plus there aren't that many people around that early, so the killer figures it's him."

Marshall was nodding and sipping his coffee.

"So he trots across the bridge, down the steps to the path, and then heads south. He's got his hands in the pouch, concealing the knife. He's getting ready to pounce, but then he realizes it's not Ritchie, so he just trots on by."

"Then he turns around and goes back to the bridge to set up again." Marshall pointed at his partner's sketch.

"A few minutes later, another runner comes down the path, only this time it really is Ritchie, and when they meet up on the lower path, it's lights out."

"Bottom line is, this wasn't some random attack. He was waiting for Ritchie."

"It sure looks that way." Marshall nodded. The two sat staring at the sketch for a while before Smith spoke.

"Guess you didn't read the *Sports Illustrated* article either, huh?"

"I had no idea he was adopted," Marshall said, shaking his head. "That's some family history. Talk about bad luck."

"More like cursed. What did you make of Saunders?"

"Pretty clear what his main concern is," Marshall said with a frown. "Who's gonna finish *his* house."

"So I wasn't the only one with that impression then."

"Pretty rich for him to talk about gold diggers. I mean, come on."

Smith nodded. "But Ritchie must have been worth more to him alive than dead."

"I guess we'll find out when we talk to the agent. He's on a four o'clock flight from Toronto, so he should be downtown at five thirty or six." Marshall checked his watch. They were due out at the Raftsmen's home rink in thirty-five minutes.

"Can you imagine what's going through their heads in the front office right now?"

Smith sat back and glanced out the window. The clouds had dispersed and it looked like the height of summer again, making the prospect of a drawn-out investigation even less appealing.

"Well," he said, returning his focus to Marshall. "On the bright side, they won't have to worry about coughing up a huge salary a couple of years from now."

"Yeah, but look at who they traded to get him. Lamer, Cotterill, and Wlodek," Marshall said, reciting the names responsible for 75 percent of the Raftsmen's offence in the past three years.

"Don't forget that young goalie, what's his name?" Smith snapped his fingers in frustration.

"Lepage. He's going to be great in a few years. Somewhere else, of course."

"McAdam's not looking like such a genius all of a sudden," Smith said, thinking of all the headlines since the brash GM had arrived in Ottawa, just after the Raftsmen had missed the playoffs for the first time in five years. If the team's owner had been looking for a shake-up, he had picked the right guy. But no one could have predicted the events of the past eighteen months. Quinn McAdam had brought a broom into town with him and, within weeks, the entire coaching staff was gone. It had taken him a year to turn his attention to the roster, but when he did, he had been no less ruthless. The first victims were the free agents, who'd been shopped without a second thought, their bloated salaries spent on younger, developing players. The general consensus was that those moves were long overdue, but a yard sale like that was based on the assumption that the core of the team would remain intact. No one had expected that two of the team's top three point-getters, and their highly coveted rushing defenceman, would be dealt for an eighteen-year-old — first overall pick or not.

Then again, there was no shortage of buzz about Curtis Ritchie, even before anyone ever mentioned his name in the same sentence with Ottawa. He had ripped through major junior like a tornado, racking up goals, points, and records along the way. A natural goal-scorer with a head for the game, Ritchie was being heralded as the best prospect the League had seen in a decade. Added to his youthful good looks, his unruly blond curls, and an impish grin, he was quite a package. Now no one would ever know if he would have delivered on the promise, and Ottawa's roster had a gaping hole in it. The fact that an eighteen-year-old life had been snuffed out seemed almost an afterthought.

"Come on, let's see how McAdam's doing in person," Marshall said, as they got up to leave. "And don't look so glum, Smitty. It's not every day you get to meet a League GM and former playing great in the flesh."

❄ ❄ ❄

Smith and Marshall stood in the reception area looking at the wall of posters, photos, and other Raftsmen memorabilia. Marshall, a diehard fan since the team's arrival in the nineties, was particularly interested in the photos and framed newspaper headlines from the early days, especially the signing of the team's longtime captain, Dennis Hearst, twelve years earlier. As for Smith, the Raftsmen had grown on him the longer he stayed in Ottawa, but he had grown up a Montreal fan, so he always found his allegiances strained whenever the two teams went head to head. He glanced at a series of newspaper headlines at the near end of the long wall, announcing the blockbuster Ritchie deal. One was a cover from the *Hockey News* that Smith remembered from the summer. The caption, "Ottawa's Saviour," topped a picture of Curtis Ritchie in a Raftsmen jersey and cap, flanked by McAdam on one side and the team's owner, James Cormier, on the other. All three wore broad smiles, Smith noticed.

Marshall wandered over to join him. Both men heard a sound behind them and turned to see Cormier standing there. "I'm sorry to keep you waiting," he said, extending his hand. "Jim Cormier."

Smith thought he looked shorter in person, but no less impressive. In fact, he seemed to radiate a general aura of confidence as he chit-chatted about the photo they had been looking at. He was dressed casually in khakis and a polo shirt, but despite the relaxed attire and easy smile, the distress of the morning's events was evident in his tanned features.

"I still can't believe it," he said, staring at the photo. "It's such a waste. Come on, let's go back to my office."

They followed him into a large office with more memorabilia on the walls and took a seat as Cormier retreated behind an oversized desk.

"Can I get you anything to drink? Coffee or a soda?"

"No, thanks," Marshall said, as he noticed a picture hanging on the wall of Cormier and the current prime minister, who was sporting a Raftsmen jersey. "We appreciate you making time for us. This can't be an easy day for you."

"I'm meeting with Curtis's mom in an hour. My problems are nothing compared to hers."

Marshall nodded. "We spoke to her earlier. Did you know Curtis well?"

"I wouldn't say well, but I met with him over the summer a few times. We had him and his family over for dinner a couple of times, and I talked to him about his future." Cormier paused and glanced out the window. "I like to think I'm a pretty good judge of people, and Curtis was a winner. That much was clear."

"Do you know if Curtis had any enemies?"

"Enemies?" Cormier paused again. "No. But I'm sure he had a lot of people jealous of him. He had a lot to be jealous of — youth, good looks, talent — not to mention his career prospects."

"About his contract," Smith said. "We understand it was just under a million. Is that right?" Everyone who hadn't spent the summer under a rock knew the amount, but the mechanics of the payments in the age of salary caps was a mystery to most, including Smith.

Cormier nodded. "Actually, it's a little over a million — we gave him the most we could for a rookie contract, but I as much as told him he could have the keys to the place three years from now if things went well." He paused, seeing Smith's raised eyebrows. "That might not seem like a good strategy to you, Detective, but I don't believe in beating around the bush — not with the guy you plan on building your future with, and that's what I had in mind for Curtis. I wanted him to know it."

"Was there any bonus, or any other type of payment, in addition to his base rate?" Smith asked. He had done a bit of research and discovered that whereas signing bonuses had been in and out of previous collective agreements, the most recent one had reinstated them, in limited circumstances.

Cormier nodded. "We had to go the league's exemptions committee and make a special case, but we managed to get him a two-million-dollar signing bonus."

Smith scribbled the numbers in his notebook. "What about death benefits?"

"My understanding is that there's a one-time payment to his beneficiary of six months' salary, but I'd ask you to check with Quinn on the details. I confess I never paid much attention to those parts of the contract. In a million years, I never thought they would come into play, especially with an eighteen-year-old kid. It's just so … tragic."

"We're probably going to want to get a copy of the contract. With your permission, of course," Marshall added.

"Quinn'll probably want to run it by media relations, not to mention legal, but I'm sure we can get you a copy. He's on his way back from the Westin with Mrs. Ritchie. When we're done here, you can meet with him too, if you like."

"So," Smith continued, looking up from his notes. "Is the team on the hook for the five hundred thousand — roughly — or is there insurance for that?"

"It should be insurance, but that's one of the things we're still trying to figure out. Like I said, no one ever thought this type of thing would happen. I've been an owner for ten years and I've never had an active player die under contract. I mean, hockey's a dangerous game and all, and you certainly have to be concerned about injuries, but something like this?" Cormier shook his head.

"And I assume none of the trades the team made to get Curtis are impacted by his death?"

"You mean, can I get my top three back? Are you asking as a detective, or a fan?" Cormier gave a grim chuckle. "I think the short answer's no, but you can bet we'll be checking. Again, Quinn would know more about the technical details. You'll probably want to talk to his daughter Melissa as well — she's the legal beagle."

Smith made a note. He didn't even know McAdam had a daughter, much less that she worked in the front office.

"So the team's not in great shape then?"

Marshall elicited another pained smile from Cormier.

"That's an understatement. We've got a gaping hole to fill, and less than two weeks before the season starts. Everyone's already made their big deals, so there's not a lot of movement out there. From the team's point of view, it's a disaster. And the vultures are already hovering, looking for Quinn's head."

"What do you mean?"

"The press has been calling our PR shop all day, asking for statements. U.S. and Toronto-based reporters, mostly. At least the local guys have a bit of class," Cormier added, with a sigh. "But these other guys, they start off with niceties, but it isn't long before they get to the point. *How do I feel about the Ritchie deal now? Do I think we should have traded our top three for him? Do I think it was wise to put all of our eggs in one basket?* That kind of shit." He paused and let out a sigh. "I feel bad for Quinn too, because this is going to be especially hard on him. With all the scrutiny of the trades over the summer, can you imagine what they're going to be saying now? They're gonna crucify him. I've already had two people ask me why I haven't fired him yet."

"I assume you don't intend to, then?"

"Hell, no. Quinn's a visionary, and as such he's always going to be on the hot seat. But I'm the owner, and none of the deals he brokered could have gone through without my approval, and I have no regrets. We'll pick up the pieces and move on." He stopped and looked at his hands. "Listen to me, complaining about the press and the team, when we're talking about the murder of a young man in his prime. I assume you're treating this as a murder?"

"It's suspected foul play at this point," Marshall said. "But I think that's kind of academic in this case."

"Do you have any idea who could have done it?"

"I'm afraid not."

"You think it could have been some crazed fan?"

"We really don't know. That's why we're trying to talk to as many people as we can, as soon as we can. We want to catch this guy as quickly as possible."

Cormier nodded and looked down at his BlackBerry.

"That's Quinn. He's back with Mrs. Ritchie. If there's nothing else, you can go over to his office."

"That would be great, thanks."

"If there's anything I can do to assist in the investigation — and I mean anything — I want you to let me know. Here's my card." He handed them each a business card. "You can call me anytime, day or night. I'll tell media relations to give you direct access, given the circumstances."

"We appreciate that," Marshall said as an assistant appeared at the door to escort them to the GM's office, just down the hall.

They rounded a corner and spotted McAdam standing at the door of his office, talking to a young woman seated at a desk outside. As they approached, he extended a massive hand toward Marshall.

"You're with the Ottawa Police?"

"David Marshall and Jack Smith," Marshall said, and they all shook hands. Smith noticed McAdam's grip was strong and cool.

"Come on in, have a seat."

McAdam arranged his large frame into a chair as the two investigators sat opposite. They had both seen plenty of him in the papers since he had come up from Florida last spring, but he was much more impressive in person. He had been a defenceman back in his playing days, with a reputation for hard hitting and the ability to drop the gloves with the best of them. Looking at him across the desk, Smith could imagine him being an imposing figure at the blue line. He noticed the scarring around the right eye and remembered hearing that McAdam's career had been cut short by an injury in his early thirties, but not before he had won a Stanley Cup with Boston.

"Thanks for seeing us. I know this has got to be a tough day," Marshall opened with his now-familiar refrain.

"I wish we were meeting under different circumstances, gentlemen." McAdam sighed and leaned forward in his chair. "Before we get started, can I ask if you have any leads?"

"We're still in the information gathering stage, but there are a few things that we need to follow up on, and I'm sure there will be more."

"You probably can't discuss it anyway. Ongoing investigation, that sort of thing. It's gotta be a murder investigation though, right? I just met with Mrs. Ritchie and she saw the body. I mean, Jesus…."

"We were at the scene when he was pulled from the canal," Marshall said.

McAdam shook his head. "It's just such a … shock, and such a goddamn waste."

"Maybe if we can ask you some questions about Curtis and his relationship with the team we can get to work, and let you get on with yours," Smith offered.

McAdam nodded. "Of course."

"How well did you know Curtis?"

"I can't say I knew him all that well, personally. In my position, you have to look at the player first, and the person second. Personality's important, don't get me wrong, but you can be the nicest guy in the world, and that's not gonna get you noticed in this league."

"So when did you become familiar with Curtis, the player?"

McAdam paused. "I started hearing about him a couple of years back, when he first broke into the OHL. I was down in Florida at the time, but all the teams have their scouts out there. It was well-known that he was someone to watch for — someone special."

"And you were instrumental in bringing him here?"

The GM gave him a bleak grin. "I can't really blame you for wanting my head on a platter, as a fan."

"I guess his death leaves you with a bit of a gap to fill."

"That's the understatement of the year. And that's what's so damn ironic," he continued. "A kid like that, you can see him going to L.A. or the Big Apple and getting himself into trouble, in over his head with a lot of money and the wrong people around him. Maybe he gets into drugs, or even it's just random crime — that's the reality of big city life in the States. But here? I would have thought Ottawa was the safest place he could possibly be. And then this happens. I still find it unbelievable."

"You mentioned the money," Smith interjected. "What happens now, with his death? I assume the team doesn't have to pay out the full contract."

"No, there's a one-time benefit of … I assume we're talking confidentially here, right? I can't have any of this getting into the press. Mrs. Ritchie's got enough on her mind."

"The press isn't going to hear it from us."

McAdam leaned forward in his chair. "Curtis named his mother as the beneficiary, so she's entitled to a half a year's salary. You may want to talk to Curtis's agent as well. He was working on some endorsement deals. I don't know if they had gotten to terms yet."

"We're due to speak to him later this afternoon."

"And the salary payout," Smith asked. "Does that come from the team, or an insurer?"

"That's a good question. In twenty years of hockey operations, I've never been in a situation like this. We're kind of in uncharted waters."

"I guess that's why you've got lawyers."

"We've got the best," McAdam said, with a genuine smile. "My daughter, Melissa, did a lot of the legal work on Curtis's contract. She'll be following up on the payouts."

"We'll probably want to talk to her as well," Marshall said.

"Sure. I can arrange that."

Marshall glanced at a picture on the wall behind McAdam, and realized the team in it was arranged around the Stanley Cup.

McAdam followed his gaze and turned to take in the picture. "What a battle that was, and what a great bunch of guys. It was a real team effort — something I'll never forget."

Marshall nodded. "How about Curtis? How did he fit in with the guys here? Did the other players get along with him, and vice versa?"

"Yeah, sure. Like any rookie, it takes a while to integrate yourself into a team, and it's even harder when you come with the kind of hype he generated. But Curtis was doing a great job. He's a … he was a likeable young man."

"The other players didn't resent his instant star status, or the trades it took to get him here?"

"There's always a period of adjustment. Some of the guys I traded were here for a long time. You have to understand, these guys go to war out there every night, and going through something like that forms bonds that go deep — they don't end just because players move on. But everyone understands hockey's a business as well as a game. Don't forget, Curtis had only been through half a training camp, he was still finding his place."

"What about off the ice? Did Curtis ever mention any trouble he was having, with other players, or fans, or in general?"

"Not to me. But our relationship really boiled down to a business one. I didn't have enough time to get to know him that well. That would have come, in time."

They were interrupted by Marshall's phone. "Excuse me."

"Do you know if Curtis had a girlfriend?" Smith asked as Marshall took the call.

McAdam shook his head. "Don't know. You should ask Peter Dunne. He was rooming with him for part of camp, and probably knew him the best among the players."

"Can you arrange for us to talk with him?"

"Of course. Let me know when you want to see him and it's done. Just so you know, we go on the road next week, for pre-season."

"Yeah, we'll want to talk with him before then."

Marshall closed his phone and glanced at Smith.

"We're going to have to cut this short, but thanks for your time. Can we get your contact info for follow-up?"

McAdam fished out two cards and handed them across the desk.

"Call anytime. My cell's on there."

"Thanks."

"And detectives," he called out, as they neared the door. "Good luck catching this guy."

Once outside, Marshall took the steps down two at a time.

"What's the rush, Marshy?"

45

"That was the station. Turns out the Palestinian General Delegation is in the building at the end of Somerset Street."

"Someone saw the perp up close?"

"Better. They've got a video camera outside."

CHAPTER 4

"That's it? That's all we've got?" Smith protested as he and Marshall sat in the briefing room of the identification lab on the ground floor of the Elgin Street station. The identification officer fiddled with a laptop and restarted the fifteen seconds of video as Smith walked up to the large screen hanging from the ceiling in the corner of the room. The intersection of Somerset Street and the Driveway appeared on screen, followed by the grainy image of someone crossing the Driveway toward the Palestinian General Delegation. The time stamp, displayed in the bottom right hand corner of the frame, read 6:42 a.m., which was consistent with Jane Emond's estimate of when she had noticed the ripple of water, and the man at the railing, from her condo balcony on the other side of Colonel By Drive.

"It's a fixed view," the identification officer explained with an irritated sigh. "It only covers that one spot."

Smith pointed to the image onscreen. "Can't you zoom in, or clear up the image?"

"Zooming in will only make the image fuzzier, but I can try. It's not the best quality to work with."

Marshall scoffed. "The amount of dough the city spends on surveillance, and this is the best we can come up with?"

"It's not even our camera, so I guess we're lucky we got anything."

The initial excitement at hearing they had video of their suspect had largely evaporated by the time they had finished their first viewing. It was clear that the poor-quality image of a large man jogging across the street, with 90 percent of his head obscured by a hat and sunglasses, wasn't going to do much to narrow their search.

"Didn't Emond say he was wearing a hoodie?" Smith said, noticing that the man in the image appeared to be wearing a long-sleeve shirt made of thinner-looking material than the heavy cotton of a hoodie, and, more importantly, with no hood. "I suppose it would be too much to hope that he tossed it in the woods on his way back up to the street."

"Is that it, around his waist?" Marshall pointed to a thickening around the man's middle, which could easily have been the arms of a hoodie.

"Shit, yeah. He must have taken it off before he got to the top of the stairs. Maybe it had blood on it."

"The size of that gash — it must have been covered."

"And no prints from the knife," Smith continued. The crime scene analysis had revealed very little so far in the way of physical evidence. No fingerprints, or any other obvious identifying marks, had been left by the attacker on either the knife or Ritchie's clothing. The concrete surface of the trail hadn't helped either — other than a disturbance of leaves and dirt in the area of the attack, and some marks on the railing that may or may not have resulted from the attack, there was nothing to go on. Yet, a one-hundred-and-ninety-five-pound man had been savagely attacked and pitched over a four-foot-high railing in a matter of seconds. There had to be something they were missing.

"There's a Mr. Avery downstairs to see you." They turned to see a young constable at the briefing room door.

"Ritchie's agent," Smith said, noticing Marshall's expression.

"Right. Tell him we'll be there in a sec."

The identification officer pointed to the screen. "I'll see if I can clean this up a bit, but it's not gonna get that much better."

Making their way down the hall toward the elevators, Smith stopped by a filing cabinet.

"How high's that rail down by the canal, Marshy?"

"I don't know. Maybe four feet."

"And Ritchie's six two?"

"If you say so."

"Just stand here for a sec." Smith arranged his partner a few feet away from the cabinet, then took a few steps back down the hall. "Now pretend you're Ritchie."

"I think I'd rather be the other guy."

"Seriously. You're out for your morning run. You're only a click from your fancy pad, where you're gonna have a nice breakfast — probably ordered in from some fancy place — then hop in your fancy car and head out to the rink for the day, playing the game you love, that you happen to be fucking great at, and which is guaranteed to pay you millions for years to come."

"Can you throw in a couple of swimsuit models for that hot tub?"

"That's the spirit. You're on top of the world, and you're relaxed. You're the *man*. You see some guy jogging along the path toward you, just like the other couple of people you've seen in the last hour or so," Smith said, starting to trot toward him. "The guy gives you a nod, maybe. You do the same…. Then …" he lunged at Marshall, grabbing his shoulder with his right hand, the palm of his left hand striking him gently over the heart as he pushed him back against the filing cabinet, stopping as Marshall's lower back made contact.

"The fuck you doing?" Marshall pushed him away, smoothing his shirt as Smith backed off.

"It was all in the momentum, and the surprise. Ritchie's tall and pretty heavy, so once he's going in the right direction and he hits that rail, he's going over. You know the saying — the bigger they are, the harder they fall?"

"Look what you did to my shirt!" Marshall pointed to the loose button.

"Sorry, but it makes sense, right?"

"Showoff." Marshall was still fussing over his shirt as they continued on toward the reception area. "Our guy'd have to be pretty powerful though, even with surprise on his side. Hockey players are strong in the legs, and not so easy to knock off balance."

"Maybe our perp's a player himself?"

Marshall considered that as they walked out into the waiting area and saw a man in his forties talking on a BlackBerry, his black hair slicked back. He saw them coming and signed off, sliding the phone into the pocket of his pinstripe suit.

"Mr. Avery?"

"Call me Dan," he said, flashing a smile and shaking their hands with a confident grip.

"David Marshall, and this is Jack Smith. Thanks for coming in."

"Normally, I'd say it's my pleasure, but ... well ... I guess everyone's still trying to take all of this in."

Marshall led the way back through the secured entrance to a small meeting room. "We'll try not to keep you too long. We know you must have a lot on your plate."

"I appreciate that."

They settled in around a rectangular table as Avery tinkered with the settings on his phone, then looked across the table. "Just putting it on vibrate."

Marshall smiled. "So, how did you find out about Curtis?"

"I got a call from Ellen this morning. She was hysterical. Poor woman."

"I can only imagine what she's going through," Marshall said, before continuing. "Part of what we're trying to establish today, through various discussions, are the financial ramifications of Curtis's death. We've talked to the team's owner and GM, and we have the broad strokes of the contract, but we'd like to ask you for some details."

"Sure. I mean, I'll answer whatever I can."

"We understand that Curtis's beneficiary gets a one-time payment in the event of his death. Is that correct?"

"Yes, that's right. The beneficiary is entitled to half of one year's worth of salary."

"And is that in addition to whatever Curtis already received under the contract?"

"Yeah. He's already been paid a signing bonus of ..." Avery paused and smiled awkwardly. "Technically, the details of the contract are confidential, between the parties and their advisers. That's the team and Curtis — his estate, now, I guess. I'm assuming the team's okay with me disclosing all of this to you?"

"The team is shipping us a copy of the contract later today, and I'd remind you that we have considerable leeway in a murder investigation. We can get a warrant if necessary, but we'd prefer your co-operation."

Avery waved his hands. "I'm happy to co-operate, believe me. I just don't want to get slapped with a lawsuit the minute I walk out of here, but it sounds like that's not going to be an issue, so I'll tell you he got a two-million-dollar signing bonus. On my reading of the contract, he's ... his estate's entitled to another five hundred K."

"Is that standard?"

"That's a good question. I remember the clause and thinking at the time it was something the lawyers dreamed up to justify their fees. I mean, this is an eighteen-year-old we're talking about. Yet, here we are." Avery sat back in his chair. "Bottom line is the family gets five hundred thousand, plus whatever's left from the bonus."

"Do you know if the team pays the five hundred thousand, or would it be the insurer?"

"You'd have to ask the team, but I would think they're going to want the insurance company to pick up the tab."

"Did Curtis have a business manager?"

"I looked after his affairs. I think he was pretty happy in that department."

"I'm sure he was." Marshall smiled. "Not too many eighteen-year-olds with a couple of mil sitting in their bank account."

"It's peanuts compared to what he would have got in a couple of years, once we were out from under the rookie cap."

"Do you mind telling us what your cut was?"

"Five percent, but I assume you'll keep that confidential."

Marshall smiled. "Of course. So, as his business manager, you would be aware of his financial affairs, other sources of income, etcetera?"

"Sure."

"So, what was the state of his affairs?"

"You mean did he blow it all on dope and hookers?" Avery gave a brief chuckle as he adjusted himself in the chair. "Not a chance. I've never seen a more level-headed eighteen-year-old. God knows there are some guys out there, a lot longer in the tooth, who would see that kind of cash and just lose it. Not Curtis. He was really grounded for a young man."

"So he didn't run out and buy a Lamborghini?"

Avery smiled and fiddled with a cufflink. "A Porsche — leased, I think — but that was really it in terms of making a splash. He didn't want to rush into buying a house or a condo, so he was renting. Now, don't get me wrong, I'm sure he was paying a bomb in rent, but it wasn't out of whack with his sudden wealth. His biggest investment was in his mom's house up around Peterborough. That says a lot about him."

"Did he have any other significant income, from endorsements or stuff like that?" Smith asked.

Avery sighed. "You can't begin to imagine what a tragedy this is, in every sense. We were this close …" he squeezed his thumb and index finger together in front of his face. "… to one of the biggest, if not *the* biggest, endorsement deals in Canadian history. I swear to God, we were less than a week away from signing. Now …"

Smith scribbled some notes, trying to determine whether Avery's anguish was more over the loss of his commission than his young client, as Marshall asked the next question.

"You knew him pretty well, then?"

Avery nodded. "He was a great kid. Like I said, very grounded. Wise beyond his years, but he still had that youthful innocence, you know? That's where I came in …"

"Do you know if he had a girlfriend?"

"Nothing serious, I don't think. You can imagine he had girls throwing themselves at him, literally. But he was even level-headed in that department. I'm not saying he was a monk or anything — let's face it, most eighteen-year-olds are walking bags of hormones. But he was very careful."

"His mom mentioned a waitress in Peterborough…."

"That was such bullshit," Avery scoffed. "Some local yokel got knocked up and tried to pin it on Curtis. She hired a lawyer but, like I said, it was BS and it never went anywhere."

"Did she actually file a lawsuit?"

"No, it never got that far. She realized Curtis wasn't just going to fold his tent, so she gave up."

"What was her name?"

"Ridgeway. Mandy Ridge — No, Nancy Ridgeway."

Smith scribbled the name in his notebook. "What about her lawyer?"

"Some small-town hack. I can't remember his name, but I've got his letters if you want copies."

"Copies would be great, thanks."

"Apart from Ms. Ridgeway, did Curtis have any enemies?"

"I'm sure he had lots: goalies with blown goals-against averages, defencemen with minus ratings. Curtis had a tendency to wreak havoc with opposing teams."

"I was thinking more of the off-the-ice variety," Marshall said.

Avery shook his head. "No, he really was a pretty likeable kid."

Smith noticed Avery had begun to fidget a bit. "What about on the ice, did he have any major run-ins?"

"Naw, nothing serious. Curtis wasn't a scrapper, and anyway, he had plenty of protection on the ice. Anyone who tried to start something with him would find themselves squaring off with the team goon. You know what I'm saying?"

Marshall continued with some more questions before wrapping up the interview, but not before Avery had asked the question of the day.

"You guys have any idea who could have done this?"

"Not yet, but we'll find him, don't you worry."

"I guess you'll be under pressure from the moment the papers come out tomorrow. I don't envy you. The media'll have a field day with this. My phone's been ringing off the hook all afternoon."

"Well, thanks for your time, Mr. Avery."

"You bet. I'll get you those lawyer's letters you mentioned ASAP. If there's anything else, feel free to give me a buzz," he said.

As he watched Avery strut out of the interview room, Smith thought he looked pretty chipper for a guy who had just lost his meal ticket.

CHAPTER 5

Smith sat in the passenger seat, sipping his coffee and looking out the window, taking in the kaleidoscope of Lanark County on the brilliant fall morning. They had left Ottawa just before seven, when it was barely light, but as they made their way west along Highway 7 toward Peterborough, the morning mist ceded to the sun's warmth and left the roadside a rolling mix of gold and green. They had stopped in Perth for coffee and had another couple of hours to go, but they would be there in plenty of time for their meeting at the OPP detachment in town. Marshall was humming along to some country tune that Smith was trying to block out by focusing on the scenery.

It had been after midnight when Smith had finally fallen into bed, exhausted after a long day of gathering information, none of which pointed them to their killer. Another runner — a University of Ottawa student — had turned up at Elgin Street claiming he had passed a large man in a hoodie, hat, and sunglasses on the lower canal path around twenty past six. The student hadn't been certain about the time, but thought he was close. If so, he was the second person to encounter the killer before Curtis Ritchie. He had noticed the other man on the opposite side of the Somerset Bridge, apparently stretching as he faced the Queen Elizabeth Drive side. Assuming the student had seen the killer, his position on the bridge overlooking the path was consistent with the other runner's statement, and the fact that the student was only five foot four and a hundred and thirty-five pounds could explain why the man on the bridge had stayed where he was, rather than descending to the path for closer inspection.

There would be follow-up interviews with as many friends, family, and teammates as possible over the next twenty-four hours, in an attempt to find out who might have known Ritchie's running schedule and route. The decision for Marshall and Smith to head to Peterborough had been made by their staff sergeant, since Nancy Ridgeway represented the only person with a documented beef against Curtis Ritchie so far. Besides, it was under three hours by car, and they would be back by late afternoon.

Smith picked up one of the morning papers and read the headline in big black letters: "Hockey Star Murdered." A photo of the crime scene, taken through the trees from the upper path and showing a plastic tarp over Ritchie's body, dominated the front page, the balance taken up with background on Ritchie's life and whatever details of the investigation media relations had allowed to be released. Smith had already read most of it, and the gist was that Ritchie had been stabbed and tossed into the canal, and that the police had no suspects. Practically all of the sports section and most of the city section was taken up with more on Ritchie's life and death. There were quotes from many of the same people Smith and Marshall had interviewed the day before, including Ellen Ritchie, James Cormier, and Quinn McAdam. Ottawa's other main daily was similarly focused on the Ritchie murder, though its headline was less restrained: "Ritchie Rich Buys It." Smith scanned some of the articles and made his way to the back of the paper, to the sports section.

"Let's see," Marshall said, glancing over.

"What?"

"What do you mean what? The girl ... lemme see...."

Smith realized he meant the full-page photo of a barely dressed young woman — a daily feature that preceded the sports section — and turned the page over so Marshall could see it without driving off the road.

"Candy. Not bad."

"Says she's into yoga," Smith said. "And older cops with beer bellies."

"Very funny. What's it say about Ritchie?"

"What doesn't it say? They've got his whole life in here, and a prediction of doom for the Raftsmen this season. I wouldn't want to be McAdam right now, that's for sure."

"Yeah, I noticed a few not-so-subtle shots at him already, questioning his choice to put all his eggs in one basket, and all that."

"As for Ritchie himself, he was apparently a saint. They got a quote from his elementary school teacher in here, for God's sake. How do they get this stuff on a Saturday morning?"

Marshall scoffed. "You didn't see the vultures outside the station yesterday?" The media crowd had swelled to a horde by the end of the day, with reporters and camera operators — mostly the out-of-town crowd — hovering around, chattering and texting while they waited for the latest update. Marshall glanced over. "You don't think he was a saint?"

"How many eighteen-year-olds with that kind of cash in their pockets wouldn't have some skeletons in their closets?"

"Well, it's the first day after his death. They're not going to print anything negative yet, but give it time. Speaking of skeletons, what do you think of the Ridgeway woman?"

"Probably just a harmless gold digger. I do think it's odd that the letters just stopped, though." Smith pulled the copies of the lawyer's letters from the file folder he had brought along. "I mean, I know the idea is to threaten and blow everything out of proportion at the beginning and settle later, but aren't they supposed to at least file a statement of claim?"

Marshall frowned. "But they were written before the draft, right? And before Ritchie signed his contract."

"Sure, but everyone knew he was going first overall, and that whoever got him was gonna pay big bucks eventually. I wonder what happened."

Marshall tapped his fingers on the steering wheel and turned the radio up a notch.

"I guess we can ask her ourselves."

✳ ✳ ✳

Nancy Ridgeway's parents' home was a rundown Victorian on the outskirts of Peterborough. But while the exterior looked in need of plenty of TLC, the inside was clean, if spartan. Smith and Marshall sat at a harvest table in the kitchen in awkward silence as Ridgeway's mother prepared the coffee and her father sat opposite, stone-faced. Ridgeway herself sat at the end of the table, eyes firmly fixed on her hands. She had a youthful, attractive face and slender arms that were in stark contrast with the round belly under a T-shirt and jean overalls. She was seventeen years old.

"So, when's the baby due?" Marshall asked, breaking the silence as Mrs. Ridgeway deposited steaming mugs of coffee in front of them. They were both jacked up already from the two cups they had consumed on the drive over, but a refusal would have been impolite. Nancy looked to her parents before speaking, and seemed to read permission in the silence.

"October thirtieth."

"Just in time for Halloween. He'll have lots of fun with that over the years." Marshall grinned, before adding, "Or she." He sipped at his coffee, and when it was clear that small talk wasn't going to work, he decided to get to the point. He was about the same age as Ridgeway's father and, with a teenage daughter of his own, he could sympathize with the other man's pained silence. He was keen to get the information they needed and leave this family alone.

"I guess the Peterborough OPP told you why we

were coming. You're aware that Curtis Ritchie was killed yesterday morning?"

"Was he murdered?" Ridgeway asked, looking up at them for the first time. Her eyes looked bloodshot, as though she were exhausted, or had been crying — maybe both.

"It's officially a homicide investigation, so yes, we think so."

"My God. Poor Curtis," she whispered, as her father shifted in his chair.

"Can't say I'm surprised."

"Why's that, Mr. Ridgeway?" Marshall asked, as Smith took note of the mother's disapproving glance toward her husband.

"He was a nasty piece of work. I told you to stay away from him, didn't I?" He was addressing his daughter, rather than Marshall's question.

"John, please," his wife scolded.

"How was he nasty?"

"He was a cocky young pig is what he was. That's about the best I can say about him. Sure, he was a great hockey player, but as a young man … You ask anyone. I reckon it was only a matter of time before someone set him straight."

"So, he was arrogant?"

Ridgeway sniffed. "He thought he walked on water. And the way they treated him around here, you'd think he was right. But I saw a little of the real Curtis Ritchie in the past few months, and he's no hometown hero as far as I'm concerned." He stopped and shook his head. "I feel bad for Ellen and all," he said, with a shake of his head. "But still."

"We've been given copies of a lawyer's letters, written on your behalf, Ms. Ridgeway," Marshall said. "Claiming that Curtis Ritchie was the father of your baby. Is that what you're referring to, Mr. Ridgeway?"

"Yes, and it's not a claim, it's the truth."

"Let me ask you, Ms. Ridgeway. Can I call you Nancy?" She nodded, and Marshall felt the need to look to her father, who did the same.

"Is it true that you alleged Curtis Ritchie was the father of your baby?"

Ridgeway nodded, eyes still downcast. Smith could see her father fidgeting in his chair as the tension in the room grew. He was about to suggest they interview her alone, but before anyone spoke again, Ridgeway's father stood up.

"I've heard this all before. If you'll excuse me, I'm going to get some air."

They all sat in silence as he left, then Mrs. Ridgeway spoke.

"This has all been very hard on him, you'll understand."

Marshall nodded. "I'm sure this is difficult for everyone. I wonder if we could speak with Nancy alone, just for a bit."

Mother and daughter exchanged a brief glance and then Mrs. Ridgeway stood and smoothed her plaid dress. "I'll be upstairs."

Nancy Ridgeway seemed visibly relieved with her parents out of the room. "Curtis and I weren't seeing each other for very long when I got pregnant," she said. "He told me he loved me, but when I told him about the baby, he turned into … someone else."

As he watched her speak, Smith could imagine how it had played out — Ridgeway, a waitress at one of the local diners, and Ritchie, the handsome young hockey player with the golden future big enough for both of them. Who could blame her for believing in his fairy tales?

"Did he deny the baby was his?"

Ridgeway looked down at her hands again. "I was seeing someone else when I met Curtis, but I know it wasn't his." She paused, as if reading their thoughts. "I was on the pill. I don't know how it happened...."

"How do you know it was Ritchie's baby, if you were seeing someone else around the same time?" Marshall asked, tiptoeing around the real question, and thankful Ridgeway's father had left the room.

"I hadn't slept with Dale in a long time."

"Dale was your boyfriend?"

Ridgeway shook her head. "No ... I mean yes, but I told you, we were broke up. Curtis was the father, I'm sure of it. And I knew right away from Curtis's reaction that he wasn't going to have anything to do with me from then on. I just wanted to drop it, but then Johnny got involved."

"Who's Johnny?" Smith asked, looking up from his notes.

"Johnny's my brother."

"Why was your brother involved?"

"He found out.... I should never have told him. Anyway, he got really mad and told my parents, and convinced them to hire the lawyer. He said Curtis was going to be rich and why shouldn't he pay for his responsibilities."

Smith and Marshall looked at each other.

"So, your lawyer wrote some letters, and what happened next?" Marshall continued.

"Curtis stopped in to the diner one night and we got in, like … an argument." She stopped and looked down at her hands again.

"What did you argue about?" Smith prompted gently.

"Curtis did most of the talking, really. He called me a whore and a slut and … I think he was drunk. He said lot of things, then Johnny showed up and they got in a fight — not a real fight, just like pushing and yelling. Then the next day I got a letter from Curtis's lawyer saying I was a liar and stuff."

"Were there any witnesses to this fight, between Curtis and your brother?"

"A few, I guess. It wasn't in the main part of the diner. We were talking out back, in the kitchen, when Johnny showed up. I didn't even know he was in the diner that night, but he must have seen Curtis come in and the two of us go into the back. I think the dishwasher was there. I was so embarrassed, I just wanted to die."

"So what happened with your lawsuit?"

"I never wanted nothin' to do with any lawsuit. And they said they were going to drag me through the mud if we didn't drop it. Mom and Dad didn't have the stomach for it, either, but Johnny kept tellin' 'em to hold out. In the end, they offered some money and we took it."

"How much money?"

"I'm not allowed to say."

Marshall's eyebrows shot up. "Nancy, you realize this is a murder investigation, don't you? If you refuse to disclose relevant information, we can charge you with obstruction of —"

"Fifty thousand. It was fifty thousand dollars, but if we told anyone, we'd have to pay it back. We're not going to have to pay it back, are we?"

Smith saw the desperation in her eyes as they welled up with tears.

"You're not going to have to pay anything back, Nancy," Marshall said. "But we're going to have to talk to your brother."

CHAPTER 6

Smith and Marshall were waiting in a conference room at the Peterborough OPP detachment when a burly constable in his late twenties entered carrying a thin file folder.

"Sorry to keep you waiting," he said as they shook hands. "Constable Mike Howard."

"David Marshall and Jack Smith, Ottawa Police."

"You're investigating the Ritchie murder? That's a tough break at this time of year. I'm a Leafs fan myself, but still."

"We'll try not to hold that against you," Marshall said, and they all shared a chuckle.

"Seriously, though. Have you got any leads?"

"Not much so far. But we were told you have a file on Ritchie?"

They had dropped in to the detachment more as a courtesy than anything else, and had been surprised to hear on arriving that there was such a file, and were eager to see just what it contained.

"It's not *on* him, exactly," Howard said, flipping through the file. "Ritchie laid a complaint for uttering threats."

"Against who?" Smith and Marshall asked in unison, both knowing the answer.

"John Ridgeway Junior. I interviewed them both myself. There was nothing to it in the end. Ridgeway's sister —"

"We just came from her place. That's why we're here."

"So you know she was claiming she was pregnant with Ritchie's baby?"

"Yeah, she mentioned her brother was pretty angry with Ritchie, and that they got in a fight — at a diner."

"The Hard Luck Cafe, yeah. It's a student place, near the Trent campus."

"So what have you got in there?" Smith pointed to Howard's file.

"Statements from both of them, the sister too, and one of the kitchen staff who saw most of it." He slid the folder toward Smith, who turned it around and started reading it as Howard continued the summary. "Ritchie admitted he was bad-mouthing the girl, and didn't know the brother was there. John heard it, and he'd had a few beers, so you can imagine he wasn't too happy. There was some yelling and shoving, and a couple of the staff broke them up, and that was it, really."

"But Ritchie wanted to press charges? You'd think he'd want to keep it as quiet as he could," Marshall pondered aloud.

"I guess it was too late for that," Howard said. "The lawyers had already started trading letters by then."

"Listen to this," Smith said, reading from one of the statements. "According to the dishwasher, Ridgeway said, and I quote, 'I'll cut your fucking heart out, you piece of shit. Just see if I don't.'"

"Lemme see that." Marshall reached for the statement.

"What's the cause of death?" Howard asked. "They didn't say in the papers."

"It's not official — the autopsy's tomorrow — but he was found with a hunting knife sticking out of the left side of his chest."

There was silence as the three cops considered the possibilities.

"Okay," Smith said, collecting his thoughts. "This was months ago, but we're still going to want to talk to the brother, and the witness, too — Stephen Gravelle. Do you know where this is?" He pointed to John Ridgeway's address.

"Sure, I can bring you if you like," Howard said. "Gravelle's place isn't far from Ridgeway's."

"Let's go then, and see what they have to say for themselves."

❋ ❋ ❋

John Ridgeway's place was an upstairs apartment located over a Chinese restaurant in a part of town that Howard described as "sketchy." It was around noon when they climbed the rickety steps to the outside entrance. The only window was covered by a blanket, and after several knocks they saw or heard no sign of movement from inside.

"Maybe he's out," Howard suggested, as Marshall rapped for the third time. He seemed ready to turn around when they heard the faint sound of footsteps. A few seconds later the door opened with a squeak and a bleary-eyed man in his early twenties with tousled hair emerged from the darkness, clad in a T-shirt and torn sweat pants.

"Yeah?"

"That's him," Howard said, as Marshall and Smith took out their identification.

"We're with the Ottawa Police," Marshall said. "I believe you know Constable Howard?"

Ridgeway squinted at the IDs and then at Howard.

"Yeah? So what do you want with me?"

"We'd like to ask you a few questions, Mr. Ridgeway."

Ridgeway grunted. "What … now?"

"We can do it here," Marshall said. "Or you can come down to the OPP detachment if you'd prefer."

Ridgeway sighed, slumping a bit before stepping back to let them in.

"Thank you," Marshall said, as they entered the cramped apartment, consisting of one living area with a small galley kitchen off to one side and the door to what they presumed was the bedroom on the other. It reeked of stale beer and cigarettes, and looked like it had been the scene of a frat house party during frosh week.

"Have a seat," Ridgeway said, motioning to a stained and dilapidated couch as he slumped into a battered brown recliner and lit a cigarette. "Ottawa, huh? I think I can guess why you're here."

"Why's that, Mr. Ridgeway?"

"Gotta be Curtis Ritchie. I know he was killed yesterday. I figured it was only a matter of time before someone came knocking."

"How did you know he was killed?"

"Are you kidding? It's all over town."

"Before we get started," Smith said, launching into a standard caution to advise him of his rights. Ridgeway looked perplexed.

"Do I need a lawyer or something?" he asked, when Smith had finished.

"You can call one if you want. And, like my partner said, we're more than happy to do this down at the detach —"

"Naw," Ridgeway said, with a wave of his hand. "I got nothin' to hide."

"All right then," Smith said. "Did you know Curtis Ritchie well?"

"Let's cut the shit, okay?" Ridgeway said. "I know you know I got in a bit of a scrap with him a few months back. I'm sure he told you all about it," he said, gesturing to Howard. "You've seen the statements and you must know about Nancy and the baby and all, so why don't you just ask me?"

"What is it you think we want to ask you, Mr. Ridgeway?"

Ridgeway chuckled and took a long drag on the cigarette before exhaling a blue cloud that lingered over them, highlighting the dust particles hovering in the stale air. "I didn't kill him, but I'm not gonna pretend I'm all broke up 'cause someone else did."

"So you don't dispute that you didn't like him."

"Why should I? He knocks up my little sister and then won't step up and do the right thing. What kinda pussy does that? Not like cash was tight or anything. Fucking cheapskate."

"We have a statement that you threatened to kill him, to cut his heart out, I think it was," Smith said, watching Ridgeway as he leaned forward to flick his ash in the general direction of an empty beer can.

"That was all bullshit. I'd had a few beers and was just pissed off. Besides, you should have heard the shit he was saying about Nancy." He shook his head. "It ain't right that the rules don't apply to him just 'cause he's some fucking hockey god."

"Where were you on Saturday morning, Mr. Ridgeway?"

"What's going on?"

They all turned to see a girl in a cotton bathrobe in the bedroom doorway. She looked a few years younger than Ridgeway, and badly hung over.

"I was in there," Ridgeway said pointing to the bedroom. "Ain't that right, Penny?"

The three cops got up and introduced themselves as she sat on the arm of Ridgeway's chair.

"Yeah," she said, her eyes dropping to her hands. "He was here, with me, yesterday morning."

"Were you doing a little celebrating last night?" Smith asked, looking around the room and taking in the empty beer cans and pizza boxes.

"You could say that, yeah," Ridgeway said, leering at the girl and crushing his cigarette out in an over-flowing ashtray.

"Everyone likes to cut loose on the weekend, right?" Smith said, playing along and looking to the girl with a disarming smile. "What about Friday night?"

"Yeah, we were here, not before we closed the Sundance down first, though," she added with a grin.

"That's a bar downtown," Howard explained. "Closes around two."

"Late night, then?"

She nodded, then glanced toward Ridgeway, whose eyes had narrowed slightly as he looked at Smith. "We told you, we were both here," he said.

"Do you own a vehicle, Mr. Ridgeway?"

Ridgeway snorted at the question. "It's the Hemi out front."

"The what?" Marshall began to say, before he saw Smith's expression.

"It's a truck," Smith said.

"It's not just a truck." Ridgeway seemed genuinely offended. "It's the most powerful full-size pickup on the market."

"How long have you had it?" Smith asked.

"Couple of months."

"Must be a killer on gas, huh?"

"It's not so bad. A hundred bucks'll fill 'er up."

"When's the last time you filled up?"

Ridgeway paused at the question. "Why're you guys so interested in my truck?"

Smith gave him a disarming smile. "Just routine questions, John."

"It's John now, is it? Maybe I shouldn't say anything else without a lawyer."

"Sure, if you want to make this official, we can head down to the detachment. Just say the word."

Ridgeway's shifty eyes panned across the three cops before settling on the cigarette pack in front of him. He took another one out and lit it. "I gassed up a week ago, give or take, not that it matters."

Marshall waited to see if Smith had any further questions before resuming his own for a few more minutes.

"We'll probably want to take a formal statement," he added, flipping his notepad shut.

Ridgeway rolled his eyes. "Fuckin' A."

"And we'll need a number where we can reach you," Smith said. "In case we have any other questions. You have a work number?"

Ridgeway shook his head. "Between jobs right now, but you can always get me on my cell." He gave them the number as they got up to leave.

"Thanks, John," Smith said on the way out. "We'll be in touch."

As they walked back down the rickety stairs, they all paused to take in the shiny black pickup parked beside the building. Its windows were darkened with tinting and the massive alloy wheels and tires were definitely aftermarket upgrades.

"That's fifty grand worth of truck," Howard said with a whistle.

"Standard fare for the unemployed," Marshall said.

"Maybe he should think about living in it," Smith added, gesturing up to the apartment. "It looks a lot cleaner than that shithole."

"Something sure doesn't add up," Marshall agreed as they got in Howard's car.

"The dishwasher lives a few blocks that way," Howard said, pulling away from the curb. "So, what did you guys think?"

"I must say, I'm curious where he got the dough for that truck," Marshall said. "But I'm not sure he's our guy. He seemed too lazy to drive all the way over to Ottawa and back just to stick a knife in Curtis Ritchie. Besides, I can't picture that slob passing as a runner to anyone."

Smith hadn't thought of that, although the poor quality of the video would make it difficult to rule him in or out. Ridgeway was a tall enough guy, and the resolution and angle of the image of the killer would make an assessment of his body weight difficult. Ridgeway was overweight, but it wasn't beyond the realm of possibility. It was certainly clear that he didn't much like Curtis Ritchie.

"There wasn't enough to charge him with uttering threats," Howard said. "What with provocation, and alcohol to factor in, it didn't seem worth worrying about."

"I'm sure it wasn't," Marshall said. "But we'll check him out, anyway."

Howard stopped the car in front of a bungalow on a quiet street in a much nicer residential area, despite being only a five-minute drive from Ridgeway's hovel.

"Don't tell me that's his," Smith said, looking at the shining Mustang parked in the driveway. "'Cause now I'm getting really curious."

They got out and walked up the front path and knocked on the door. A woman in her sixties answered the door, looking wide-eyed at the three men on her doorstep.

"We're looking for Stephen Gravelle," Howard said. He showed her his identification, although his uniform left no room for doubt as to who was calling.

"Stevie? He's not here. I … I'm his mother. He stayed over at a friend's last night. Is he in trouble?"

"No ma'am, we just want to ask him a few questions about a witness statement he gave a few months ago. Stephen lives here, at home, then?"

"Yes. Should I tell him to call you as soon as he gets in?"

"That'll be fine." Howard gave her his card.

Smith pointed to the Mustang. "Is that your son's car?"

Mrs. Gravelle frowned. "Yes, it's his. Spends more time polishing that thing than doing anything useful around here, that's for sure."

"Well he's doing a good job. It looks brand new."

"It should. He's only had it a few months."

"You don't say." Smith glanced at Marshall as they turned to leave. "Thanks for your time, Mrs. Gravelle."

"Thank you, officers. I'll make sure to tell Stevie to call you as soon as he gets back."

Smith took note of the dealer sticker on the back of the car, and wrote it in his notebook. "Can we spin by Ridgeway's again on our way back?" he said, as they got in the car.

"Sure," Howard said as he turned the car around.

Approaching Ridgeway's apartment a few minutes later, they could see the truck backing out of the driveway.

"Block him off, will you?"

"What are you up to, Smitty?" Marshall said, as Howard honked and pulled up behind Ridgeway's truck.

"You'll see." Smith jumped out of the back seat and walked up to the driver's side of the truck, just as the smoked glass window came down to reveal Ridgeway's face, his irritation obvious.

"What'd you forget to ask me whether it takes regular or unleaded?"

Smith laughed and stepped up onto the running board and looked into the cab. Ridgeway leaned back, surprised by the gesture.

"Sorry, I just couldn't resist having a look inside. I've been thinking of getting one of these myself. How many horses she got?"

Enjoying the admiration for his vehicle, Ridgeway relaxed. "The base model's got two-fifty, but the Hemi's got almost three hundred," he said, as Smith took in the instrument panel.

"And I guess towing's not a problem?"

"You kidding?"

"It really is quite a truck. I'm sorry to bother you, John. I'll let you get on your way now."

"All right then," Ridgeway said awkwardly as Smith jumped back down, glanced at the tailgate, and got back in the car.

"What the fuck was that all about?" Marshall said, as they pulled ahead and Ridgeway drove off.

"Maybe nothing. What do you say we grab a bite?"

CHAPTER 7

"What do you think of our odds of getting a warrant for Ridgeway's finances?" Smith said as they all sat around the booth. Howard had recommended the little diner for lunch because of its food, and its proximity to the detachment office.

"He's the only person of interest we've got so far, in the biggest murder in Ottawa's history. Pretty good, I'd say." Marshall plucked the laminated menus from the end of the table and passed them out. "What do you think you're gonna find?"

"Not sure, but did you notice the keychain by the door?"

"Not really. Why?"

"It's got one of those Easypass gizmos on it. For gas, you know?"

Marshall put the menu down. "You're thinking he might have lied about when he last gassed up?"

"If he was in Ottawa on the morning of Ritchie's murder, that truck is his most likely method of transport. And he doesn't strike me as the sharpest knife in the drawer."

"Even he wouldn't be dumb enough to gas up with a credit card — or whatever — near Ottawa, if he was our guy."

"People can surprise you."

"So, you were looking at his gas gauge?"

"Just under a quarter-tank. Here to Ottawa and back would be about three quarters of a tank, wouldn't it?"

"About that." Marshall was grinning. "Not bad, Smitty. If he's lying about when he filled up last, you might be onto something. Call it in."

As Smith stepped out to make the call to set the warrant in motion, Marshall chatted with Howard. They were soon back to the investigation.

"You think it might be Ridgeway?" The young constable's excitement was obvious.

"I don't think we're that lucky," Marshall said. "But you never know. Guys tend to be protective of little sisters."

"So, where to next?" Howard said, as the waitress arrived to take their orders.

"Ridgeway's lawyer, Derek Bell. You know him?"

"Doesn't sound familiar, but I guess he's not a criminal lawyer."

"Generalist, I think," Marshall said, as Smith returned.

"What'd you get me?"

"Burger."

"Cheese?"

"Of course, cheese. What's the word?"

"I talked to Beaudoin. He thinks it'll be a slam dunk."

"Good."

Smith yawned and looked at his watch. "So we've got the lawyer at one-thirty, and then it's just the dishwasher. He should be back to us by the end of that meeting."

"If it's okay with you," Howard said, "I'll drop you back at the station after lunch. I've got to be in the other end of town for a two o'clock. The lawyer's office is across the street."

"Perfect. Thanks for taking us around this morning."

"No worries. So what do you guys think? If it's not Ridgeway, do you think it could be some crazy fan?"

"Anything's possible right now," Marshall said. "I meant to ask you, since Ritchie played his junior hockey here, did you ever see him in action?"

Howard nodded. "Sure. He was amazing. I've never seen anyone with a nose for the net like that. He wasn't a big hitter, or much of a backchecker. But he was fast, and man, did he ever know how to put the puck in the net. He woulda broken some records, that's for sure."

"I guess we'll never know."

❄ ❄ ❄

Smith and Marshall sat at a round table in a little library off the main reception area at Derek Bell and Associates. According to the directory by the front door, the converted two-storey housed a handful of lawyers, practising everything from property law, wills, and estates to family and criminal law. Bell himself was listed as a property expert, Smith noticed, looking at a certificate on the wall. He glanced at the adjacent print, depicting a man in Victorian clothes standing before a mirror with a legal text in one hand, the other raised dramatically. The caption below read: The lawyer who represents himself has a fool for a client.

"Hey, Marsh, check it out," Smith said, pointing to the print as Bell, who had already greeted them and ushered them into the library himself — the office being closed for the holiday — came through the door with a file in his hand. He was wearing jeans and a polo shirt, but didn't seem too put out by their arrival, given he was already working anyway. The rest of the building seemed empty.

"That one's my favourite," he said, following Smith's gaze.

"It's a great line," Smith agreed as Bell sat and opened the file folder.

"So, what can I help you with, detectives?" They had kept the explanation for their visit vague on the phone, but Bell had obviously come to his own conclusions about the purpose.

"We're investigating Curtis Ritchie's murder, and our inquiries led us to Nancy Ridgeway. We understand you represented her."

Bell nodded. "Yes, I did. But surely you don't think she's a suspect. She wouldn't harm a fly."

"No, she's not a suspect at this time, but we are interested in her paternity claim."

Bell crossed his arms and leaned back in his chair. "It's a bit of a sad story, really. She's basically a good kid who got mixed up with the wrong guy."

"You mean Curtis Ritchie?"

Bell nodded.

"So you think he's the father of Nancy Ridgeway's child?"

"I have no doubt."

"Then why didn't she pursue the claim?"

"You'd have to ask her that, but I suspect it had a lot to do with family pressure, and appearances."

Smith looked up from his notes. "We met her parents this morning, and I can see what you mean about their not wanting the claim going through the courts. Who could blame them?"

"Yeah. I've known John Senior for twenty years. He's a good man, and I know he's crushed by this whole thing. Since Nancy's still a minor, he had the final say on the litigation."

"What about John Junior?" Marshall asked.

Bell's face hardened at the sound of the name. "What about him?"

"Do you know him well?"

"Not really."

"Was he involved in the claim?"

"Most of the meetings were at the family home, and he was there, though I think he's moved out since."

Smith nodded. "Yeah, we've been to his place. He should probably have toughed it out at home for a few more years."

Bell grinned. "To be honest with you, I always felt that it was John Junior who convinced Nancy's folks to file the claim in the first place. I took instructions from the father, as Nancy's legal guardian, but I think his son was egging them on."

"Nancy mentioned it settled for fifty thousand. That doesn't sound like a lot of money."

"It's not. I advised them against accepting it, but by then I think John Senior had stopped listening to his son, and Nancy had lost heart. It had already started to become unpleasant."

"How so?"

"Ritchie's lawyers wanted Nancy examined by an independent gynecologist, and they sent out a letter threatening all sorts of things, including a counterclaim for defamation, recovery of astronomical medical costs, that sort of thing. It was all smoke and mirrors, but it was clear they were going to fight the thing to the end." Bell unfolded his arms and leaned over the table. "Like I said, I advised him against settling for that amount, as I think it was my duty to do. But deep down I was glad he didn't listen. It would have torn them apart."

"What about John Junior? How did he feel about the settlement?"

"He wasn't really in the mix by the time it got to settlement. He wasn't at the last meeting we had to discuss it."

"Were you surprised?"

"A little, I guess. He certainly seemed to be pushing it in the beginning."

"So when, exactly, did you settle?"

Bell reached for the file folder, opened it, and flipped to a lawyer's letter with a cheque stub on top. Even looking at it upside down, Smith could see the amount of fifty thousand dollars, and the name of the payee: Derek Bell and Associates.

"Who's the cheque from?" he asked.

Bell looked at the stub, and his eyebrows rose just a little. "I was assuming it was the other lawyer's trust account — my paralegal processes all of the cheques — but it's actually from a numbered company."

"Is that unusual?"

"Not really, though it's usually either from the opposing firm or directly from an insurance company."

"And this isn't?"

"I don't think so, but to be honest, I never checked. Like I said, I don't really get involved in processing the cheques. Besides, the funds cleared and everyone was happy. Well, sort of."

"Can we get the number?"

"I don't see why not. It's 819640 Ontario Ltd."

"Thanks." Smith scribbled the name in his notebook. "I see the cheque was made out to your firm. Is that normal?"

"Yes. Our fees and disbursements are deducted, and the balance is paid to the plaintiff. In this case, it was to John Senior, because of Nancy's age. I can give you the exact amount, if you think it might be relevant. I only charged them ten percent."

"If you wouldn't mind."

"It was forty-three thousand, even."

Smith pictured the Ridgeways around the kitchen table looking at the cheque, which seemed like a paltry sum for all their troubles.

"Any idea what they planned to do with the money?"

"None of my business, but if I know John Senior, it will be put away for the benefit of his daughter and her baby."

"And John Junior wouldn't have any right to any of it?"

"Not unless they had some kind of agreement within the family, but I doubt it."

Marshall resumed with a few more questions before they thanked Bell and headed out into the warm afternoon sunshine.

"So?" Marshall said, as Smith fumbled with his notebook, feeling a sudden and powerful urge to smoke. He tried to focus on the case instead.

"I'm gonna give commercial crimes this company and see what comes back. If it's not an insurer, who would be paying Ritchie's debts?"

"Lifestyles of the rich and famous…. Maybe some slush fund in the Caymans."

"But this was before he was drafted, remember?"

"True."

Smith placed the call as they began strolling back toward the OPP detachment. Smith had just finished his call when his phone rang again. He said a few words, looked at his watch, then hung up.

"What's up?"

"That was Howard. Gravelle — the dishwasher — called. He's on his way to the station. Howard's going to meet us there," he added.

They were less than a hundred feet from the detachment, almost at the crosswalk, when the air filled with the throaty roar of a sports car's engine.

"There he is now," Smith said, turning to see the shiny new Mustang pull up at the light.

❋ ❋ ❋

"Thanks for coming in," Smith said as he took a seat between Marshall and Howard. Stephen Gravelle sat opposite, looking decidedly hung over, and nervous.

"Do you prefer Steve or Stephen?"

"Steve's fine."

Smith pointed to the little black ball affixed to the wall by the door. "Just so you know, that's recording video and audio."

Gravelle shrugged. "Uh, okay."

"I understand you work at the Hard Luck Cafe, is that right, Steve?"

"Used to, yeah." Gravelle was dressed in shorts and a checkered shirt, and Smith's well-trained nose picked up the smell of stale smoke from the cotton.

"You don't work there anymore?"

"No, I quit. I'm going to Trent now."

"When did you quit?"

"I don't know. Around the beginning of May, I guess."

"Summer off, huh? Nice. What are you studying at Trent?"

"Psychology."

Good luck finding a job with that one, Smith thought, as he made a note. "But you did work at the Hard Luck, back in the spring of this year?"

"Yeah."

"And you did witness an altercation between Curtis Ritchie and John Ridgeway?"

"Yeah."

"Can you tell us about that?"

Gravelle fidgeted in his chair. "Look, is this to do with Curtis Ritchie's ... murder?"

"Yes, as we said at the start, we're investigating his death."

"Should I have a lawyer here, with me, I mean ..."

"Steve, we might be getting a little ahead of ourselves here. You signed a statement regarding the incident at the Hard Luck. That's what we want to ask you about. You're not a suspect in his murder, and you don't need a lawyer, but if you want one, you're perfectly within your rights to call one right now if you'd like."

Gravelle's shoulders dropped a couple of inches and the tension in his posture seemed to flow out of him.

"Would you like to get a lawyer, Steve?"

"No, that's fine."

"Okay, why don't you just tell us what you saw?"

"Nancy and Curtis Ritchie came through the kitchen doors, yelling at each other. I guess it had started out front."

"What were they yelling about?"

"She was crying," Gravelle said, leaning back in his chair. "Saying why don't you love me anymore, that sort of thing. He was calling her names."

"Like what?"

"He called her a slut, and a whore, I think. He said the baby wasn't his and she was just a gold digger. That's when Johnny came in."

"Her brother, John Ridgeway?"

Gravelle nodded. "He must have been out front when they started arguing, and followed them in."

"Go on," Smith prompted.

"He and Ritchie had some words, and then Nancy was saying something and Ritchie shoved her and called her a whore again. That's when Johnny lost it."

"How'd he lose it?"

"He took a swing at Ritchie, but he missed. I think he was kinda drunk. Ritchie just shoved him to the floor and pinned him down."

"What was Nancy doing?"

"She was crying, telling him to leave her brother alone. That's when Johnny said he was gonna kill him."

"Do you remember what he said, exactly?"

"It's in my statement, but I think he said he was gonna cut his heart out, something like that."

"You don't remember?"

Gravelle paused, looking first at Marshall then back to Smith. "Yeah, I remember. He said he was gonna cut his fucking heart out."

"What did Ritchie do?"

"He just laughed. Nancy begged him to leave, and he did."

"He didn't say anything else?"

"No ... well, he called John a loser and then he got off him, then he left. That was pretty much it."

Smith nodded. Given the fact that it was Ritchie pinning Ridgeway down when the threat was uttered, not to mention the obvious provocation, he could understand why no charges were laid. Gravelle's recollection was in line with his statement, as well. He decided to try a different tack.

"So you quit your job ... when was that again?"

"Early May, I guess."

"So, a few weeks after the incident at the Hard Luck?"

"I guess so, yeah."

"I couldn't help admiring your Mustang earlier today. Your mom said you got it this summer."

"Um-hmm," Gravelle muttered, shifting his weight on the chair and crossing his arms.

"Anyone else talk to you about the incident at the Hard Luck, besides the OPP?"

"No," he replied quickly.

"You sure about that?"

Gravelle paused, looked down at the table, then up at Smith. "Well, there was one guy."

"This guy, did he get in touch with you, or the other way around?"

"Naw, he called me…. Look … I can't … if I …" Gravelle stopped and squirmed some more. Smith let the silence linger for a few more seconds before continuing.

"I'm only going to say this once, Steve. A young man is dead, quite probably murdered. This is an official investigation and I expect answers to my questions. If you hold out on me, you're going to find yourself in a whole lot of trouble, real quick. Do we understand each other?"

Gravelle nodded, his eyes pleading.

"Did someone pay you to keep quiet about what you saw at the Hard Luck?"

"If I tell, I'll have to give it back." Gravelle was in obvious distress, blurting out the words.

"Someone paid you and told you that if you ever said who it was from, you'd have to pay it back?"

Gravelle nodded.

"Who was it that you talked to?"

"He said he represented Curtis."

"Was he a lawyer?"

"I don't think so."

"An agent?"

"Maybe. I think so…. I really don't know. I only ever talked to him on the phone. He told me I could never tell anyone, or I'd have to pay it back. What am I gonna do?"

"How much money did he pay you, this agent?"

"Fifty thousand dollars."

Smith looked at Marshall.

"Do you know if this agent paid anything to John or Nancy Ridgeway?"

Gravelle shook his head. "I don't know. I haven't talked to Johnny since that night. I don't really like him."

"What about Nancy?"

"She didn't say, and I lost touch with her after I quit."

"How'd you get the money?"

"They couriered a cheque. It was here two days after I talked to the guy."

"You still have the stub?"

"I doubt it … maybe. I don't know. Are you gonna charge me?"

Smith sighed and stood up, motioning for Marshall and Howard to join him. "Relax, Steve. You haven't done anything wrong, as far as I can tell. Just sit tight for a sec. I'll be right back."

Marshall was first to speak when the door was closed behind them. "That fucking agent's got some explaining to do, that's for sure."

Smith nodded. "And I want to talk to John Ridgeway again. I got a feeling he was paid off by the same person, which is why he lost interest in his sister's claim so easily."

"So Ridgeway buys a truck and Gravelle a Mustang. Not exactly low-profile. Then again, like you told him," Marshall gestured toward the door to the interview room. "There's nothing illegal about taking the money."

"Yeah, I'm not sure any of this really helps us, but I'd love to know more about Ridgeway before we cross him off our list. I'm also curious to know whether the payments to Gravelle and Nancy Ridgeway came from the same source. I wonder where we are on the warrant."

"What about him?" Marshall gestured toward Gravelle. "Poor kid's probably shitting himself in there."

"I guess we cut him loose, but maybe we can find out who the payee on the cheque was first."

"I can go back home with him, see if he's got the stub," Howard offered.

Smith was about to respond when his phone rang. Marshall and Howard discussed how to deal with Gravelle as Smith wandered off, phone at his ear. He was back a few minutes later.

"What?" Marshall could tell from his partner's expression that there was news.

"That was Beaudoin. Turns out a teammate of Ritchie's from Peterborough came in to give a statement."

"Sayin' what?"

"About a death threat he witnessed being uttered against Ritchie at a Toronto hotel back in March."

"Who threatened him?"

"You're gonna love this," Smith said, putting his phone back in his pocket. "Tom Saunders."

CHAPTER 8

"Wait'll I get my hands on Avery," Marshall said, gripping the wheel as they sped along Highway 7, the early evening sunshine casting the scenic views in an auburn glow. They had filled in some of the details of the Peterborough teammate's testimony since hitting the road, most notably that the argument that led to the threat had to do with Ritchie cutting Saunders loose as his agent, a fact that came as a complete surprise to both investigators.

"Take it easy, will you," Smith said as they came up fast behind a camper trailer with a pair of bicycles strapped to the back. "There'll be plenty of time for you to kick the shit out of Avery when we get back. Not that he's actually done anything."

"What are you talking about?"

"Well, he left some stuff out, there's no question. But in fairness, we didn't ask him how long he'd been representing Ritchie, or who he might have stabbed in the back to get the gig." Smith was sketching on his notebook, drawing lines jutting out from a central circle representing Curtis Ritchie, connecting to everyone that they had come into contact with in the past twenty-four hours. One of the lines led to a circle with a question mark at its centre, representing the man from the video — presumably the killer. He drew another line from the middle circle to a new one, in which he wrote Dan Avery's name.

"What about the payments to Gravelle and John Ridgeway?" Marshall rapped his knuckles on the steering wheel in frustration. "Kind of important information to leave out, no?"

Smith had a few questions of his own for Avery, and he was certain there was a sordid story lurking behind the agent, Gravelle, and especially John Ridgeway, but he wasn't at all sure it was going to lead them any closer to finding Curtis Ritchie's killer. The stepfather had potential though, Smith thought, as he recalled the instant impression the man had made when they first met him with Ellen Ritchie. All Smith could think of was that damning question near the end of the interview: How were they going to pay for the rest of the house? He looked up from his sketch.

"What did Avery say the mother was going to see from the contract? Five hundred grand plus whatever's left of the bonus money?"

"You're thinking it's enough for Saunders to kill him over?"

"Not a bad payday. But he doesn't strike me as being the brightest guy, for some reason. If he did do it, he'll have left clues."

"Maybe." Marshall swung the car over the centre line and pulled it back just as quickly as on oncoming semi rattled by.

"Besides," Smith put the notebook down in his lap, "what if money wasn't the motive, or at least not the main motive?"

"What do you mean?"

"Well, imagine you're the stepdad. Maybe Ritchie wasn't the easiest kid in the world to handle, right? Add to that the fact that both adoptive parents are dead and you're adoptive mom number two's new boyfriend. Probably led to some complications."

"I agree his family history's a fucking mess. Then again, that seems to be the norm these days."

"Fair enough," Smith said. "But then imagine things take a turn for the better. The kid's suddenly on the fast track to the pros, as a number one pick, no less. And who's there to look after his interests? Good ole Stepdad. He's a couple of months from Ritchie getting snapped up in the first round — the beginning of a pretty short road, at the end of which is a contract for millions, and the commission that goes with it — and he gets cut loose. How pissed would *you* be?"

Marshall pulled out to pass the camper as they reached a stretch of double-lane highway. "Pretty pissed. But why'd he wait five months? Besides, as long as Saunders stayed with the mom, he was gonna do okay. Shit, that reminds me; we never got a chance to check out the house they were building."

"I got a feeling we'll be back before long," Smith said

as the shrill ring of his phone pierced the quiet of the car's interior.

"Yeah, Smith here." He scrambled for his pen and started scribbling in his notebook. "No shit? What for?" He scratched a few more notes, then looked over at Marshall. "When on Friday?" There was another pause, followed by more scribbling. "Okay, let me know if you find out anything about the Delaware company."

Marshall stifled a yawn with the back of his hand as Smith ended the call.

"I'm gonna have to stop in Perth for a coffee or I'm gonna drive off the road. What was all that about?"

"John Ridgeway lied to us, for starters. His Easypass account shows he gassed up on Friday evening, around six — almost seventy bucks worth. He told us it had been a week."

"And you said there was only a quarter tank left on the fuel gauge? That means he burned three-quarters of a tank in less than forty-eight hours. That's about what we'll have used by the time we get back to Ottawa."

Smith nodded. "They also accessed his bank account and found a deposit of fifty grand, around the same time Gravelle got his money. Same payee — the Ontario numbered company. They're still checking it out, but one of the shareholders is another numbered company, to which Curtis Ritchie has been making some pretty hefty payments since he signed on with Ottawa."

"This is getting interesting." Marshall glanced at his watch. "When do we interview Avery again?"

"He'll be at the station at seven thirty. We should be there by then. You've even got time for your coffee,"

Smith added, as they passed a giant Tim Horton's billboard, indicating that salvation lay ten kilometres ahead.

❉ ❉ ❉

"So, Dan," Marshall said, as they sat around the table in the same meeting room where they had first interviewed Avery the day before. "We just got back from Peterborough, and we learned all kinds of interesting things."

"Oh yeah?" The interview was only seconds old and the confident façade was already starting to erode. Avery was wearing the same suit as the day before, with a different shirt unbuttoned at the crisp collar.

"You said Nancy Ridgeway's claim was bullshit, and that she dropped it when she realized Ritchie was going to fight it."

"Yeah."

"That's still your understanding of what happened?"

"Look fellas, I don't know what you're getting at. I told you the truth."

"Well, we spoke to Nancy's lawyer, Derek Bell, and he told us the case was settled — for fifty thousand dollars."

"What?"

Marshall nodded. "Do you know Stephen Gravelle?"

Avery was still stung by the figure. It took him a few seconds to shake his head. "I don't think so."

"What about John Ridgeway, Nancy's brother? You ever talk to him?"

"No, Curtis told me about a scuffle he got into with Nancy's brother, but I don't think I've ever heard his first name, to be honest."

"Since we're being honest, I'll tell you who Stephen Gravelle is. He's the dishwasher at the Hard Luck Cafe who witnessed the scuffle between Curtis and John Ridgeway. Turns out he got paid fifty grand, too. So did John."

Avery was looking like the last kid standing at a game of musical chairs as Marshall continued.

"It was hush money, Dan," Marshall said, putting his elbows on the table and leaning toward Avery. "And Gravelle told us the offer was made by Curtis Ritchie's agent. Care to comment?"

Avery was ashen-faced. "I really don't understand. I have never spoken with … never even heard of this Gravelle person. And I certainly didn't offer to pay him anything."

"Have you ever heard of 819640 Ontario Inc.?" Smith asked.

Avery frowned. "No."

"You said you were Curtis Ritchie's business manager as well as his agent. Is that right?"

"Yeah, that's right."

"So you would know about any significant payments he was making, on a regular basis, wouldn't you?"

"I guess so, but it's not like I was his banker or anything." Avery squirmed in his chair. "I didn't supervise his account. I mean, it was his money, after all."

"What about 169421 Ontario Inc. Ever hear of it?"

Avery looked as puzzled to hear of the second numbered company as the first. "No. Listen, guys …"

"Curtis Ritchie made a series of payments to that company totalling more than a hundred and fifty thousand dollars between May and July of this year. Are you telling us that as his business manager you had no idea about those payments?"

Avery had a blank expression on his face. "I … I guess so. I really don't know anything about those payments, and I've never heard of those two companies."

Smith looked at Marshall and nodded toward the door.

"We're gonna take a minute, Dan. You sit tight."

They left the room, stepping into the hallway and closing the door to the interview room.

"He's either a very good liar," Smith said, "or he really doesn't know about the hush money, or the large chunks of dough coming out of Ritchie's account."

Marshall nodded. "Something's weird. It's not the reaction I was looking for."

"You don't suppose Ritchie had another agent?"

"Why would he have two? Why would he want to *pay* for two, apart from anything else?"

"I don't know. It doesn't add up. I was wondering if it was just me." Smith checked his phone for messages and seeing nothing from commercial crimes, he patted Marshall on the shoulder. "Sorry to interrupt. You gonna ask him about the stepfather next?"

"Yeah," Marshall said, opening the door. Avery looked up expectantly as they re-entered the room and took their seats.

"I really don't know why you're asking all these questions about numbered companies, but I'm telling you the truth. I'm starting to wonder if I should have a lawyer here, though."

Marshall smiled. "You're not under arrest, Dan, and this is a voluntary statement."

"But you said it's being recorded," Avery said, his Adam's apple bobbing.

"Standard procedure. This is a homicide investigation."

"So I don't need a lawyer?"

Marshall shrugged his shoulders. "You can call a lawyer anytime you want, but like I said, this is just a statement."

Avery seemed to consider his position for a moment, then nodded. "All right."

"We're just trying to put the pieces of a puzzle together, Dan," Marshall continued. "We hear that Ritchie's agent contacted two people who witnessed a scuffle and paid them significant sums of money for their silence. We're not suggesting that you're lying, but you can understand why we're a little confused right now. Same goes for the payments from Ritchie's account."

Marshall paused, as Avery's brow furrowed in thought.

"I don't suppose it was someone from Ashcroft?" he said, after a long pause.

"Who's Ashcroft?"

"It's a PR firm. A lot of the pros use them."

"You mean to cover stuff up, like that golfer?" Smith had scribbled the name in his book and circled it.

Avery shrugged his shoulders. "I don't know if they represent him — they're pretty secretive — but yeah, that sort of thing would be up their alley."

"Would paying people off to be quiet about events that might damage a professional athlete's reputation be up their alley, too?" Marshall continued.

"You'd have to ask them that."

"Where can we find out more about Ashcroft?"

"I think they're based in DC, but like I said, they're fairly secretive."

"They don't advertise their services?"

"They don't need to. Ask any big-time pro athlete who does their PR, and chances are it's Ashcroft."

"All right," Marshall said, standing to stretch. The five hours he had spent at the wheel were having their effect on his lower back. "What do you know about Tom Saunders?"

Avery gave a grim chuckle. "He's Ellen Ritchie's boyfriend."

"We're told he was representing Curtis, up until around this past March, anyway."

"If he told you that, I wouldn't be surprised, but I don't think *Curtis* ever thought he was representing him."

"How about you, Dan? When did you become Curtis's agent?"

"I've been in touch with him for the past eighteen months or so. We met at an OHL awards banquet."

"When did you sign him up as a client? Officially, I mean."

"Last March."

"That's pretty good timing," Smith commented. "You come on board just in time for him to go number one. You pick up the commission for his rookie contract, and put yourself in position for the big payday in a couple of years, not to mention the commissions on all the endorsement deals. Saunders can't have been too happy."

"Saunders is a moron," Avery sneered. "He's a retired paralegal who thinks he's an agent. As if challenging parking tickets in small claims court somehow qualified him to negotiate complicated multi-million-dollar pro sports contracts."

"But Saunders *did* think he was acting for Ritchie?" Marshall asked, returning to the table.

"I have no idea what he thought he was doing — there was never any agreement between them — but the result sure wasn't of any benefit to Curtis. I spent weeks trying to smooth over Saunders' fuck-ups. He pissed off just about everyone who was interested in Curtis. I know what you're thinking — that I swooped in after he'd done all the work — but it wasn't like that at all." Avery paused to catch his breath.

"Tell us how it was, then," Marshall said, keen to have Avery continue his venting.

"He was like this toxic personality or something. He thought he knew what he was doing, going in tough and holding out. But you need a little honey to catch flies and he was all vinegar. He just irritated everyone, plus he had no idea what he was doing. He was generally a disaster. He pissed off this one hockey equipment maker — I'm talking the biggest one in North America, if not the whole world — so bad that it took me months just to get them back at the table. Curtis would have been signed to a huge endorsement deal by now if it wasn't for Tom Saunders."

"So you acknowledge that Saunders was angry in March, when Curtis formally hired you as his agent and effectively cut him out of any fee he might have gotten from his signing?" Marshall asked.

"Sure. He called me and started mouthing off, saying he was going to sue me for all he was worth. It was all bullshit, and I knew it. I just let him say his piece."

"Did he threaten you physically?"

"No, not really. I mean, the first time he called he was pretty steamed. He's a real hothead, too — another drawback for dealing in the big leagues. I wouldn't be surprised if he threatened to do all sorts of stuff, but I never took it seriously. I knew he was just blowing smoke."

"Did you and Curtis discuss him at all, either before or after you two formally contracted with each other."

"Sure. He told me Saunders just kind of imposed himself on his career ever since he hooked up with Ellen, which is exactly the impression I had. Curtis warned me Saunders'd be pissed off, but to ignore him. He said he'd get over it."

"Did Curtis say whether Saunders was pissed off at him? Or mention any altercation between them, about him signing you up as his agent?"

Avery shook his head. "No. Like I said, he told me I could expect him to be pissed, but he didn't seem concerned himself about Saunders, or mention anything like that."

Marshall looked down at his notes. "We're told Saunders showed up late one night at Curtis's hotel in Toronto and had a blowout — started screaming at Curtis outside his room. Curtis ever mention that?"

Avery shook his head. "No. That's news to me." His expression changed subtly before he spoke again. "Are you guys thinking Saunders may have done this?"

Marshall sighed. "Why don't you let us worry about that, Dan. Right now, we're just looking for straight answers from you."

"Of course."

Smith glanced at the clock and stifled a yawn. They still had a lot of ground to cover, and he could sense his partner's irritation.

"What about Ritchie's contract?" he asked. "Why don't you take us through the details."

❊ ❊ ❊

Smith sat at a table in the corner while Marshall stood at the bar waiting to order their beers. He had his notebook open, and was tracing over the line between the circle at the centre of the page and the name Ashcroft. Commercial crimes had already connected it to a Delaware LLP that owned a hundred percent of one of the numbered Ontario companies that had issued the cheque to John Ridgeway, and he had a feeling the connection to Gravelle's cheque was next. It had been almost 9:00 p.m. by the time they had established the link — too late for further inquiries today — but a call to Ashcroft's head office in DC was the first order of business for the morning.

Staff Sergeant Beaudoin had made the decision to hold off on re-interviewing Tom Saunders until they had done some more legwork. A couple of investigators had left for Toronto, around the time Smith and Marshall were returning from Peterborough, to interview hotel staff and anyone else who might have witnessed the late-night altercation in March between Saunders and Ritchie. Ritchie's autopsy was also scheduled for eleven the next morning, and it was thought wise to have the results in hand before they decided to take a hard look at Saunders.

Smith yawned and stretched his arms over his head. It had been a long day indeed, and he was eager for the first sip of cold lager. He looked toward the bar, unusually crowded for a Sunday night, and thought of his cancelled trip to Toronto, where his buddies were no doubt three sheets to the wind by now. As he continued his scan of the room, he noticed a trio of women at the far end of the bar. When the blonde turned, he felt the air leave his chest as he saw recognition in her eyes. He looked desperately for Marshall, still chatting with the bartender. Looking back at the blonde, she was talking to her friends, and then … heading his way.

"Hi, Jack. How are you?"

It always amazed him how at ease she seemed in his presence, when the sight of her sent him into such turmoil. He had first laid eyes on Lisa White in a courtroom in St. John's, where she was defending a client Smith had arrested for impaired driving. White was a keen young lawyer then, just a couple of years out of law school and looking to make her mark. And the vigour of her cross-examination made it very clear that no one was going to get in the way of that goal. She had spent thirty minutes excoriating him before finally letting Smith down from the stand. Despite the ferocity of her attack, though, he had harboured no ill will toward her. He liked to credit this benevolence to his good-natured spirit, but it likely had more to do with the fact that Lisa White was the most beautiful lawyer he had ever seen. And so, when they bumped into each other down in the coffee line of the nearby food court after the trial was over, he graciously accepted her offer to buy him a cup, just to show that what she had put him through upstairs wasn't personal.

But from that initial encounter, things had quickly become personal, indeed. For Smith, and he was sure she felt the same, those first two years were the happiest of his life. They were well on their way to marriage, kids, a dog, and a picket fence when she suddenly decided that St. John's was too small for her. Although he didn't really understand what it was she was after, it was clear to Smith that she couldn't be happy until she at least tried to find it. So, when a job at a law firm in Ottawa came up, Smith had left his home, family, and friends and a job that he truly loved so that she could follow her dream. The possibility that he might not be a part of it had never even occurred to him.

"Lisa. I haven't seen you in … it's been a while. How you doing?"

"Great. I took the summer off. I was travelling for a while, spent a couple of weeks in St. John's."

"Guess that explains why I haven't seen you around," he said, although they didn't exactly travel in the same social circles. "How'd you manage to take the whole summer off? I thought you lawyers were all obsessed with billing time."

She grinned. "I wasn't off the whole time, just working remotely."

"I'll have to try that sometime."

"So, I guess you're working this Ritchie thing?"

He nodded. "Everyone's working it. I was supposed to be in Toronto this weekend."

"Getting shitfaced with the old gang?"

"Something like that, yeah. Instead, I have to drink with this guy," he said, as Marshall returned with a couple of beers.

"Hi, Lisa."

"Hi, Dave. Listen, I've gotta get going, so I'll leave you two to your beers. I'm sure you've earned them."

"I need a new deodorant or something?" Marshall asked, once she had left.

"Well, I wasn't gonna say anything, Marsh, but …"

"Very funny. What'd she want?"

"Just saying hello. Cheers," Smith said, taking a long sip of the cold beer. They chatted for a while, about things unrelated to the investigation, before they got to the Raftsmen's prospects for the new season. Eventually, they were back to the case, where they both knew they'd end up.

"Still doodling, huh?" Marshall pointed at the diagram on Smith's notebook, sitting open on the table. Apart from a bunch of circles with lines connecting them, the average person would have a hard time making any sense of the chicken scratches.

"We're forty hours in, Marsh, and what have we got?"

"I don't know. I kinda like Saunders for it, don't you?"

"He's a selfish arsehole, but not necessarily a killer."

"Don't you have to be one to be the other?" Marshall chuckled, then grimaced as he leaned back on the seat. "Jeez, my back is killin' me. All that driving."

"You want a hot water bottle, gramps?"

"Don't get smart, or I'll put in a disability claim. You'd probably like that, wouldn't you. You'd try and get partnered up with Giroux," he added, referring to the newest investigator in the major crimes unit, who had just arrived from Montreal. She was young and attractive and, by all accounts, unmarried. "How's your *français*?"

"Fuck you." Smith sipped his beer. He had gone on language training several times in the last few years, and as Marshall well knew, he just didn't seem to have the aptitude for languages. Marshall had been around long enough that the bilingual requirement wasn't formally part of his job description, but, even so, he understood and spoke the language better than his younger colleague.

"So what's on the agenda tomorrow, besides the autopsy?"

"Follow up on Ashcroft, and John Ridgeway's alibi, and flesh out Tom Saunders. That reminds me. I want to talk to Ritchie's junior teammate, Jordan Connolly — find out more about this argument."

"Well, that sounds like a full day right there," Marshall said, draining his beer. "I'm gonna head home and get some shut-eye. You want a ride?"

"Naw, I'm gonna stick around here for a bit and think."

Marshall laughed. "Hell of a place to think, but to each his own. I'll swing by around eight?"

Smith nodded. "Thanks for the beer."

"I just started a tab," Marshall said, as he got up to leave and patted him on the shoulder.

CHAPTER 9

Smith awoke to the sound of a door slamming shut and turned toward his bedside clock radio, squinting as he tried to make out the time. He hadn't heard the alarm, and was trying to remember if he had even set it, when the fog around his brain began to lift and he turned to see the outline of a human form under the comforter next to him. He gently pulled back the covers to reveal a tangle of blonde hair and bare shoulders.

His surprised pleasure was interrupted by the sound of footsteps in the hallway and the jangling of keys.

"Jack? You in there?"

Panic seized him as the familiar voice from the hallway registered and images from the previous evening flooded his mind: the encounter with Lisa … sitting at her table … leaving the bar with her just after midnight.

"I brought coffee, two creams, one sugar — just the way you like it. I figured you're …"

The voice trailed off as its speaker arrived at the bedroom door and took in the sight of Smith sitting up in bed, shirtless, next to the slowly rousing figure next to him, then the rumpled clothing and discarded lingerie on a bedside chair.

"What the *fuck*?"

White stirred, opening her eyes just in time to see the launch of the coffee cup, and to duck back under the covers before it exploded on the headboard, sending scalding coffee splattering everywhere.

"Jesus!" Smith yelped, clutching at his neck.

"You piece of shit!" The voice breaking as the woman turned from the bedroom door.

"Alison, wait!" Smith bolted out of bed, grabbing a T-shirt to cover himself as he raced down the hallway, just in time to see the front door slam. He jerked it open and saw her at the end of the hall. "Alison! I can explain. I just …" He set off after her as she disappeared into the stairwell, and was gaining on her by the time they reached the ground floor.

"Just let me talk to you."

"Stay away from me, you bastard," she yelled over her shoulder, as she swung the front door open and fled into the cool morning air. Smith stopped on the top step, seeing no point in pursuing her further. What was there to say, really? Besides, he was suddenly aware of the seasonal shift to autumn as he clutched the T-shirt closer to his privates and turned to go back inside, just as he caught sight of Marshall's car pulling into the parking lot, and his partner's wide-eyed expression.

Returning to his apartment, Smith checked the damage in the mirror by the front door. There was an angry red blotch on the right side of his neck, where the coffee had splattered, and the initial sting was morphing into a raw ache. He shook his head as he padded back down the hall. When he reached the bedroom, Lisa was sitting on the edge of the bed, buttoning her blouse.

"Guess that was Alison?"

"Yeah, she's … anyway, she's gone."

"I can see that," White said, getting up to slip on her jeans. "You all right?" She was looking at his neck, and the growing patch of red.

"I'll survive. Listen, you don't have to rush off. We could get some breakfast…."

She waved a hand. "Listen, Jack. Last night was fun, but I really think I should go now."

"Come on, don't be like that," he said, as he held her in his arms. She looked up at him, kissed him on the cheek, and then gently pushed him away.

"I'll see you around, Jack."

"Well, let's at least have lunch or a drink or something soon," he called after her as he threw on a pair of shorts.

"I'm kinda busy the next couple of days," she replied, reaching the door to the apartment and finding her shoes. "You know, back to work and all that. But sure, let's talk later in the week."

She blew him a kiss and opened the door to reveal Marshall standing there with a tray of coffees and an even more surprised look on his face than the one he had sported in the parking lot.

"Hi, David." She glanced at the coffee. "You're not gonna toss those at him, are you?"

"What?"

"See you, guys."

Smith could only smile as he watched her leave. "You don't want to know, believe me," he said, stepping aside to let his partner in.

Marshall handed him one of the coffee cups and headed toward the sofa, where he settled in, took a sip of his own coffee, and smiled. "Oh, yes I do."

❄ ❄ ❄

Smith sat at his desk, tapping his fingers in frustration as he waited with the phone at his ear. He had been on the line with Ashcroft for at least fifteen minutes and gotten precisely nowhere, despite progressing through an automated telephone tree and two actual people. He was running out of patience as a third voice came on the line.

"Yes?"

"Look, I'm calling from the Ottawa Police, and I'm getting ..."

"Where?"

"The Ott — Who am I speaking with, please?"

"Customer service." Smith detected a slight drawl in the woman's voice.

"Where did you say you were calling from?"

"Canada," Smith said, casting a broader geographic reference and hoping she had heard of the country immediately to her north.

"Yes, sir. What can I do for you?"

"I'd like to speak to someone regarding one of your firm's clients."

"I'm sorry, sir, we don't disclose any information about our clients."

"This is a homicide investigation, ma'am. I'm sure you don't want to be obstructing —"

"I'll refer you to legal."

"Wait —" The muzak returned and Smith banged his forehead on his arm as Marshall came over.

"What's goin' on? You've been on the phone forever."

"These people are unbelievable. Talking to someone in authority is like getting an audience with the Pope."

"I'm gonna grab a coffee. You want me to throw one your way?"

Smith looked up to see his partner's smile.

"That's good, Marshy. You been working on that one all morning?"

"Just think how lucky you are that you take two creams, otherwise you might be spending the morning at the burn unit."

"You're a fucking riot … hello? Yes, this is Detective Jack Smith, Ottawa Police. Is this the legal department? I'm an investigator in Ottawa, Canada. I'm trying to get in touch with someone in your firm who can answer some questions relating to one of your clients. These questions are part of an active homicide investigation and I've been getting nothing but —"

"Detective, I'm sure your questions are important, but we have very strict disclosure rules," a cool voice at the other end replied.

"Are you refusing to co-operate?"

"We'd be more than happy to co-operate, sir," the woman replied, her voice taking on a superior tone, indicative of someone used to slamming the door shut on inquiries. "But only with a subpoena. You'll understand, our discretion regarding client data is the cornerstone of our business."

"You want me to get a warrant?"

"As I said, we'd be happy to comply with a subpoena."

Smith stared at the clock. It was almost nine. He had wasted forty minutes just to be politely told to go screw himself. "Fine, I'll get a warrant. Before you go, can you at least confirm Curtis Ritchie is one of your clients?"

"Like I said, Detective, I can't disclose any —"

"Are you guys like the CIA or something?"

"Have a great day, Detective."

Smith slammed down the phone in frustration.

"Take it easy on the office equipment, Smith." He looked up to see Staff Sergeant Al Beaudoin's enormous frame looming over him. His top button, as usual, was undone and his tie askew.

"That was Ritchie's PR firm, who won't tell me a friggin' thing without a warrant."

"So get one."

"They're in Washington. Isn't that going to be complicated?"

"We do it all the time. Talk to … who did that, not long ago?" Beaudoin asked, his brow creasing in thought. "Schneider," he said, snapping his fingers. "You're talking about the outfit commercial crimes linked to the cheques paid to the Peterborough witnesses?"

Smith nodded.

"Get on it, then. Go to DC yourself if you have to. I want everything they've got on Ritchie. I have a feeling it's lots."

❊ ❊ ❊

Smith stood in the viewing gallery, feeling his stomach churn as the pathologist began his examination of Curtis Ritchie's lifeless body. The skin had a greyish tint, flawless in the fluorescent light but for the scar that crossed the left side of his chest. It had looked a vibrant pink when they had dragged Ritchie from the canal on the morning of his death, blood still oozing out around the knife. Now the murder weapon was safely bagged and sitting in the evidence room, and the scar itself looked less dramatic, edged in bluish-grey. Ritchie's face had a restful expression, again in stark contrast to the wide-eyed stare that had greeted them when they had pulled back the waterlogged mess of hair covering it that morning. The tabloids had dissed Ritchie's unruly mop, calling it a prime example of helmet-hair gone wild. For some reason, as he stood there staring at Ritchie's corpse, Smith recalled a particular headline: "Can't Ritchie Rich Afford a Barber?"

"Eighteen-year-old male, Caucasian," Dr. Greg Lake began, snapping on rubber gloves and approaching the table. He seemed to pause as the age was uttered aloud, the same thought likely running through everyone's mind: *What a waste*. Lake proceeded with the examination of Ritchie's hands and feet, noting the lack of any obvious defensive wounds.

"There's nothing visible under the fingernails, and we've already swabbed and found no foreign skin or hair. That's not to say it wasn't washed off by his time in the canal. Apparently, the water in there's got some fairly astringent properties. Not a bad place to dump a body if you want to wash off physical evidence, according to the identification officers," he said, looking up to viewing gallery. "But I digress."

Lake turned his attention to Ritchie's head and neck area, feeling his scalp and looking in his ears, nose, and throat with a flashlight. "No bruising or other signs of trauma," he said, as he completed the examination of the head and moved to the wound on Ritchie's chest. "Wound of approximately six inches in length, starting laterally at the third intercostal space and traversing medially — that's right to left," he said, looking up at his audience before continuing. "Transecting all great vessels and myocardium and lung parenchyma in its lethal course. The location of the wound, its angle and depth — indicative of extreme force — all suggest a left-handed attacker. The wound ends where steel met bone and the knife became permanently lodged on the left side of the sternum, where it remained until the body was removed from the water."

Lake paused and looked up at his audience.

"Said weapon being a filleting knife — extremely sharp, and with a blade of approximately six inches. It was lodged in the soft tissue above the ventricular cavity. We'll be able to be a little more precise as to the internal damage caused in a few moments."

Smith had heard enough about the knife already — that it was sharp, that it lacked any fingerprints or other identifying marks, and that it had been mass-produced before being discontinued and removed from most retail shelves at least three years before. To the best of the knowledge of the ident officer who'd done the legwork, there was no way to narrow the list of possible owners in any meaningful way. In short, the knife was a dead end.

"I'm assuming that's the cause of death, is it, Doc?" Marshall piped up.

Lake frowned. "We should never assume, though you're probably half right."

Marshall looked puzzled.

"I suspect cause of death was actually drowning. Do we know if he could swim?"

Marshall looked at Smith, who shrugged his shoulders.

"Sorry to interrupt, Doc," Marshall said, as Lake began prodding at the wound with an assortment of tools.

"My, my," the pathologist muttered as he craned to look into the opening. "Whoever did this was capable of extreme force. The blade seems to have been embedded into the sternum. I'm guessing his aorta was severed as the blade made its way across, but either way, the tract slashed by the passage of the knife, and the resulting massive blood loss would have been instantly lethal."

Lake turned to a side table, from which he selected a little handsaw. "And now," he said, looking at Marshall as he hit the power switch and the blade whirred into action. "Let's find out if his lungs are dry."

❈ ❈ ❈

Smith sat at his desk, poring over the autopsy report, jotting notes of Ritchie's height, weight, and eye colour as well as scribbling a little diagram of the chest wound. As he read the words, the high-pitched whirr of the bone saw and the sickening sound and smell it made as it cut through Curtis Ritchie's chest returned in vivid detail. He had been to dozens of autopsies, and he had grown somewhat used to the sight of watching a human body being torn apart like some laboratory frog, but that sound never failed to unsettle him. He knew he would never get used to it, and maybe that wasn't a bad thing.

"Hungry?"

Smith looked up at Marshall. He seemed serious.

"How can you even think of eating?"

"Ah, come on. We got a full afternoon, you know. Can't work on an empty stomach."

"You go ahead. I'll grab something later — much later."

"Suit yourself. I just bumped into Schneider. He says his American contact told him we can execute a warrant in DC same day, no problem."

"I didn't think you could do anything cross-border on the same day."

"Yeah, who would of thought, huh? Anyway, we should get the warrant later this afternoon. We could take the early flight tomorrow and be back in time for dinner."

"Is that all you ever think about, food?"

"I'll bring you back a sandwich. You know you're gonna be starving later. What time's the interview with Connolly?"

Smith looked at his watch. "Half an hour."

"I'll hurry back."

119

❄ ❄ ❄

Smith picked up his cellphone and read the text for the tenth time. It was from Lisa, and he'd received it just after Marshall had gone for lunch. He was running out of time if he wanted to get back to her before the interview. The message was on the wordy side — always a bad sign with her — but the gist was clear. Last night was a mistake and should not be misinterpreted as a possible reconciliation. He had known it himself, of course, but the familiar warmth at the memory of her lying in his bed this morning, in the apartment they had shared until a couple of years ago, was hard to resist. So was the illusion that they could just pick up where they had left off. Was he so easy to read that she felt the need to nip the idea in the bud? He had long ago given up on trying to stick to any strategy with her — he knew it was hopeless. He punched her number in and was about to hit the dial button, but he hesitated. What was he supposed to say? Let's give it another shot?

The night before, after he had manoeuvred himself into her path at the bar, she had revealed that her on-again, off-again relationship was off again. That was all it had taken to keep him at the bar instead of home catching some much-needed sleep, or repairing the faltering relationship with Alison that was now over for good. But there was no comparison, as evidenced by the ease with which he and Lisa had laughed about old times together — the transition to his bed being seamless. But they were each retreating to established patterns for very different reasons. He knew she was using him to get over someone else, and he had even told himself that he couldn't expect more, but it didn't matter. He redialed her number just as Marshall appeared over his shoulder.

"He's here."

"Who?" Smith hit the button to abort the call.

"Who do you think? Jordan Connolly. I bumped into him downstairs."

"I'm coming." Smith reached for his notebook and realized he hadn't finished preparing his questions. He was annoyed at himself as they arrived at the interview room. He had neither the time nor the energy to devote to a romantic reunion he knew was hopeless. He would send Lisa a reply later.

Don't worry, it meant nothing to me either....

Smith was surprised to see two people waiting in the room. Next to a shaggy-haired kid, who looked like he should be out delivering papers, sat a man in his late fifties. Then he remembered Connolly was still a minor.

"You're Jordan's father?" Marshall asked as the two Connollys stood.

"Keith Connolly," he said, offering a hand across the table. "Jordan's my boy." Marshall shook hands and introduced Smith, and they all took a seat.

"Thanks for coming in," Smith began. "They explained on the phone why we wanted to talk to your son, Mr. Connolly?"

"Call me Keith. Yes, I spoke to another detective, and he said you had some more questions for Jordan, about Curtis."

"That's right," Smith said. "And just so you know, we're going to be recording this statement — standard procedure."

Connolly Senior looked at his son and nodded. "That's fine."

Smith smiled at Jordan Connolly. "So, I understand that you witnessed an incident between Curtis and his stepfather, is that right, Jordan?"

"Well, my dad called it in, actually, after I mentioned it to him. We were talking about what happened to Curtis and everything, and well, it made me think of that night."

"Okay, we'll get to that night, but why don't we start with the basics. How did you know Curtis Ritchie?"

Jordan Connolly looked to his father and waited for his nod before he started to speak. "We were teammates in Peterborough — linemates, actually — and we roomed together on the road last year."

Smith nodded. "So you knew him pretty well, then?"

"Yeah, I guess so. It was his last year and my first, so it was just the one season, but I'd say we got to know each other pretty good."

"What did you think of him?"

"He was a good guy. I mean, he was an amazing hockey player, obviously, but he was nice too, you know?"

"All those goals, and all those scouts drooling over him, didn't go to his head, just a little?" Smith smiled.

Connolly shuffled in his chair. "Well, he was very … confident. I know some people said he was kind of, like, arrogant. He sure was always in the spotlight, wherever we played, but like I said, he was always pretty good with me."

"How did he feel about being in the spotlight, as you put it?"

"I think he found it tiring sometimes, having everyone crowding around after every game, asking about every play he made, about his future, whatever."

"Did Curtis talk to you about his future at all?"

"Not really. I mean, we all knew he was gonna go number one, but it was just a question of where. Everyone knew Florida had the first pick, but that they were probably going to trade it — they're rebuilding and need a whole new roster, not just one player."

"Did Curtis ever mention Ottawa to you as a possible destination?"

"No." Connolly laughed. "I don't think anyone would have predicted he'd end up here."

Smith remembered the rumours around the time of the draft, when most of the pundits were picking either New York or Chicago to make a play for Ritchie. There was even a theory that Toronto might go after him, but no one thought Ottawa was in the mix.

"Let's talk about that night in Toronto. Do you recall what the date was?"

"Yeah, I looked it up on a calendar before I came in today — the fifteenth of March. We were in Toronto for a Saturday night game and we were going on to Ottawa on Sunday, so we stayed the night in a hotel instead of bussing out right after the game. I think it was kinda like a reward for playing well. We won the game four-three in overtime. Curtis scored the game winner. I got one in the third, too, so I remember it well."

"So, did you have a bit of a celebration afterward?"

"Yeah, a bunch of us went out, had a bit of fun." Connolly looked down at his hands, glancing quickly to his side.

Smith smiled. "Listen, Jordan. We know you're underage, but we're not looking to get you or anyone else in any trouble if you had a beer or two. Your dad's probably not gonna be too shocked either," he added, with a wink at Keith Connolly, who patted his son on the shoulder.

"Boys will be boys."

"So you hit a few bars before heading back to the hotel?" Smith prompted.

"Yeah, we hit a few places, had a couple of beers. It was probably after one by the time we got back."

"What happened then?"

"Well, Curtis and me were heading down the hall toward our room, when someone called out from behind us. Turned out to be his stepdad, or whatever — his mom's boyfriend."

"Tom Saunders?"

"Yeah."

"Had you ever met him before? Did you recognize him?"

"Yeah, I'd seen him at games, and practices. But not like this. He was coming down the hall, yelling at Curtis and looking … kinda drunk, I guess. He wasn't walking straight, and he was slurring some of his words."

"What was he yelling about?"

"He was mad, I guess. He was calling Curtis names."

"What kind of names?"

"He called him an ungrateful bastard." Connolly paused, looking at his father.

"It's okay," Keith Connolly assured him. "Tell them what you heard."

"He called him a slimy little fucker, and he said if he thought he was going to get away with it, he had another thing coming."

"What was Curtis's reaction?"

"Scared, I think. I know I was, kind of. He's a pretty big guy, and he didn't look too happy. We kind of ran to the door but Curtis couldn't get the key to work — the light kept coming up red every time he swiped the card."

"What happened then?"

"When Saunders got to us, he grabbed Curtis by the shirt and pushed him up against the wall and just kept yelling."

"What did Curtis do?"

"He just threw up his hands, to protect himself, you know. I was trying to pull the guy off, but it wasn't working. He shoved me and I fell, then he turned to Curtis and I thought he was gonna hit him, but he didn't."

"What'd he do?"

"He let him go, and he started shaking. He was still talking but he was, like crying, almost, or something."

"What was he saying?"

"Just stuff like I can't believe you did this, and how could you." Connolly shrugged. "While he was doing that, I picked up the card off the floor and got the room door open. Curtis saw me and managed to slip away from Saunders, and we slammed the door shut and bolted it."

"What did Saunders do?"

"He pounded on the door, started swearing again, then stopped. I was watching through the peephole as he stood there. He wasn't crying anymore. He was mad again. He yelled out he was gonna kill him and then he left."

"What exactly did he say?"

"He said 'I'll fucking kill you for this, Curtis, I swear to God.'"

Smith looked up from his notes. "And then he left?"

"Yeah."

"Did you call for help or anything?"

"No. We figured he wasn't coming back. I don't know why. We probably should have called someone, but we didn't."

"Was there anyone else around, in other rooms, when this was going on?"

"There was a guy down the hall, poked his head out when Saunders had Curtis pinned against the wall, but Saunders told him to get lost ... or whatever, and he went back inside."

"What about your other teammates? Any of them witness this?"

"No." Connolly shook his head. "We were the only ones in that section of the hotel. Everyone else was in a different wing."

"Do you know what they were arguing about? Why Saunders was so upset?"

"After Saunders left, Curtis told me it had to do with him hiring Avery as his agent. Curtis said it was all bullshit, that it would blow over and that he wasn't worried."

Smith paused to write some notes, then looked up at Connolly. "What about you, Jordan. Were you worried?"

"I wouldn't have been, if I hadn't seen his eyes."

"What did you see in Saunders' eyes?"

"Murder," Connolly said, looking to his father, then back at Smith. "I saw murder."

CHAPTER 10

Smith lay back in bed listening to the sounds of day-break outside the open window. His hand caressed the blonde hair fanned out over his chest as Lisa slept next to him, her head resting on his chest and rising with his every breath. He didn't want to get up, ever, but there was something weighing on his conscience — something was wrong. He closed his eyes to escape the nagging fear, but was confronted by Curtis Ritchie's vacant stare as his waterlogged body was dragged from the canal. Ritchie's eyes kept their fixed gaze but his lips, blue from oxygen deprivation and the cold of the water, were moving, struggling to utter unintelligible words. Smith was back in his bed again, but Lisa was headed for the door, and no matter how he tried to catch up to her or make her listen, he couldn't reach her.

"We're getting ready to land," the flight attendant said, her hand on the button that had jolted his seat-back upright again.

Smith rubbed his eyes as he adjusted to the bright sunlight streaming in through the windows.

"Good snooze?"

"Yeah, I guess so." He registered Marshall sitting next to him, flipping through a magazine.

"You were having some kinda dream, by the sounds of it."

"What?" Smith was suddenly wary of what his subconscious might have revealed in his sleep.

"You were jerking around like a piñata, and you were babbling about something."

"What, were you taking notes?" He stretched his arms overhead. "I don't suppose I solved the case, did I?"

Marshall snorted. "Fat chance. You kept saying no, but that was about all I could understand."

"Man, I needed that." Smith looked out the window, glad to have slept through most of the early morning flight. He only wished he had stayed out for the landing. His stomach lurched as the plane bumped its way through a cloud and the ground came into view again, cars streaming down the freeway below like toys on a track. He looked at his watch. "We're gonna be early."

"Not really. It's been a while since my last time in DC, but I think it's like forty minutes into town from Dulles."

"I'm gonna need a coffee before we hit the —" Smith was interrupted by a loud thud from somewhere beneath them, followed by a mechanical whirr. "What the fuck was that?"

"Relax, will you? It's the landing gear."

Smith laughed to conceal his racing heart. The plane was a little inter-city job with its best years behind it from what he could tell, and he didn't like the noises it was making, or its jerky descent. He pretended to look out the window and closed his eyes as Marshall chatted away, but Curtis Ritchie's vacant stare was waiting for him. Maybe it was better than the sight of Lisa leaving him behind for the last time.

❊ ❊ ❊

They sat in the reception at Ashcroft, stunned into silence by the opulence of their surroundings. The vastness of the triple-height atrium was impressive in itself, and no expense had been spared in the decoration. An assortment of magazines lay in meticulous order on one of the enormous glass tables, cut flowers in a crystal vase on another. The muted air was punctuated by the distant clicking of heels on the marble floors and by the subtle tone of the receptionist's phone. Located on E Street, just around the corner from the Hoover building, the six-storey mix of glass and metal bore no indication of the identity of its occupant, other than a subtle etching of the name into the glass behind the reception desk. The sound of approaching footsteps alerted them to the arrival of their host, Chad McCleod, whose voice Smith instantly recognized from the brief phone call from the Canadian Embassy, an hour before.

"Welcome to Washington," McCleod said, greeting them with a firm handshake. In his early forties and well over six feet, with prematurely grey hair that looked shellacked in place, McCleod was as immaculate as the décor, clad as he was in a blue pinstripe suit, crisp white shirt, and lavender tie. "I hope you had a good flight."

They made small talk as McCleod led them past the reception desk, though Smith couldn't shake his irritation at all of the niceties when the only reason they were here was that Ashcroft had refused to even acknowledge Ritchie as a client over the phone. They arrived at a meeting room where another suit sat waiting.

"This is Dick Watkins," McCleod said, as the other man got up to greet them, "from legal."

"I guess this is for you, then," Marshall said, handing over the subpoena. They had gone straight to the Canadian Embassy from the airport, where they had met with an RCMP liaison officer who had helped them through the process of having the warrant certified for service in DC.

McCleod seemed to sense the tension. "I want to say two things before we get started," he said, glancing toward the lawyer, who scanned the document and gave a quick nod. "First, I want to apologize for having to be so formal, but in our business it really is unavoidable. The last thing I want to do is waste your time and I can assure you we will do everything in our power to assist you in your investigation. Second, of course, is to say how horrified I was to hear of what happened to Curtis, and to again offer you whatever help I can in your efforts to find his killer."

"Well, we appreciate that, Mr. Mc —"

"Call me Chad, please."

"Chad, right. Anyway, I'm glad everything's in order now," Marshall said, looking to the lawyer, who tucked the subpoena into a buff folder and stood.

"It is, and we appreciate your understanding, gentlemen. With this on file, Chad can now provide full disclosure. I wish you the best of luck with your investigation. Now, if you'll excuse me."

As Watkins left, McCleod pointed to a side table with a pair of silver decanters, and a selection of juices and waters in a large silver bowl filled with ice. "Please help yourself to coffee, or something else."

"We're good, thanks."

"So, where would you like me to start?"

"Maybe you could tell us what you do, exactly."

"Sure. We're a public relations firm, so we look after the media and public relations of our clients. Given the breadth of our client base — Ashcroft's the largest PR firm in the world — that can mean a lot of things. We represent business and political leaders, TV and film celebrities, and, of course, pro athletes."

"So what did you do for Curtis Ritchie?"

"With a client like Curtis, we start by developing a custom-made media strategy," McCleod began, with an enthusiasm that made it clear he enjoyed hearing himself talk. "I worked with him on media messaging … that just means defining the kind of message you want to get out there on a consistent basis, and controlling the venue, like post-game press conferences, radio, television, and print interviews, that sort of thing."

"Isn't that part of what the agent's supposed to do?"

McCleod shook his head. "We're not agents. We're specialized consultants, though we do work hand in hand with agents on some aspects of the overall PR program."

"So you know Dan Avery, then?"

"Yes, he's … he was Curtis's agent."

"Would it surprise you if we told you he never mentioned you, or Ashcroft, when we spoke with him in connection with this investigation?"

McCleod adjusted the perfect knot in his tie. "Not really. Like I said, while there is some interaction between the services we each provide, we do operate independently. I don't know what questions you were asking him, but unless you specifically asked about PR, I don't see why he would have mentioned me, or Ashcroft."

Smith had to hand it to McCleod — he was smooth. Marshall smiled. "You mentioned you look after media messaging and other services. Can you tell us a little more about those other services?"

"Sure. Apart from establishing an overall PR program, we also on occasion respond to particular situations as they arise."

"You mean damage control?" Smith said.

McCleod gave him a thin smile. "That's one way of putting it, but it really just means further tailoring the messaging program to respond to specific situations."

Beginning to tire of the double-speak, Smith decided to ask a more straightforward question and see what McCleod came back with. "Have you ever heard of Nancy Ridgeway?"

"Yes, she was the woman who claimed Curtis had fathered her child."

"What about her brother, John?"

McCleod nodded.

"Is it true you paid John Ridgeway and another witness, Stephen Gravelle, fifty thousand dollars each, to keep quiet about the incident between John and Nancy Ridgeway and Curtis Ritchie, up in Peterborough?"

"Yes, those two individuals received co-operation payments. There's nothing illegal about that, as I'm sure you know."

"That depends on what the money was for, as I'm sure *you* know, Mr. McCleod."

"It's Chad. Look, detectives, it's not like we interfered with their evidence in any way. They both gave statements to the police before we spoke to them. The payments they received were related only to media inquiries, certainly not to any testimony they might be asked to give in a court of law, whether in connection with any criminal charge or a civil suit."

"So you were aware of Nancy Ridgeway's paternity suit?"

"Of course, though my understanding is it was settled between the lawyers. We really weren't involved." McCleod paused, perhaps sensing Marshall's growing irritation. "Look, I know this may seem unusual to you, but this is the norm these days, with the media the way it is, and everyone tweeting and posting real-time camera-phone pictures. Without people like us, none of our clients would be able to accomplish anything. They'd be too busy fighting off bogus claims, whether in print, on TV, or in the courts."

"Like that golfer, you mean?" Smith said, watching McCleod's reaction to the reference to a year-long media frenzy surrounding a married pro golfer and a string of hookers and porn stars. "Sorry, you probably represent him, too."

"I'm afraid I can't comment on that."

"Let's get back to Curtis Ritchie," Marshall said. "Were there other Nancy Ridgeways we should know about?"

"There were no other paternity allegations that I was aware of."

"Let me rephrase the question," Marshall said, leaning forward over the table. "You know why we're here. Curtis Ritchie was killed — we believe murdered — and we want to know who did it, and we're particularly interested in finding out about anyone who might have had an axe to grind with him. Given that information, were there any other 'situations' you were asked to 'manage' for Curtis?"

McCleod smiled, then stood. "Let me get my file."

CHAPTER 11

Smith sat in the rear of the church, scanning the crowd and slotting each of the people into Curtis Ritchie's life. It had been Marshall's idea to come to the funeral, and he had secured approval before they boarded the flight home from Washington the day before. At the time, the prospect of getting back in the car early on Wednesday morning had seemed unnecessarily cruel punishment, but he was glad they were here now.

As he scanned the front row opposite, he took in Ellen Ritchie in a black two-piece suit, complete with a hat and veil. Smith knew little about funeral fashion, but he sensed it was probably a choice, and expensive, outfit. She dabbed under the veil with a handkerchief from time to time, leaning against a sober-looking Tom Saunders. Apparently ill at ease in a dark suit, he kept pulling at his collar as though the starched fabric were choking him. Smith tried to imagine what was going through his mind as the crowd assembled behind him. Was this a moment of quiet relief, after which he was free to enjoy the fruits of Ritchie's labour — specifically, what was left of the signing bonus and the half-million insurance payout? Or was he saying goodbye to the golden goose, having only a cracked egg to hold onto? It still was far from clear, as were a lot of things about the case.

They had left Ashcroft's offices the day before, after three gruelling hours of collecting evidence that had floored them both. Smith had been under no illusions about the kind of trouble an eighteen-year-old jock with too much money could get into, but in his wildest dreams he never would have imagined the debauchery they had uncovered courtesy of the slick Chad McCleod. Apparently, the couple of hundred grand that Ritchie had sent Ashcroft's way had been money well spent. The files were filled with references to Ritchie's numerous interactions with strippers and prostitutes, mostly in Toronto and Miami, where Ritchie had spent part of the summer with a personal trainer. There were also some ill-advised barroom scuffles, not to mention a string of accusations of generally questionable conduct. Ashcroft had been concerned enough by the prospect of Ritchie being unleashed on thirty cities over the course of a season to recommend a personal PR escort to be assigned full time to keep him out of trouble.

So much for the clean-cut kid image that Ritchie had still managed to project — with the help of Ashcroft's expert media messaging advice, of course. The more important question, for Smith and Marshall, was whether there was someone among all of these encounters who felt aggrieved enough by their interaction with Ritchie to want to stick a knife in his chest.

There were no obvious contenders, but the Ashcroft files were going to generate a lot of follow-up work. There was even someone in Toronto who claimed to be Ritchie's biological mother, but there was nothing to support her claim and her motives had become clearer once her addiction to heroin and crack became evident.

"There's Cormier," Marshall whispered, as the Raftsmen's owner passed them in the aisle and made his way toward the front, with an attractive woman a couple of decades younger on his arm whom Smith recognized as his wife from newspaper pictures of her posing with her favourite charity.

"And McAdam," Smith added, as they saw the GM turn to greet Cormier and his wife. Smith noticed a tall blonde woman at McAdam's side. Even from afar, she was striking. Smith saw her in profile as she moved along the pew to accommodate the new arrivals. As she swept the crowd behind her, she caught Smith staring and he thought he saw a demure smile before she turned back.

"Wow." Marshall had obviously noticed her as well. "McAdam's taking the trophy wife thing to another level."

Smith spotted most of the current roster of the Raftsmen in the crowd, along with another, younger group of athletic types that included Jordan Connolly and many of his other teammates from Peterborough. As the organ played its sombre notes and the last of the funeral-goers pressed into the remaining standing room at the back, Smith turned his attention to the front of the church, and a huge, framed picture of Curtis Ritchie to the right of a lectern, surrounded by flowers. Ritchie's impish grin, framed by his trademark unruly blonde locks, was how most people pictured the young star. No doubt this was the way Ellen Ritchie wanted him remembered, too, whether she knew about the troubled young man in the Ashcroft files or not. He hoped for her sake that she never found out.

❋ ❋ ❋

Filing out of the church into the bright fall sunshine, Smith scanned the sea of media jostling at the security perimeter, television cameras and telephoto lenses trained on the church doors. James Cormier had arranged for the bulk of the Raftsmen's arena staff to attend the funeral, with strict instructions to prevent it turning into the media circus that everyone anticipated. For the most part, their efforts had been successful, though no one could prevent the shouts from behind the perimeter for a pose for a photo, or for a quotable sound bite. Smith spotted a familiar face standing at the foot of the steps, talking to one of the Raftsmen defencemen, recognizing him from the little black and white picture that always accompanied his bylines in the sports page of the main Ottawa paper. Obviously, he was on good enough terms with Cormier to have earned an exemption from his peers' banishment from the entrance. Smith was about to head over when he heard a distinctive voice behind him, and he turned to see McAdam standing by the railing.

"Afternoon, detectives."

"Mr. McAdam …"

"Quinn, please. It was good of you to make the trip."

"It was a moving service," Marshall said.

"Yeah. I still have a hard time believing he's gone."

Marshall nodded. "He was far too young, that's for sure."

"How's your investigation going?"

"It's coming along," Smith said.

"I guess you can't really say much," the big GM added, pausing just in case they wanted to correct him before continuing. "But I wanted to repeat what I told you when we first met — that my door's always open. If there's anything I, or anyone on the team, can do to assist your investigation, please tell me."

"We will, and thanks," Marshall said, as Smith watched the striking blonde he had noticed inside walk up to McAdam.

"Oh, there you are. I believe you've already spoken to Detective Smith," he said, as Smith's curiosity was piqued. "This is my daughter, Melissa."

"Oh, right. You helped us out with Curtis's contract." Smith shook her hand. Her grip was firmer than he had expected, and her emerald eyes were almost level with his as they took stock of each other. "Thanks for that."

"My pleasure," she said. A grin teased the corners of her mouth before she turned to Marshall and shook his hand.

"I was just asking how the investigation was going," McAdam Senior continued.

"And?" His daughter seemed genuinely interested.

"It's making progress."

"But you haven't arrested anyone yet?" This seemed to be her only measure of success.

"Not yet, no," Smith said. In fact, after four full days, while they had uncovered a lot of leads, and identified Tom Saunders and, to a lesser extent, John Ridgeway Junior as persons of interest, he had the feeling this was going to be a complicated investigation.

"Isn't it true that the more time elapses after a murder, the harder it is to find a killer?"

"Sometimes, yes, but in this case I think it's more a question of the volume of information slowing things down. It'll take a while to sift through all the facts, but I'm confident we'll get our man soon enough."

"So, you're sure it's a man?"

Smith paused before answering, eliciting a smile from Melissa McAdam.

"It's okay, Detective, I assume you've got evidence that leads you to your assumption, but I'm not going to ask what it is."

"You could say that," Smith said, noticing Marshall and McAdam Senior were deep in conversation about something.

"It must be fascinating," she said, inching closer, "to be involved in a case like this, from your perspective. Criminal procedure was one of my favourite law school classes."

"It never interested you as a career?"

"I'm afraid I took a different route — a shorter, more conventional one, with a bigger payoff." She smiled. "I guess that makes me shallow."

"I don't know about that. Working in the front office sounds like a pretty interesting career, with or without the money. Interesting work, interesting people. Speaking of which, did you know Curtis well?"

Melissa McAdam's eyebrows lifted slightly. "Are you going to interrogate me now?"

"Of course not, I just wondered…."

"So formal." She was grinning again. "I was just kidding, Detect —"

"Call me Jack. There, you see? Not so formal."

Quinn McAdam was patting his daughter on the shoulder.

"We'd better get going," he said, as the lineup of cars heading for the interment formed in the parking lot.

"I take it you're not going?" Melissa asked, as her father said his goodbyes and set off down the steps.

"No, we weren't planning on it. We've got some work to do before we head back."

"Well, it was nice to meet you, Jack."

"Pleasure was mine."

She stopped halfway down the stairs. "I didn't get a chance to answer your question."

"That's okay. I know where to find you."

"Why don't you come out to the rink on Friday, it's the pre-season home opener."

"I can't accept —"

"I'm not talking about giving you freebies to watch the game. I just thought I'd show you around backstage, so to speak, and answer whatever questions you might have."

Smith hesitated as Marshall returned from chatting with James Cormier. "Sure. Why not."

"See you Friday then."

Smith watched her as she set off to join her father.

"Got a date?" Marshall whispered.

"We both do."

Marshall looked at him with a sideways glance. "Oh yeah?"

"She's going to show us around the Raftsmen's front office, and tell us what she knows about Ritchie."

"If you say so. I don't know about you, but I'm starving. What do you say we hit a greasy spoon?"

Smith nodded and they headed down the steps. Nearing the bottom, Smith saw the Ottawa sports-writer again.

"Steve Hunter, right?"

The other man nodded.

"I like your stuff, especially that series on rec leagues."

"Thanks."

"I'm Jack Smith, and this is my partner, David Marshall. We're with the Ottawa Police."

"Are you guys investigating Ritchie's murder?"

"Care to comment?" Smith said, in his best impression of a reporter.

"Not here." Hunter looked around and Smith could see him eyeing a cluster of Raftsmen players on the other side of the steps.

"We were going to grab a bite, if you want to join us."

"Naw, I've got to work on my story."

"Maybe we could meet another time?"

"Are you heading back to Ottawa today?"

Smith nodded.

"I could meet you for a beer, say around six?"

Smith looked at Marshall, who nodded.

"How about the Lieutenant's Pump? We'll see you there."

❋ ❋ ❋

After a greasy burger and fries, Smith and Marshall made their way to the Peterborough OPP detachment, where Mike Howard was waiting, with John Ridgeway and his girlfriend cooling their heels in the waiting area. They had decided to make use of the trip to re-interview Ridgeway in light of what they had discovered at Ashcroft, and on his Easypass account.

"They ready to go?" Smith asked, after they met with Howard and decided their strategy — they would interview the girlfriend first.

Howard nodded. "I told them the interview was going to be under oath, and warned them about perjury and obstruction. I think Ridgeway got the message."

"What about her?"

"I think she's scared shitless, but I get the feeling that what he says goes."

"All right, let's get her in."

Smith and Marshall sat in the interview room as the girlfriend was led in and they put her under oath, repeating dire warnings of the consequences of per-juring herself or obstructing a homicide investigation. She sniffed at the warnings.

"And just so you know, this interview is being taped," Marshall said, looking up at the little black globe that recorded audio and video from the corner of the room.

"Whatever."

"Can you please state your name, age, and address before we get started?"

"Penny Scott. 31A Deslaurier Drive, Peterborough. I'm nineteen years old."

"Do you work, Ms. Sco — Can I call you Penny?"

"Sure."

"Do you work, or go to school, Penny?"

"I work at Value Plus, as a checker."

"That's a grocery store, here in Peterborough?"

"Yeah."

"And how long have you been dating John Ridgeway?"

"Coupla months."

"How'd you meet?"

"I was checkin' his groceries and we got to talkin'."

Marshall smiled. "All right then. Did you work last weekend?"

"No, well, I worked Friday afternoon, then I was off until Tuesday. I traded a shift so I wouldn't have to work Saturday."

"Why'd you do that?"

"I knew we were going to be partying Friday night. I didn't want to go into work hung over. Nothin' worse."

"Who do you mean by 'we'?"

"John already told you, I was with him all weekend."

"Well, we're interested in your statement right now, not John's."

"Okay then." She shrugged her shoulders. "I was with John. We went to the Anvil after I got off work on Friday and stayed 'til closing."

"Where did you go then?"

"Back to John's place."

"Was there anyone else, or was it just the two of you?"

"Just us."

"And would you normally go back to his place after a night on the town, or …"

Scott raised an eyebrow and smiled. "You wanna know what we did, is that it?"

"Look, Penny. We're not interested in your personal life, other than to establish John's whereabouts."

"I get it." She waved a hand. "I was pulling your chain. Truth is, we didn't get up to much. John was pretty drunk. He's more of a morning-after guy anyway."

Smith was watching Scott as she spoke. She had a pretty face, and he couldn't imagine what she saw in John Ridgeway, or why she would want to go back to that filthy hovel that he called home. Then again, who knew what her home life was like, and she had met Ridgeway around the time he had come into his fifty grand. Maybe some free drinks and the shiny truck were enough to impress her. He hoped for her sake that it wouldn't for long.

"So, what time did you get back to John's apartment?" Marshall continued.

"The bar closes at two. It was probably two thirty before they kicked us out. We were back there by quarter to three, I guess."

"So you went to sleep as soon as you got back?"

"John passed out on the couch. He was out five minutes after we got home. I went to bed."

"And what time did you wake up the next morning — Saturday morning?"

"I don't know, maybe one, one thirty."

"And where was John?"

"He was in bed next to me. He must have come in from the couch while I was sleeping."

"What was he wearing?"

"Wearing?" She laughed. "I told you, he's a morning guy. He wasn't wearing anything."

Marshall seemed embarrassed, so Smith stepped in.

"Any chance John could have left the apartment while you were asleep, Penny?"

"And do what? Drive to Ottawa, kill Curtis Ritchie, and drive back? I told you, he was shitfaced. There's no way he would have made it down the front steps. I practically had to carry him in from the cab."

Smith had to admit, the more he heard, the less likely it sounded.

"We're gonna step out for a minute, Penny, if that's all right. You wait here."

She sighed as they left the room and crossed the hall to another interview room, where Howard had John Ridgeway all ready to go, having been through the same warnings about perjury and obstruction. As they entered, Ridgeway seemed annoyed.

"I don't know why we're going through this all over again. I told you everything two days ago."

"Is that so?" Marshall said, as he took his seat. "Did you tell us about the fifty thousand dollars Ashcroft paid you?"

147

Ridgeway looked stunned. "What's that got to do —"

"I'll remind you that this is a murder investigation, Mr. Ridgeway, and we expect full disclosure. Anything less just makes us more curious — and we're going to find out everything, sooner or later, so you might as well tell us what you know."

Ridgeway sighed and looked down at his hands. "Look, they told me I wasn't allowed to mention that, or I'd have to pay it back. Besides, I still don't know what it has to do with Ritchie's death."

Marshall asked him about his whereabouts on Friday and Saturday, the responses to which corresponded pretty well with what Penny Scott had already told them. Smith flipped through his notes from their interview with Ridgeway two days before.

"You told us you hadn't gassed up your truck in over a week the last time we talked. Is that still your version of events?" he said, pulling a printout from the file and putting it on the table, for effect.

Ridgeway looked puzzled. "Yeah, why?"

"We noticed your key chain has an Easypass key. Is that how you buy gas usually?"

"Yeah, so?"

"Well, maybe you can explain why there's a seventy-five-dollar purchase from a local gas station on the Friday afternoon. That's less than two days before we asked you the question, not a week. It's also the day before Curtis Ritchie was murdered."

They watched his reaction for signs of guilt, but were surprised to see genuine surprise, bordering on outrage.

"I didn't buy any friggin' gas. I bought some smokes, and mix, and a few other things. Does it say that on your little sheet?" he said, pointing to the paper. Smith felt a wave of unease as he saw only the total amount at the top of the page, but no description whatsoever of what had been purchased. Neither he, nor the constable in commercial crimes, had bothered to check, but it was Smith's responsibility. Still, seventy-five bucks was a lot for cigarettes and mix. Then he remembered Ridgeway's apartment, with its overflowing ashtrays, and noticed his orange-stained fingers and the stale smell of smoke in the little interview room.

"How many packs of cigarettes did you buy, do you remember?"

"Four," Ridgeway replied, without hesitation. "I usually buy 'em by the carton, but I was in a rush. You get a better deal at the gas station if you buy in twos, so I bought four packs, enough for the weekend."

"That would have been about forty bucks then?"

"Roughly, yeah."

"And the other thirty-five dollars?"

"A bunch of two-litres, for mix — I knew we were having some people over Saturday night. Some chips 'n stuff, too."

Smith nodded, but it still didn't add up. He looked at Ridgeway and tried to imagine what in the average gas station would have snared his last twenty bucks and thought he knew before asking the question. "Anything else?"

"Coupla those magazines," he said, lowering his eyes momentarily. "You know."

"Right," Smith said, as John Ridgeway slid a few spots down on the list of suspects before his eyes. "The ones on the top shelf."

❊ ❊ ❊

Smith sat at the bar, sipping his beer as he waited for Steve Hunter to arrive. The drive back from Peterborough had been uneventful, and after a couple of hours going over the growing pile of evidence the case had generated so far, he and Marshall had agreed that he would take the meeting with the reporter while Marshall worked on the questions for the interview tomorrow morning with Tom Saunders. They had decided to bring him in again and confront him about the encounter with Ritchie in the Toronto hotel, to see how he reacted. John Ridgeway's slide down the list of persons of interest necessarily buoyed Saunders right to the top.

He turned in response to a tap on the shoulder.

"Jack, right?"

Instead of the reporter Smith expected, he found himself looking at a pretty brunette. She looked familiar, but despite a concentrated effort on his part, he couldn't recall from where. The good news was that she was smiling.

"I'm a friend of Lisa's." She held out a delicate hand. "Valerie."

"Right," he said, remembering her from the bar the other night.

"How are you doing?"

He sipped his beer and smiled. "Good."

"Alone tonight?"

"You ask a lot of questions," Smith said, with a grin. "Are you a lawyer, too?"

"I guess I'm busted."

"Actually, I'm here to meet someone."

Her smile withered a bit. "I'll get out of your way," she said.

"I didn't mean you had to leave," he added quickly, noticing Steve Hunter's arrival at the other end of the bar.

"I can take a hint, believe me," she said. "Have a nice evening."

Hunter looked at the departing woman, then at Smith.

"Hope I didn't interrupt anything," he said, taking a seat.

"Not at all. Can I get you a beer?"

"I'll have the same as him," Hunter said to the bartender. "Sorry I'm late. What a day."

"I guess you've got plenty to write about these days."

Hunter grimaced as his beer arrived. "Yeah, the start of the season is busy enough, but this is just crazy. Then again, I guess I shouldn't be whining on a day when we went to an eighteen-year-old's funeral."

"To Curtis Ritchie." Smith raised his bottle and Hunter did the same.

"Listen, I'm sorry if I was less than a hundred percent co-operative in Peterborough," Hunter said, after a long pull on the beer.

"It's okay. I know you've got a job to do."

"It's just that I've worked hard over the years to establish a certain rapport with the players, you know?"

Smith nodded, wondering what it was that Hunter wanted off his chest so obviously.

"And I don't want them doubting what off the record means."

"I understand." Smith took a sip of beer. "How well did you know Ritchie? He was relatively new in town, but I noticed you've devoted a number of articles to him in the past few weeks. Sounds like you did a fair bit of research."

Hunter nodded. "Yeah, I did. I can't say I got to know him that well, and you never really know whether you're getting the full story out of these guys when you're talking to them with a reporter's hat on. Probably a lot like talking to the cops — people tend to have their guard up."

"I hear that."

"He was a helluva player, from what I got to see at practice, and even in talking to some of the veterans. He really did have that scoring touch. Could have been one of the greats."

"That's what everyone talks about — the money he was going to make, the records he was going to shatter. I'm more interested in the real Curtis Ritchie, though."

Hunter sipped his beer and kept his eyes looking ahead. "What do you mean?"

"Come on, you're around these guys on a regular basis. It's not a normal life they lead. I know everyone likes the myth of the clean-cut kid from Peterborough, but we both know he wasn't helping too many old ladies to cross the street."

"Someone's been telling you he had a bit of a dark side?"

"I've learned a lot about the dark side of pro sports in general in the past few days — a real education. As for Ritchie, I would say it's pretty clear he had some issues. All I'm trying to find out is whether any of his extracurricular activities might have led him down the wrong path."

Hunter nodded. "This is gonna sound crazy — not to mention ass-backwards — but I've got to ask. If I did tell you something, would you have to reveal your source?"

"If you're the only witness and you had to testify first hand, then there's not much I could do. But if you can direct me to other witnesses, I can try to keep you out of it. I'll be honest with you, though. I'm trying to catch a killer — the guy who put that eighteen-year-old kid in the ground today. That's got to be my first priority."

Hunter nodded and took a sip of beer before continuing. "There were rumours about Ritchie's extra-curricular activities, as you put it, over the summer and in camp."

"What kind of rumours?"

"That Ritchie couldn't keep his dick in his pants."

"What, he was screwing one of the other player's wives?" Smith asked, knowing it was the sort of cliché that happened all the time. In fact, if you looked behind some of the trades over the years that led the public at large to scratch their heads, locker room discord was often at the root — more specifically, the kind involving wayward wives and girlfriends.

"There were a couple of on-ice incidents that had us wondering. One was a scuffle between Ritchie and O'Neill."

"O'Neill?" Smith's eyebrows shot up. "What'd Ritchie have a death wish?" Tanner O'Neill, or 'TKO' as he was affectionately referred to by Raftsmen faithful, though Smith couldn't remember whether his middle initial really was K, was the team's longstanding goon, and a fan favourite of the past five years. He was one of a handful of tough guys who inspired fear among other enforcers, not to mention the regular players. He rarely lost a fight, other than to his arch-enemy in Toronto, with whom the decision could go either way from one game to the next. Smith had only ever seen him from the nosebleed seats, and even from there he was an imposing man at six-five and two-thirty. He could only imagine what he might do if someone tried to challenge his manhood, on or off the ice.

"In Ritchie's defence, O'Neill's girlfriend is a bit of a flirt — and you didn't hear that from me. I don't want to be the next one found floating in the canal." He paused. "That was in bad taste."

Smith responded with a grim chuckle. "I know what you mean. Did you ever get any confirmation that Ritchie was fooling around with ... what's her name?"

"Tammy something. They're not married."

"I'm thinking big hair and big tits. Am I warm?"

"She's a former dancer, and I'm not talking about the kind of ballet you wear a tux to, you know?" Hunter grinned. "None of the players said so for sure, but they didn't deny it either. These guys are like the mafia when it comes to team unity — they have their own code of silence."

"So what was the rumour?"

"They were at some team barbeque at Dennis Hearst's place and Ritchie and O'Neill's girlfriend were getting a little too cozy, to the point that Hearst and Ritchie had words." The mention of the Raftsmen's captain caught Smith's attention.

"What about O'Neill?" he asked, after a pause.

"I'm not sure he was there, or maybe he showed up late or something."

"Were there other incidents?"

Hunter shook his head. "Not that I know of, directly."

"So you say this barbeque was during training camp? That's a hell of a way to introduce yourself to your teammates." Smith whistled. "Though I can't say I'm surprised from everything else we've found out about Ritchie in the last few days."

"I think we're gonna hear more as time goes on. There was an awful lot of out of town press at the funeral — some of them less reputable than others. The respect for the dead thing only lasts for so long."

"Like how long?"

"I'd give it about a day."

They drank in silence for a moment while Smith collected his thoughts.

"What about this on-ice incident? I assume you weren't the only guy in the stands."

"No, there were a dozen media people watching practice that day. If you wanted to ask O'Neill about it you wouldn't be putting me at risk."

They chatted generally about Ritchie's performance at camp, and what moves the Raftsmen might make to try to replace him, then Hunter looked at his watch.

"Listen, I'm trying to get home to tuck my kids in, if you're done with me," he said, pulling out his wallet.

"Of course. And put that away. You can get the next one."

"All right. I'll see you around, and good luck with the investigation."

Smith waved him off, then pulled out his notebook and scribbled Tanner O'Neill's name onto his little diagram, connecting the circle around it with a dotted line to Curtis Ritchie. He picked up his phone to call Marshall and noticed he had a text. His breath caught as he recognized Lisa's number. He clicked it open and read the short note. *Jack. Let's not make the same mistake again, and pretend we aren't better off apart. Your friend, Lisa.*

Smith read it over a few times, set the phone down on the bar, and ordered another beer. Catching sight of Valerie, seated in the corner with a couple of girlfriends, he leaned toward the bartender.

"See the brunette over at the table in the corner?"

"Yeah."

"I'd like to buy her one of whatever she's drinking."

❋ ❋ ❋

Smith stood on the balcony in the cool night air, enjoying a few seconds of total silence before a distant siren ruined it. Even at three in the morning, silence was a relative concept in his neighbourhood. In a few hours, the sun would rise over yet another day without any hard evidence to a suspect in the Ritchie murder. The pressure would start to build from here on in, Smith was sure of it. Beaudoin would do his best to shield his investigators from its brunt, but it was only a matter of time before they would feel it themselves.

Going over his diagram in his head, Smith crossed John Ridgeway off and replaced him with Tanner O'Neill. Maybe he should add Dennis Hearst, as well, given what Hunter had said about the Raftsmen's captain confronting him at the barbeque, but he was reluctant to add the name to his chart. Was it the handful of Lady Byng trophies he had accumulated over the years — for most gentlemanly player — as opposed to the record number of penalty minutes accumulated by O'Neill? Did a player's conduct on the ice necessarily dictate how they behaved away from the rink? He had scribbled in a few unnamed circles for the people mentioned in the Ashcroft files, but he didn't really think they would amount to much. A few of them had already been ruled out for one reason or another. Then there was Tom Saunders. The interview later today would be interesting, for sure, but Smith still couldn't see him doing it, which left no one else at the top of the list of suspects. He felt disappointed by their progress so far, as he was sure a lot of others were, from Beaudoin to Ritchie's family. They all deserved better.

But there was another reason for the hollow feeling in the pit of his stomach as he stood alone on his balcony in the pre-dawn stillness, wishing he still smoked, as another stranger lay sleeping in his bed.

CHAPTER 12

Marshall had already prepped Tom Saunders for the interview, advising him that it was being recorded and confirming that Saunders had already spoken to a lawyer beforehand, and had no further need to consult.

"I got nothing to hide," Saunders said, sitting with his arms crossed, wearing jeans and a plaid shirt and looking like he would rather be somewhere else. Smith had spent a couple of hours going over the various statements and other information collected on Saunders to date, and it made for interesting reading. After spending fifteen years in construction in the Toronto area, he had put himself through a college paralegal program and moved to Peterborough to hang out his shingle, challenging parking tickets and scrapping it out in small claims court. Smith admired anyone who was able to put themselves through school in midlife, and apparently Saunders had done well for himself. But there was something very unpleasant about the man — in the way he carried himself and spoke — that betrayed an underlying anger at the world. Perhaps it was bitterness over what might have been. Smith imagined that paralegal work could get pretty draining after a while, especially when the lawyers he rubbed shoulders with were making three times what he was able to bill. Saunders had also tried his hand at politics ten years ago, but had abandoned any further political aspirations after a failed bid for a seat on municipal council.

Then he had met Ellen Ritchie and apparently found a new outlet for his energy: her son's budding hockey career. With the interview of Ritchie's Peterborough teammate, Jordan Connolly, fresh in his mind, the idea of Saunders as the ultimate extreme hockey parent was a natural progression. As Curtis's career progressed through minor hockey into junior and the stakes became higher, Smith could picture Saunders reading up on sports contracts and putting himself in position for the ultimate prize when young Curtis turned pro. It didn't take much imagination to see the anger and disappointment that Curtis's decision to hire a super agent just weeks before signing on with the Raftsmen must have caused after all those invested years.

"That was a really nice funeral service," Marshall said, to open the interview.

"Yeah, thanks for coming out."

"I understand you're in Ottawa for some meetings with the Raftsmen?"

"The Raftsmen, Curtis's agent, the lawyer, you name it. Quinn McAdam invited Ellen and me to the home opener, but she can't bear to go…."

"I'm sure it's a very difficult time for her. For you all."

Saunders nodded.

"Well, we won't take too much of your time this morning, but we did want to ask you some follow-up questions. I understand you spent most of last week in Ottawa, is that right?"

"Yeah. I told one of the other detectives," he said, nodding toward the door. "I was setting up a new line of sportswear with an Ottawa-based company. Curtis was going to do some promotional stuff for us."

"So you were here all last week?"

"Yeah, from Monday until … well, I was in a meeting on Saturday when I got the call about Curtis."

"That was from Ellen?"

"Yeah."

"And where were you staying while you were here?"

"My sister's place. Her and her husband live here."

"Downtown?"

Saunders sniffed in disapproval. "I don't know why they don't move out to the suburbs. They got a big old house that's falling apart, a boarding house on one side and some kind of shelter across the street. It's like livin' in the Bronx or something."

"Where's that?"

"Gloucester Street."

Marshall nodded. He could picture the area. There were nice pockets, but plenty of seedy parts as well.

"Is that where you were meeting, when you got the call?"

"No, I was out in Kanata."

"So had you seen Curtis during the week?"

He shook his head. "Not much — he was busy with camp. I talked to him on Monday, just to line up some promotional photo shoots for later in the month, and we went out for dinner on Wednesday night, but that was the last time I saw him."

"When were the photo shoots going to happen?"

"I don't know … it was gonna be sometime this week. Thursday, I think."

"So you stayed at your sister's place Friday night?"

"Yeah."

"And when were you headed back to Peterborough?"

"I was supposed to go after the Saturday meeting. 'Course I never did, cause Ellen ended up coming here."

"And what time was your meeting on Saturday?"

"Ten-thir —" Saunders looked at Marshall, then Smith. "Why are you guys so interested in my meeting on Saturday, or where I stayed…?" He stopped, answering his own question. Despite his proximity to the courts over the years, he obviously hadn't learned much about criminal investigations, because he seemed genuinely shocked at the realization. "You guys aren't thinking *I* had something to do with Curtis's death, are you?"

"We're just getting the record straight, Tom."

"He was like a son to me. How could you even think …?"

"Look, we have to follow standard procedure, as I'm sure you know. You were one of many people who was in contact with Curtis in the last couple of days of his life. We need to know as much as we can about that contact."

"So you can rule me out, like?"

"Yeah," Marshall said, as Smith watched the tension in Saunders' neck muscles subside. "Why don't you tell us about your relationship with Curtis. It must have been tough at first, as the new man around the house. Curtis would have been, how old?"

"Twelve or thirteen, I guess."

"So, how did you guys get along?"

"It wasn't really that big of a deal. His dad — well, adoptive dad — had been dead a couple of years."

"Bob Ritchie."

"Right. And I didn't try to replace him or anything. I knew that wouldn't be a good idea, so I just sort of gradually got more involved in his life. Hockey was good for that."

Marshall nodded. "You took him to hockey, and all that?"

"Yeah. I tried to give him a few pointers, but he didn't need much, even then. It was obvious he had something special."

"So hockey was good for bonding, then?"

"You could say that, yeah."

"I understand you worked as a paralegal up in Peterborough," Marshall said, looked down at his notes.

"Up until about a year ago, that's right."

"What happened a year ago?"

"I sold my business."

"This was your paralegal business?"

"PCS, yeah — Peterborough Court Services. I took on a partner a few years back, and he bought me out."

"Business was good, then?"

Saunders shrugged his shoulders. "Yeah, I'd just had enough. I wanted to do something different."

"What did you want to do?"

"I had a few ideas for businesses. I'm doing the clothing line now."

"Even without Curtis?"

"His endorsement would have been great, but it's still a good product. It's a line of breathable warm-up gear, good for hockey coaches and team wear."

"Did you have any other plans, with Curtis?"

"Nothing formal," Saunders said, adjusting himself in the chair.

"Did you ever think about maybe helping Curtis out with his career? You having some business savvy and all that," Marshall asked.

"Well, we had some discussions about that, but Curtis wanted to use a high profile agent for his contract talks."

"You didn't agree with him hiring Dan Avery?"

"I didn't say that." Saunders gave a bitter smile. "Let's just say I'm not sure Avery earned his hefty fee."

"You mean you could have done as well for less?"

"Probably, but I can understand why Curtis thought he needed someone like Avery. He was young, and pretty green about the business side of hockey."

"Did his hiring Avery cause any kind of rift between you and Curtis?"

"Naw." Saunders crossed his arms again. "I was mad at first, but like I said, I couldn't really blame him. Avery's got a silver tongue, and looks the part. That was enough for Curtis, I guess."

"We understand you had an altercation with Curtis, in a Toronto hotel."

Saunders looked at Marshall for a moment, his

features clouding as his glance diverted downward for a moment. "Who told you that?"

"Do you want to tell us what happened?"

Saunders stared hard at the table for a few seconds before speaking again. "Look, it's not something I'm proud of, you know? I was in town for business, and I was staying near Curtis's hotel, so I decided, with a few drinks aboard, that it would be good idea to go see him. It was stupid, and I said some things I didn't mean, but it was just the booze talking."

"What did you say to him?"

"I don't know. Stupid stuff. I told him he was making a mistake with Avery."

"Anything else?"

"You must have been talking to Connolly," Saunders said, looking up at Marshall, whose expression remained inscrutable.

"Did you tell him you'd kill him?"

"I don't know. I think I might have shoved him. I was drunk and it was the day after he told me he'd hired Avery. I honestly don't know what I said. Whatever it was though, I didn't mean it."

Smith could see the emotion in his face, but he wasn't sure if it was embarrassment at whatever drunken vitriol he had spewed, or discomfort at the incident coming to light now. Either way, one thing was clear to Smith as he sat there assessing him — Saunders had a temper.

CHAPTER 13

"You sure this is about more than you trying to get into Melissa McAdam's pants?" Marshall said, as he and Smith rode up the dedicated elevator that would deliver them to the owner's box on the top level of the Raftsmen's home rink.

Smith sighed. "You have such a low opinion of me, Marshy. I find it really hurtful."

"It's just that I couldn't help noticing at the funeral, she really is quite a looker. I'd be careful if I were you, though. Quinn McAdam had a reputation for always playing with a bit of an edge in his day, and he could drop the gloves with the best of 'em. I'd hate to think what he might do if he thought someone was messing with his little girl."

"Who's messin' with her? We're looking for information, and she's offering it."

"As long as that's all she's offering."

"Relax," Smith said, as the elevator doors swung open. "I'm not her type. She spent the last few years on Bay Street, and now she's being groomed for the front office. Pretty sure dating a lowly cop isn't really part of her plan."

They showed their ID for the fourth time since entering the building, and were allowed to pass only after their names were checked against a list in the enormous hand of a red-jacketed security guard, who led them to a large door with the Raftsmen's familiar logo. It opened to the sound of applause from nineteen thousand fans as the players hit the ice below.

"Glad you could make it." Melissa appeared with a glass of wine in her hand. She had to shout over the sound of the blaring rock music mingled with the crowd noise as the players began their warm-up skate. They followed her to the front of the booth, where the Raftsmen's owner and general manager were sitting, with an assortment of people Smith didn't know, though some looked familiar.

"I think you've already met Jim," Melissa said, as Cormier stood and shook their hands.

"Good to see you again, detectives," he said, clapping Marshall on the shoulder, without introducing him to the other guests, who then resumed a conversation with Quinn McAdam. "Can we get you something to drink?"

"No, thanks," Marshall said.

"We'll go to my office to talk, where it's a little less distracting," Melissa said. "I just thought they should check out the view while they're here."

"Of course. How's the investigation going?" Cormier said, as the music faded in the background.

"We're making progress, but there's a lot of ground to cover," Marshall said. "There are a lot of people we need to talk to, including some of Curtis's teammates. That's one of the reasons we're here."

166

"Melissa can set that up. We're on the road in a few days, just so you know," Cormier added, as the lights in the arena dimmed and the announcer began a special tribute to Curtis Ritchie. "We're gonna want to take this in," he said, as the giant screen above the score-board displayed a picture of a smiling Curtis Ritchie and a hush fell over the crowd. They watched as a collage of pictures and video of Ritchie's life flashed by on the giant screen; wobbling down the ice as a six-year-old, through his minor hockey years, and up to the press conference at the draft, grinning as he pulled on the Raftsmen jersey and hat. Smith noticed Melissa McAdam's discomfort at the video, and thought maybe he had misjudged her — she hadn't struck him as the type to coo over babies or cry at weddings, or be affected by occasions like this. When the video came to an end, the announcer called for a moment of silence and nineteen thousand fans stood in deafening quiet for what seemed an eternity. But when the time was up, the lights came back on and the starting lineup was announced: business as usual.

They watched the first ten minutes of the game from the comfort of the box, Smith and Marshall finally accepting a cola after the third offer from the circling waitress. After Ottawa scored its second goal, and seemed in a comfortable lead, Melissa turned to them and pointed toward the door.

"Do you want to go talk some business now?"

"Sure," Smith said, as they said goodbye to the owner and McAdam Senior, then followed the GM's daughter to the back of the box and out into the hallway.

"My office is downstairs," she said, as she led them back to the elevator, waving them through security.

"You must see a lot of games in the course of a season," Smith said, as the elevator doors slid shut and they started their descent to the basement, where the suite of management offices was located.

"I catch parts of most of the home games. I don't often go on the road, though, unless I have business wherever they are," she said, as they stepped out of the elevator. She led them through another secure door before they reached her office, "or I want to do some shopping. Come on in."

The office was small, but well-appointed. McAdam eased into a high-backed leather chair as Smith and Marshall took their seats in front of the dark-wood desk. There were framed prints on the wall, as well as McAdam's undergraduate and law degrees. Smith noticed she had gone to Harvard, then Osgoode Hall. She followed Smith's gaze to the wall.

"Dad spent five years with Boston as a player, then went back after he hung up the skates and spent another three in the front office. I always wanted to go to Harvard for some reason."

"I hear it's not a bad school," Smith said with a grin.

"There's that, of course. But I've got a real soft spot for Cambridge. We lived not far from the campus. I was ten or eleven, and it was the happiest time in my life. Then my parents got divorced and Dad got traded, all at the same time."

"Must have been tough, to be on the road like that, as a kid."

"I shouldn't complain." She smiled. "Anyway, how can I help you with your investigation? You want to interview some of the players?"

Smith nodded. "We thought we should have a word with Dennis Hearst."

McAdam nodded and jotted down the captain's name. "He's a super guy, and a natural leader in the room. Anyone else?"

"Who did Curtis room with?"

"He was paired up with Peter Dunne for camp, I think."

"I don't think I've heard of him," Marshall said.

"Rookie. He's not in the lineup tonight, but he's here, if you want to talk to him."

"That'd be great," Smith said. "And Tanner O'Neill?"

McAdam looked up. "What do you want to talk to him for?"

"We thought we should get a cross-section of the team," Smith lied, not wanting to make unnecessary waves.

She shrugged her shoulders and wrote down the name. "Anyone else?"

"If we think of anyone else, we'll let you know."

"Like I said, you can talk to Dunne tonight. Is tomorrow okay for the other two?"

Smith nodded. "So, what's the plan for the season, without Ritchie?"

"You mean can we get Cotterill, Lamer, and Wlodek back?" McAdam sighed. "Dad has never been afraid of risks, and he knew this trade would be scrutinized closely. But who could have predicted this? We'll just have to try to make the best of it. We could make a few moves, but we'll probably just draw on our existing talent pool, maybe bring up a few players earlier than we had originally planned. We'll be okay."

Smith wasn't so sure. Those three players had put up an awful lot of points in the past few years. Cotterill was no spring chicken, and his numbers had declined a little the previous season, but Wlodek was in his prime, and Smith had a hard time understanding his trade for an eighteen-year-old rookie, no matter what the scouting report said.

"Wlodek, right?" McAdam said, a grin appearing at the edges of her pert mouth. "You're thinking we should never have traded him."

Smith was impressed. "He did have pretty good numbers."

"The score sheet isn't everything. There were issues, that's all I'm gonna say. You know hockey, Detective? Ever play?"

"I played a little in my younger days."

"He's being modest," Marshall chimed in. "He's the Blues' best player."

"The Blues?"

"It's our tournament team," Marshall explained. "Hey, maybe while we're here, we should ask if there's any chance we can get a friendly with the Raftsmen — for charity."

"You guys any good?" McAdam looked at Smith.

"We're not big-league calibre, but we do okay."

"Not a bad idea. It'd have to be in the off-season, but I'll run it by our community liaison folks," McAdam said.

"You were talking about Wlodek," Smith reminded her.

"Since you play the game," she said, "you know about team chemistry. It's either there, or it isn't. And if it isn't, you're going to have problems."

"What about Ritchie? How was he fitting into the team's chemistry?"

McAdam's eyes narrowed slightly. "Fine, although training camp is one thing, the regular season's another."

"The other players liked him?"

"Sure, but the locker room isn't really my area of expertise, for obvious reasons." She seemed amused by Smith's puzzled expression. "I'm a woman, and some of these guys are pretty backward, if you know what I mean. They see a woman and think of one, maybe two uses for me. Once they know they're out of the question, they lose interest, along with any desire to admit me into the group."

"Sounds like you're in a tough profession."

"There aren't a lot of women in the front office, other than token ones," she said, the grin returning. "And I realize the fact that I'm the GM's daughter doesn't necessarily improve my credibility. But they're not all cavemen, by any means. Hearst, for example, is an intelligent guy."

"What about Ritchie? What was he like?"

"He was young and cocky, but you'd have to expect all that hype was going to create some attitude."

"Did you get a chance to know him at all?"

"I met him a few times. I went to a dinner with him and my dad out at Jim's place, after we signed him."

"Was he one of the cavemen?"

"He was an eighteen-year-old with a history of puck bunnies throwing themselves at him. What do you think?"

"Puck bunnies." Marshall grinned. "I like that."

"We understand Curtis had some issues with some of the women he interacted with," Smith tried again.

"You mean the one in Peterborough? Yeah, I heard about the paternity claim."

"I have a feeling she's the tip of the iceberg." Smith noticed her expression change a little. "Have you heard of Ashcroft?"

"The PR firm? Sure."

"Did you know Curtis was a client?"

"No, but it doesn't surprise me."

"So Curtis's ... how should I put it ... sexual exploits ... weren't an issue for you, then?" He noticed her eyebrows creep up slightly and quickly added: "I mean, from the team's perspective."

"We were aware of the Peterborough incident, and we discussed it with Curtis and his agent during the contract negotiations, as well as our expectations for conduct in general — being a part of the community here, public appearances and charity work — all that. But again, you have to remember, we're talking about an eighteen-year-old kid with a pile of money and an assortment of groupies waiting to jump into his bed at every stop. He was an adult and to a certain extent, his personal life was just that — none of our concern, unless it became detrimental to the team as a whole."

"So Curtis wasn't a liability in that regard, as far as you were aware?"

"No more than any other rookie. Part of the learning curve is how to handle yourself off the ice, and it's something the older players have a lot of influence over, especially on the road. A guy like Hearst would have been a great influence on Curtis." She picked up her buzzing BlackBerry and read the incoming message. "That's Peter Dunne. You want me to bring him here or would you rather meet him by the dressing room, after we're done here?"

"Did you have anything else for now?" Smith looked to Marshall, as Quinn McAdam appeared at the door behind them.

"No, I think we're good."

"Not interrupting, am I?" McAdam said, entering and sitting on the edge of his daughter's desk.

"They were going to talk to Peter Dunne."

"We understand he was rooming with Curtis Ritchie," Marshall said.

McAdam nodded. "Yeah, for part of camp. There's a boardroom next door, if you want to meet with him there."

"So, I'll set up the other interviews for tomorrow and get back to you with times?" Melissa McAdam was thumbing on her BlackBerry as a ringtone sounded — the refrain from a popular song that had been played constantly on the radio over the past few weeks.

"Do you think we could do the player interviews out here?" Quinn McAdam asked as they paused by the door. "I just think it would be better than having them at the police station, what with the media buzzing about the murder already. I've got a road trip coming up that

I have to think about. The last thing I need is half the team with their head somewhere else, you understand?"

"I don't see any reason we can't do the interviews out here," Marshall said. "But you'll understand that we have a murder investigation to run."

"I didn't mean to suggest that wasn't the priority," McAdam said, with a deferential wave of the hand. "Melissa'll have Peter come down," he added, as he led them out into the hall.

"I'll be in touch," McAdam called out from behind her desk, her BlackBerry still at her ear as she gave Smith a smile.

"Thanks for your time," Smith replied, as he and Marshall followed her father a few doors down into a spacious boardroom, where he turned on the lights and they all took a seat.

"Before Peter gets here," McAdam began, twisting an oversize ring on the third finger of his left hand — Smith hadn't noticed it before, but assumed it was a Cup ring. "There's something I thought I should tell you."

"About Dunne?"

"What? God, no. Dunne's pure as the driven snow. It's just that I know you're interested in anyone who might have had an axe to grind with Curtis." He paused.

"Yes?"

"Have you heard of Dmitri Kurtisov?"

Smith looked to Marshall and they both shook their heads.

"He's the owner of the Sochi Dynamo, an RHL team."

"Is that the one Doucette and Larmer played for?" Smith said, remembering the name of the team that had lured a pair of one-time greats to play in the upstart Russian league a couple of seasons before. From what he recalled, neither had stayed for long, but he remembered their salaries sounding astronomical for a couple of guys with their best years behind them.

McAdam nodded. "Those guys put the RHL on the map."

"Didn't they get, like, ten million each or something crazy like that, for one season?"

"It was all publicity, and they didn't see a fraction of that money — that's why they were back within a few months. But Kurtisov got what he wanted: a shitload of press."

"So, what's Kurtisov got to do with Curtis Ritchie?" Smith asked.

"He was talking to Curtis last winter — his reps were, anyway. They wanted him to go over to Russia for his first year. He was trying to sell it as a good transitional year for Curtis, plus I'm sure he offered a lot of money."

"Was Curtis interested?"

"No." McAdam shook his head. "He was never serious, but I think he might have strung them along a bit, maybe the agent told him to do it, to bump up our offering price, who knows, but I'm sure Curtis never had any intention of going to Russia."

"So why do you mention it?"

McAdam paused and rubbed a finger over his top lip. "Let's just say Kurtisov isn't a guy you want to cross, you know what I mean? He's supposedly connected to some pretty scary dudes. One of the reasons they're having a hard time with recruitment in that league is some of the shit that's gone on over the years."

Smith had heard the rumours. "You mean threatening Russian players and their families if they leave to play in North America?"

McAdam nodded. "There was enough of a chill to make players think twice about getting involved. Anyway, I got a call from someone on behalf of Kurtisov just after we started talking to Curtis. They told me to back off, that Kurtisov had a right of first refusal over Curtis. It sounded like bullshit, and when I checked with Dan Avery he confirmed there were no such rights in place. He wasn't aware that there were any discussions at all with Kurtisov, or the RHL, so I just ignored it."

Smith was scribbling in his notebook as McAdam paused and began fiddling with his ring again.

"The next day, someone slashed my tires."

"You think it was Kurtisov's people?"

"I know I've made some unpopular decisions in my time in management, but that's never happened before. I can't think of any other explanation. And there's more," McAdam continued. "I mentioned the tire incident to Ritchie, after we had signed him, and asked him if anything weird had ever happened to him."

"And had it?"

"He said he had a meeting with Kurtisov's people in Toronto and told them — nicely, as he put it — that he didn't think playing a season in Russia was in his best interest, thanked them for the offer, and brought their discussions to an end. A couple of nights later, someone broke into his hotel room and left a little surprise."

"What was it?"

"A coffin — a miniature."

"A coffin?" Marshall looked at Smith, then back at McAdam. "Did he report it?"

"Are you kidding? Would you? If you weren't cops, I mean."

"So he was scared, then?"

"I'd say so, yeah."

"And this was when, exactly?" Smith held his pen at the ready.

"March, I guess."

"When he told you about it, did he mention anything else? Any other visits or nasty surprises?"

"No."

McAdam looked up in response to a light rap on the door.

"That'll be Dunne. I'll leave you guys to it," he said, heading to the door. "Look, there's probably nothing to the Kurtisov thing, but I thought I should mention it for what it's worth."

"Thanks. We'll certainly look into it," Marshall said, as he and Smith exchanged glances. McAdam opened the door and invited Peter Dunne inside. He was over six feet tall and dressed in his best suit, but he still looked like he should be delivering pizzas.

"Peter, this is Detective Marshall and Detective Smith, with the Ottawa Police. They'd like to ask you some questions," McAdam said, retreating to the hallway. "If there's anything else you need, let me or Melissa know, okay?"

❆ ❆ ❆

"So what do you make of the Kurtisov angle?" Marshall asked, as they headed back to the car after an uneventful interview with Peter Dunne.

"It's like everything with this case — a teaser."

"You mean the timing?"

Smith nodded. "If it had happened last week, we'd maybe have something, but we're talking about March. Same with Saunders. There's gotta be something we're missing. Something more recent."

"Well, let's start with what we've got so far. A grainy video of a large male who we think is the perp, wearing a hoodie, hat, and sunglasses on an overcast morning. We've got a cocky eighteen-year-old millionaire who liked to put his dick in everything that moved, and a banker's box full of bad news at a PR firm to prove it. We've got Nancy Ridgeway's brother, who's got a motive, fits the general physical description, and has a less than watertight alibi."

"Are we still looking at Ridgeway? I thought we had pretty much ruled him out. If nothing else, he's too fat. I don't care how big a hoodie he was wearing, or how bad the video is, I don't see him passing as a jogger."

"Which leaves Tom Saunders."

"I kinda like Saunders for it," Smith said, as Marshall scanned the lot.

"Where'd we park again?"

"Think about it, Marsh. Saunders is the type of guy I can see bottling up a lifetime of rage. Starts out in construction — that's got to be tough sledding. Then he goes into the paralegal business, where he gets to spend his time hanging out with lawyers all day — enough said. Then his big chance comes along to ditch it all. Saunders is so close to a tidy commission, not to mention the big one in a couple of years that'll set him up for life, and the ungrateful little bastard cuts him loose. It's a pretty powerful motive."

"I'm not sayin' he's not worth a hard look," Marshall said, spotting the car. "I just don't see him as our guy."

"Well, so far we've got fuck-all else to go on."

Marshall shrugged. "That's true. Who knows, maybe O'Neill caught his girlfriend doing a little extracurricular pole dancing at Ritchie's fancy condo. I wouldn't want to be the other guy in that love triangle. I can't wait to interview him tomorrow."

"Yeah, I'll let you ask him the questions about his girlfriend," Smith said, as they reached the car and he pulled out his phone to check his messages. There was an assortment of work emails, including one from Melissa McAdam.

"She's set us up for ten tomorrow with O'Neill, then it's Hearst, right after."

"Already? What'd she ask them between periods?"

"The girl's got pull."

"That's not all she's got," Marshall added, with a whistle. "And don't start thinking about interfering with a possible witness, either."

Smith ignored him, as he noticed a pair of text messages. The first was from Lisa. He felt his cheeks flush as he read it, either out of anger or embarrassment, or perhaps a combination of the two: "Jack, I know you're pissed at me, but don't take it out on Valerie. She doesn't deserve to get screwed over."

"Everything okay?"

"What?" Smith looked across the roof of the car at Marshall and realized his expression, even in the dim lighting of the parking lot, must have betrayed him. "Women," he said, as they got in the car.

"That's not the coffee-chucker, is it? I'd stay away from her if I were you, unless you're taking her for ice cream."

"That's good, Marsh," Smith said with an elaborate sigh. "You're definitely improving."

"I don't know how you do it," he said, starting up the car. "Trying to manage that revolving door at your apartment, with the job we've got."

"Last time I looked, my door was the same as yours."

"Whatever happened with you and … what was her name?"

"Andrea?"

"Yeah, Andrea."

Smith looked out the window as Marshall pulled out of the lot. He wasn't sure himself, really. They had dated for about six months and had a lot of fun. He still had fond memories of the ski trip they had taken to Mont Tremblant between Christmas and New Year's. She had started to leave more and more stuff at his apartment, and he was fine with the gradually increasing permanence of their relationship, and came to see it as comforting, somehow. But then they had gotten into a fight over something stupid — he could barely remember what now, but it had been the beginning of the end. The trip they had been considering taking south in the spring had fizzled, and then that was it. He had seen her a few times over the summer and it had occurred to him that he should try to resurrect their relationship. Then he ran into her one August night in the Byward Market and discovered that she had met a Mountie and was moving to the West Coast with him on a three-year posting.

"She moved away. Shipped out with a Horseman from Vancouver, or somewhere out there."

"Too bad. I liked her."

"What are you gonna do?" Smith returned his focus to the glowing text message and re-read it. Why was it that Lisa assumed everything revolved around her? Was it so unthinkable that he might be interested in Valerie for some other reason than to get back at her? It pissed him off that she felt she had such a hold over him. He clicked on the second text, read it, and smiled. It was from Valerie, and it had only come in fifteen minutes ago: "Hoping we can connect tonight — your place or mine?"

"I'm done for today, I think. Wanna swing by around nine tomorrow, we'll grab a bite on the way out here?"

"Yeah, sure. You wanna grab a beer?" Marshall started the car.

"Naw, I'm beat," he said, thumbing a response to Valerie: "Mine in 30."

CHAPTER 14

Smith lay in bed watching Valerie sleep. He had another fifteen minutes before he had to get up, but something had woken him early. As he lay there, the remnants of a dream returned and he closed his eyes, welcoming it back. He was running down the canal path, toward the copper spires of the Château Laurier in the distance. But then he was in the water, and for all his thrashing, he couldn't stay afloat. He slipped under the surface, the murky, cold liquid closing around him. As he went deeper and deeper, and his lungs felt ready to burst, he noticed an approaching form. Barely discernible at first, he made out the shape of a human figure lolling in the murk. He steeled himself for Ritchie's bloated features and lifeless, wide eyes, but not what he saw when a ray of sunlight from beyond the surface illuminated the face before him....

He bolted upright out of his half-sleep, startling Valerie awake.

"What's the matter?"

"Jesus, I ... nothing. Go back to sleep," he muttered, getting up and sitting on the edge of the bed.

"Are you okay?"

"It was just a dream. I'm fine." He ran a hand through his hair.

She pulled herself up onto one elbow and rubbed her eyes, looking at the clock. "I should get going. I'm gonna be late for work."

"Can I get you some breakfast, or maybe you want to grab a shower here?"

"No, I'll swing by my place," she said, slipping into her clothes and searching the floor for something.

"Your shoes are out front," he said, as he stood up and pulled on his boxers.

"Right."

"Don't forget your keys." He pointed to the side table.

"When will I see you again?" she asked, fixing her hair in the mirror.

"I don't know. I wish I could say, but with this case …"

"I understand," she said, as they made their way to the front door.

"You sure I can't make you some coffee or something?"

"I'll get one on the way home." She stopped at the door to give him a kiss. "But thanks for the offer, and for last night. I had fun."

"Likewise," he said, as she slid out the door.

He made his way to the bathroom and turned on the shower. He stepped under the warm water and closed his eyes, the face from his dream returning in all its horror — Lisa White's face.

❈ ❈ ❈

When Marshall and Smith arrived at the rink, Tanner O'Neill was waiting in the same room where they had interviewed Peter Dunne the night before. Smith was expecting him to be taller, but he was no less imposing as he stood to shake their hands, his massive, scarred mitt enveloping Smith's not insubstantial hand in a firm grip.

"Jack Smith, and this is David Marshall, with the Ottawa Police."

"Morning."

"That was a good game last night," Marshall said, as they sat around the table. He had caught the third period at home, and watched as the home team fought off a final rally in the dying minutes.

"Yeah, we really wanted to stay away from OT," O'Neill said. "I thought we put in a good effort."

"You go on the road later today?"

"Toronto, Chicago, and Montreal," he said with a grin. "Tough teams, but they'll be good games."

"Be good for team morale to get out of town for a few days, I guess," Marshall said. "What with all that's happened in the past week."

O'Neill nodded. "Yeah. It's a real shame." He looked at Marshall, then at Smith as he said it, as though sizing up an enemy before deciding whether to drop the gloves. Up close like this, Smith could see the scars that criss-crossed his face. There was an especially big one on the bottom right of his chin that dissected the dark stubble sprouting around it. There was a coldness in O'Neill's dark eyes — like those of a prowling great white shark — that was unnerving in a meeting room. He could only imagine the effect out on the ice.

"Did you know Curtis well?" he asked, as O'Neill looked away.

"No, not really. Camp was the first time I saw him. I mean, I heard about him and all, but I didn't know him. That's why I was kinda surprised you guys wanted to talk to me."

"Well, we're talking to lots of people," Marshall interjected. "Teammates included, as you can understand."

"Right."

Smith gave him a reassuring smile before continuing. "Are you saying you didn't have much to do with him — on the ice, I mean?"

O'Neill chuckled. "I wasn't gonna play on his line, that's for sure. I couldn't keep up. The kid was *fast*." He shook his head. "But seriously, we all have different roles on the team. His and mine were 'bout as different as you can get. He was there to score goals. I'm there to protect guys like him."

"In case anyone on the other team thinks about giving him a shot."

"Yeah. Obviously, he's worth a lot of money, but there's also team pride on the line."

"Must be kind of strange, when an eighteen-year-old comes in with all this fanfare, and talk about the big contract he's gonna land in a couple of years, what with the salary cap and all."

O'Neill shrugged his shoulders. "It's the game. Do I think I should be getting the same money?" He paused for a little laugh. "That's not the way it works, but I'm not complaining."

"Was there any resentment among the rest of the team?"

"Nah. We're all pros at the end of the day. The kid had some attitude, but you gotta have it to make it this far."

"How about off the ice?"

There was a distinctive flash in O'Neill's dark eyes. "What do you mean?"

"Did he get along with everyone? There must be team social events, aren't there?" Smith prompted. "You guys have team dinners, barbeques, that kind of thing?"

O'Neill scratched an ear and adjusted his weight in the chair. "Sure, we do some bonding stuff during camp. If you're asking if we were best buds, the answer's no, but like I said, we're different. Plus, the kid's eighteen. He can't even have a friggin' beer yet. I got a nephew almost that old."

"What about spouses?" Smith continued, casually. "Would they normally attend these bonding events?"

"Sometimes, I guess."

Smith could sense the heightened tension in the silence following O'Neill's response. He was surveying them again with those eyes, narrowed slightly, and dark as coal.

"We've heard Ritchie was quite a player. I just wonder if he was mature enough to know where the boundaries lie."

"What are you sayin'?"

"Look, Tanner," Marshall intervened. "We understand there was some friction between Ritchie and some of the Raftsmen, maybe an altercation or two, possibly related to Ritchie getting a little too cozy with some of his teammates' wives, or girlfriends."

"You gonna say somethin' about my old lady now?" A vein had begun to throb above O'Neill's left eye, and his shoulders were hunched. Smith had visions of him leaping across the table and beating Marshall to a pulp.

"We weren't referring to you, or your ... girlfriend. We heard Hearst was the one who confronted him, maybe at a party? You know anything about that?"

O'Neill seemed to relax a little, his shoulders dropping slightly as he shook his head. "Nope."

"I know you and Hearst have been teammates for a long time, and you probably respect him."

"Fuckin' right."

"Right, so we understand you want to protect him, off the ice and on. But this is a murder investigation. Ritchie might have been a nice kid, or a cocky little bastard, but the point is someone killed him, and we've got to find out who."

O'Neill sat motionless in the chair.

"We know you're tight with your team, but whatever notion you've got — a code or whatever else — you've got to remember what's at stake here, and we're not just talking about your relationship with your teammates. If you're withholding evidence in a murder investigation, that's a very serious matter," Smith added, as Marshall leaned forward over the table.

"Let's try this again. Did you witness an altercation between Curtis Ritchie and Dennis Hearst, or any of the other Raftsmen players?"

"Fuckin' skank," he said, after an awkward silence. "I told her to stay the fuck away from him."

"Who?"

"Tammy. My girlfriend. She was all over him at a party at Hearst's house, at the start of camp. She can be a real cock tease when she's drunk. I was late getting there, so I didn't see it — she's not that stupid. Anyway, Hearst stepped in and told Ritchie to smarten up. I shoulda straightened him out myself when I got there and found out."

"So you weren't there when Hearst confronted him?"

"No, some of the guys told me."

"Who told you? Who witnessed it?"

"Aw fuck. Now you're gonna make a rat out of me."

"We'll keep what you tell us as confidential as we can."

O'Neill didn't look convinced, and Smith had to admit he had a point.

"Jonesy told me. He saw Tammy sittin' on Ritchie's lap, and he was there when Hearst gave him a blast of shit."

"Matt Jones?" Smith asked, referring to the up-and-coming tough guy on the Raftsmen's roster. He imagined Jones looked up to O'Neill as a mentor.

"Yeah," O'Neill sighed.

"Did Ritchie back off?"

"Yeah, he sure stayed clear of me the rest of the night."

"And the next day in practice?"

"I let him know what I was thinking." O'Neill looked up with a wide grin that revealed chipped teeth. It vanished as quickly as it had appeared.

"And what were you thinking?"

"That he should stay the fuck away from my girl."

"Did you threaten him?" Smith realized the question was ridiculous under the circumstances, addressed as it was to one the NHL's most feared enforcers. But he had to ask it anyway.

"You're goddamned right I did."

Given the direction the interview was taking, Smith decided to give O'Neill a caution, just in case. After he had read out the standard text, O'Neill sat in silence.

"Do you understand, Tanner?"

"What? Yeah, I understand. I got nothin' to hide."

"Where were you on Saturday morning?"

O'Neill looked puzzled. "I was at home, why?"

"Where's home?"

"Kanata Lakes. Why you askin' me that?" He paused, the dark eyes going from Marshall to Smith and back. "You guys aren't thinking —"

"What should we be thinking, Tanner?"

"Look, maybe I had a mind to give him a shit-kickin', but that don't mean I'm gonna go and kill him." He shook his head. "This is nuts."

"You said you were at home on Saturday morning. Until when?"

"What?" O'Neill seemed to be reassessing his situation.

"What time did you first leave the house on Saturday?" Smith tried again.

"I don't know. Ten? Had a late night Friday."

"Anyone home with you?"

"Yeah, Tammy was there."

"She's your girlfriend, you said. Does she live with you?"

O'Neill nodded. "Look, fellas, maybe I should talk to a lawyer after all —"

"One more question," Marshall interrupted. "What way do you shoot?"

O'Neill looked puzzled.

"It's a simple question, Tanner, and then we're done."

"Left. I shoot left."

"All right, that's it for now, though we might have some follow-up questions. And we're going to want to talk to Tammy."

"Whatever."

Marshall was taking down O'Neill's address and cell number when Smith's phone went off. He had it at his ear as the burly enforcer left the room.

"Yeah, I'm listening," he said, as Marshall closed the door and stretched. "Really? Anything like uttering threats, intimid — You don't say?" Marshall was looking on with interest as Smith's conversation went on.

As Smith ended the call, he noticed there was a new text from Lisa. He ignored it.

"What was all that about?" Marshall asked.

"It seems Dmitri Kurtisov has been living up to his gangster reputation. The Toronto guys have a file on him the size of a phone book."

"What kind of stuff?"

"Everything from fraud, to extortion, to uttering threats and assault. They've never had enough to charge him with, of course, but they're also looking at taking a run at him under the anti-gang legislation."

"Sounds like a guy you don't want to cross."

"Looks that way, yeah."

"What did you make of him?" Marshall pointed toward the door.

"Another guy I wouldn't want to cross, but more in an ass-kickin' kind of way."

"You mean you don't see him sticking a knife in Ritchie."

"Do you?"

"Not really." Marshall shook his head. "We'll run it down, talk to the girlfriend and Matt Jones. We ready for Hearst? He's out in the hall."

"One more thing," Smith said, as Marshall went to the door. "Beaudoin wants a status report after we're done here."

"Great," he said, opening the door and leaning out into the hallway. "Come on in."

Dennis Hearst was wearing warm-up pants and a form-fitting shirt that revealed an upper body chiselled by years of workouts. The longest-serving member of the Raftsmen took a seat and pointed to the door.

"What'd you guys say to TK? I haven't seen him like that since he lost a bout with Gruber," he said, referring to O'Neill's nemesis in Toronto. The light note didn't conceal the tension in Hearst's body language, even though his face was a mask of calm.

Marshall smiled. "I think I saw that one, and it was definitely worse than our interview. Thanks for giving us some of your time. I guess you're on the ice this morning."

"In forty-five. But we've got all the time you need."

They spent a few minutes on chit-chat, then Marshall began to take him through the same line of questioning as with O'Neill. Marshall got up for a stretch when they got to the subject of Ritchie's integration with the Raftsmen.

"You'll have to excuse me. My back won't let me stay seated for too long."

"I should hook you up with one of our physio guys downstairs. They can work wonders."

Marshall smiled. "I just might take you up on that. Now, I know you didn't know Ritchie that well, other than a few meetings, and you mentioned a dinner out at James Cormier's house over the summer."

Hearst nodded.

"But I assume part of your role as captain is to make sure the new players fit in with the rest of the team."

"For sure. We're all about teamwork here. On and off the ice."

"I'm gonna be frank, Dennis," Marshall said, taking his seat again. "We've heard that Ritchie might have had a bit of an attitude. And maybe his integration wasn't as smooth as it could have been. Would you say that's a fair comment?"

Hearst sighed. "He was only with us for a matter of weeks. Start of training camp was the first time most of the guys had ever met him. I've been through a lot of camps over the years, and I've seen a lot of guys come and go. Some ease right in from the start, others take a little longer, but I don't think we can really judge anything based on a couple of weeks. I've seen guys walk through the door with all kinds of baggage — big ego, big salary, maybe traded because they couldn't get along with their old coach, or were disrupting the room, whatever. Couple of months into the season, they're the most popular guy on the roster. Sure, it can go the other way, but it's the exception, not the rule. And I didn't see anything like that with Curtis." He paused, as Smith and Marshall looked on. "Sure, the kid had some pluck, but you want that, especially in a guy who's gonna be the future of the franchise. I'd be more concerned if he was a wallflower, you know?"

"What if we told you we'd heard Ritchie had taken some liberties with some of the other players' girlfriends, or wives?"

Hearst's shoulders sagged slightly as his eyes darted back and forth between the two cops. "There was one incident, with Tanner's girlfriend. I guess he told you?" Realizing he wasn't going to get any confirmation, he continued. "It was a party, just after camp started up — kind of an ice breaker for the new guys. Tammy — Tanner's girlfriend — had a little too much to drink, and she was making a bit of a scene, with Curtis."

"So you two had words?"

"Yeah, I guess so."

"Did he know she was with O'Neill?"

"I honestly don't know, but that was what I wanted to make clear. The last thing you want is friction over women — it's ruined team chemistry often enough that it's something you watch for if you're in my position."

"So how did Curtis react?"

"He was fine. We worked it out."

"We heard you two had to be broken up."

"That's overblown." Hearst gave a dismissive wave. "We had some words, sure, maybe it was a bit heated, but it was no big deal. It's not like he left in a huff or anything. He stayed the rest of the evening. We talked when he left, and it was all smoothed out."

"You said you didn't want the team chemistry messed up. We just spoke with O'Neill, and he's an imposing guy. Not someone I would want pissed off at me, personally," Marshall said. "Were you concerned at all about what he might do if he showed up and saw his girlfriend sitting on Ritchie's lap?"

"Well, that's what I'm talking about — hard to have chemistry when that's in the way."

"So you don't think O'Neill would have been mad?"

Heart frowned. "I didn't say that. Of course he'd have been mad."

"I've seen him in action on the ice, and we've probably all heard he has a bit of a temper," Smith said, recalling an incident he had heard about a couple of years ago, when a booze-fuelled O'Neill had reportedly taken a hotel room apart after a big loss on the road. He had been fined and benched for a couple of games, and the press had made a big deal of it for a few weeks.

"He's two different people. There's the guy on the ice, who'll take down anyone who threatens one of his teammates, and yeah, I wouldn't recommend crossing him in that mode. But his off-ice personality couldn't be more different. He's the first one with a joke, or to prank a rookie. He's not the animal people think he is, really. Now, I'm not saying he and Ritchie couldn't have traded some punches in the situation we're talking about, but that's it."

Smith looked at him and scribbled something in his notebook.

"You don't really think he had something to do with Curtis's death, do you?" Hearst said, looking at Smith, then Marshall.

"What about the incident at practice — the next day, was it?"

"You guys are well-informed." Hearst shook his head, and Smith hoped he wouldn't make the connection to Steve Hunter. "That's what I'm saying, though. A guy like Tanner has a problem with someone on the team, that's where he's going to work it out — on the ice. He's not going to wait a few days and then stick a knife in him when he's out for his morning run."

Smith looked up from his notes.

"Did Curtis always run in the morning?"

Hearst nodded. "Yeah, we talked about his conditioning. He was in good shape, but there was room for improvement, so he mentioned he was going to increase his cardiovascular work, starting with a run every day, bright and early."

"Did he mention where he was running?"

"He said he liked running along the canal. Not a lot of traffic before sev —" he stopped, his eyes meeting Smith's.

"What's the matter?"

"The way you're looking at me, I'm starting to wonder if you suspect *me*."

"Why would we suspect you?"

"Look." Hearst gave a nervous laugh. "Should I have my lawyer here?"

"Do you have a criminal lawyer on retainer?" Smith said.

"No, no. I mean —"

"Relax, we're not going to lock you up, we're just asking questions. Who else knew about Curtis's running route?"

"I don't know. He might have told one of the conditioning coaches, but I can't think who else."

"Did he have a girlfriend that you knew of, or anyone else who spent time at his place — slept over, I mean?"

"Not that I know of, but I don't think I'm the best one to ask about that."

"Do you know if he ever ran with someone else, like a training partner?"

"I don't think so."

Marshall nodded to Smith, who glanced at his notes, before shaking his head.

"Well, we'll let you get out on the ice now," he said. "We do appreciate your time."

"No problem. If there's anything else, don't hesitate. I hope you catch this guy soon."

"Thanks." Marshall stood to shake his hand and pulled a folded program from the previous night's game out of his jacket pocket. "I feel kind of stupid asking this, but I've got a twelve-year-old who idolizes you. If he finds out I met you and didn't at least ask …"

"It'd be my pleasure," Hearst said, with his first genuine smile, as Marshall handed him a pen. "What's your son's name?"

"Bobby."

Hearst scribbled something below a full picture of him at the back of the program, followed by his autograph, and handed it back. "There you go."

They watched him go and shut the door.

"You notice what I did?" Smith asked.

"I may be old, but I'm not stupid," Marshall retorted. "He signed with his left hand."

Smith nodded. "Another southpaw. This just gets more and more interesting."

CHAPTER 15

Smith was going over his notes when his cellphone rang. Expecting a call back from the Peterborough OPP, and preoccupied with what they were going to tell Beaudoin in a few minutes, he answered it without checking the caller ID. He was surprised by the voice.

"Oh, you're actually answering your phone."

He stopped reading. "Lisa?"

"We need to talk, Jack."

"What's up?"

"Can I buy you lunch?"

"I'm kinda busy right now."

"When, then?"

"Look, Lisa, I really am tied up. Why don't I —"

"Don't give me that, Jack. Don't think I don't know what you're doing. I know how your mind works."

"Really?" Smith could feel the colour rising in his cheeks.

"Valerie thinks you're for real, and I haven't told her otherwise, yet."

"What business is it of yours, anyway?"

"I know you're just using her."

"Ever occur to you that I might like her?" he said, lowering his voice and looking around.

"She's not your type, Jack, and she's going to be heartbroken, and she doesn't deserve that. She just came out of a really bad relat —"

"Why are you doing this? Why do you always assume everything revolves around you?"

"Valerie's a friend, Jack. A good one. And I don't want to see her hurt. I'm asking you, also as a friend —"

"So we're friends now? A couple of days ago you didn't think coffee was a good idea, now you want lunch, and you want to tell me who I can and can't date? Where do you get off?" He saw Marshall headed his way with a folder under his arm. "Anyway, I gotta go. Why don't you worry about your own love life."

"Jack, listen to —"

He ended the call just as Marshall arrived at his desk. "Ready?"

Beaudoin was on the phone when they rapped on the door and he waved them in. As he concluded his call, they took their seats.

"That was the Chief's office. I've got a briefing in an hour. You guys better have something good."

Marshall shook his head. "I don't want to disappoint, but there's still no obvious suspect."

Beaudoin frowned and moved his considerable bulk back in his chair, stretching his arms behind his head. "That's not a good start. Tell me what we do have."

Marshall took him through the evidence collected so far, and the list of people who were at least worth a second look, topped by Tom Saunders. Beaudoin frowned when Marshall recounted Jordan Connolly's statement about the late-night encounter at the Toronto hotel between Saunders and Ritchie.

"How's his alibi for Saturday morning?"

"It's loose," Marshall said, looking down at his notes. "He was in town, staying at his sister's place on Gladstone. The sister and the husband confirmed he was there when they went to bed Friday night and when they got up the next morning, but they didn't get up until nine or nine-thirty. Ritchie was killed about six-thirty, so Saunders would have had plenty of time to sneak back while they were sleeping."

"What's he got to say for himself?"

"Says the Toronto thing was just the booze talking — the threat, that is. He says he got over it and moved on. He was working with Curtis on some promotional stuff for his new business. A line of sports gear or something."

Beaudoin rubbed a finger over his top lip. "So Ritchie screws him out of a sizeable agent's commission at the last minute and he 'gets over it and moves on,' and it's all sweetness and light? Sounds pretty thin to me. I'd be pretty pissed off in his shoes."

"We thought the same thing, but the timing's throwing us off. This happened in March. Why wait until September?"

"Mmm," Beaudoin growled. "And this business of his, it checks out?"

Smith nodded. He had looked up the company online himself, though he noticed no mention anywhere of Curtis Ritchie's name. "I talked to someone at the photography studio Saunders referred us to and they confirmed a photo shoot was booked for Curtis this week. Who knows if Saunders would have turned a profit, but it definitely seems as if they were working together. Ellen Ritchie said the same thing."

"Then there's the house in Peterborough," Marshall said.

"What house?" Beaudoin was rubbing his eyes.

"Ritchie was building his mother and Saunders a house in Peterborough worth a couple of mil. Includes a special workshop for Saunders that he had custom spec'ed."

"You mean Ritchie was making amends? Maybe Saunders realized he didn't have it so bad after all?"

Smith nodded. "You can say that again. Turns out it wasn't a construction mortgage, where the bank advances as the house goes up. They just advanced the money to Ritchie and he paid the builder up front. They must have been counting on doing a lot of business with him in future."

Beaudoin looked puzzled.

"It means the bank, or more likely the insurer, is on the hook for the full amount, and Ellen Ritchie will take possession of a two-million-dollar house when it's finished in November."

Beaudoin nodded. "Have we canvassed the sister's neighbourhood to confirm Saunders' whereabouts Saturday morning?"

"Yeah, but it's kind of a shitty neighbourhood. There's a couple of rooming houses nearby — not a whole lot of people up and about at six or seven on Saturday morning, you know?"

Beaudoin frowned and adjusted himself in his chair. "What about this RHL owner?"

"Kurtisov. McAdam mentioned him, said he had been talking to Curtis around the end of last season about spending a year playing in Russia. He said Curtis was threatened after he broke off talks. We haven't really had a chance to take a good look at him yet."

"You should," Beaudoin said. "I talked to a friend on Toronto's organized crime task force. They've been trying to put something together on him for a couple of years."

"Yeah, we heard he might be connected to organized crime in Toronto."

"I'll give you the name of my contact and he can tell you himself. I guess we have the same timing issue with Kurtisov though, huh?"

Smith nodded. "They fell out about the same time Curtis ditched Saunders as his agent. I guess you never know. People can hold grudges for a long time."

"But you don't think it fits either one of them?"

"I'd prefer a more recently triggered motive," Smith said, as Beaudoin rubbed his temples. "But we'll give them both a full look."

"Anyone *with* a more recently triggered motive I should know about before I meet with the Chief?"

Smith hesitated. "Apparently, there was an incident at a Raftsmen's practice between Ritchie and O'Neill."

"*Tanner* O'Neill? You serious?"

Marshall nodded.

"When?"

"During training camp. It was the day after a team

party at Dennis Hearst's place, where O'Neill's girl-friend was getting a little too friendly with the new kid in town."

"Was she screwing him?"

"Not sure, but Hearst had to tell Ritchie to stay away from her, so as not to ruin team chemistry — that's how he put it."

"You mean, so O'Neill wouldn't rip his head off." Beaudoin gave a throaty chuckle. "You talk to O'Neill?"

"Yeah. He says he straightened him out on the ice, and that was the end of it, in his mind."

"You believe him?"

"We kind of got the impression he knew his girl was a bit of a flirt. It seemed like he was more pissed off at her than Ritchie, but who knows? We've got to talk to the girlfriend, and one of the other players — Matt Jones. He witnessed Hearst and Ritchie's 'chat.' He had to break them up."

"What, Hearst and Ritchie?"

"Yeah."

"Boy, the kid was really making a name for himself, wasn't he? Your first pro camp and you try to fuck the goon's girl and get in a scrap with the captain." Beaudoin crossed his massive forearms across his chest. "I'm trying to picture O'Neill…. Is he a leftie?"

"Shoots left, so I doubt it. We'll confirm though."

"And what about the Ashcroft files? I understand Ritchie was a busy little boy over the summer."

"You could say that. He paid them a pile of dough to keep his indiscretions discreet, and it looks like they were earning it."

"Shit, maybe *they* had him clipped — too much trouble."

They shared a laugh as Marshall laid out the next steps.

"We'll keep running down all of the leads from Ashcroft, but no obvious suspects yet. If that changes, we'll let you know. In the meantime, we plan to focus on Saunders, Kurtisov, and O'Neill, in that order."

Beaudoin scribbled on a Post-it Note and handed it to Marshall. "That's my contact on Toronto's OC task force."

"We'll get in touch right away," Marshall said, taking the note.

"I don't have to tell you guys that time's a wastin'," Beaudoin said, leaning forward and placing his massive forearms on the desk. "We're a week in now, and from the sounds of it, we're not quite there. You've read the papers, right? It's only gonna get worse."

"We're doing everything we can," Marshall said.

"I know you are. Keep me posted."

"Will do," Marshall said, as they took their leave and Beaudoin picked up his phone.

"He didn't seem as pissed as I thought he'd be," Smith said, as they made their way back to their desks.

"That's what I'm worried about. I think we better catch a break soon."

"Or what?" Smith said, as his phone rang and he saw Valerie's number on the display. He considered letting it go to voicemail but he knew she had already sent several texts. "Just a sec," he said, detouring toward the hallway and taking the call.

"Jack, how come you're not answering my texts?"

"I've been in a meeting."

"All morning? You're gonna give me the wrong idea here." She softened the line with a little laugh, but Smith could sense an underlying tension.

"What do you mean?"

"Well, I don't want you think I'm just some booty call."

"Valerie, I'm in the middle of a murder investigation. I told you, it gets kind of crazy."

"I know, but how long does it take to respond to a text?

"Look, I don't have time for this now."

"Well, excuse me." The laughter was gone. "You know, I was warned about you."

"What's that supposed to mean?"

"That you're only really interested in one thing."

"I really don't know what this is all about. I'm not in some nine-to-five where we can schedule in lunch dates, I told you that. And what are you talking about, you were warned?"

"Never mind. Maybe this wasn't a good idea."

He knew she was talking about Lisa. They had probably met for coffee, and spent half an hour skewering him over lattes. He considered a counter-argument, but was quickly losing interest, and he didn't have the time anyway. "Maybe you're right," he said, ending the call and returning to his desk, where a black cloud settled over his head.

"What's up?" Marshall said, watching his partner sit heavily in his chair.

"Nothing. So, how do you want to take it from here?"

"I'm thinking we divide the labour. If you want to call Beaudoin's guy in Toronto, I'll follow up with O'Neill's girlfriend and try to talk to Matt Jones. I got a message from Peter Dunne. Said he wanted to add something to what he told us the other night."

"The rookie?"

"Yeah. He said he'd prefer to speak in person."

"That sounds promising," Smith said, with a nod. "I've got the name of a Peterborough sportswriter who covered Curtis's junior team for years. I'll touch base and see if he knows anything about Saunders. I was thinking of talking to someone in the front office there, as well." He looked at his watch. "If you're gonna talk to Dunne, you'd better hurry. Aren't they going on the road this afternoon?"

Marshall shook his head. "He's not making the trip."

"Sucks to be a rookie, I guess. All right, let's make some calls and catch up in a couple of hours."

CHAPTER 16

Smith took his seat on the plane and sighed. It had only taken a fifteen-minute conversation with Beaudoin's task force contact to convince him that Dmitri Kurtisov was worth further attention. In addition to his active involvement with several organized crime-connected business interests in Toronto, the task force was working on trying to connect Kurtisov to three gang-related murders in the past twenty-four months. Also, contrary to Smith's assumption that he spent most of his time in Russia, Kurtisov had a house in Toronto and spent at least five months of the year there, including the past four. Smith also learned that Kurtisov was booked on a flight to Moscow in three days, so the window for pulling him in for a chat was narrowing quickly.

It had been late afternoon before Smith had gotten the chance to talk to Beaudoin again, at which point he had been ordered onto the next flight for Toronto, while Marshall followed up with Tanner O'Neill's girlfriend and Peter Dunne. By the time Smith had gotten his paperwork in place and spun by his apartment for an overnight bag, he had been stuck in gridlock all the way out to the airport, and he had barely made his flight. He looked at the empty seat next to him as they announced that boarding was complete and realized he would have some room to stretch out during the brief flight.

A last check of his messages revealed a confirmation from the Peterborough reporter of a meeting the next day. He had gotten Don Brooks's name from Steve Hunter, and when he had called earlier, he had discovered that Brooks would be in Toronto for the weekend to cover Peterborough's first road game. He was still waiting for a call back from the team's communications director about trying to set up a talk with someone in the front office. He called Marshall as a flight attendant roamed the aisle checking seatbelts and frowned at him.

"I'll just be a second," he said, as Marshall picked up on the second ring.

"You about the leave?"

"Yeah, I just called to let you know I got a response from Brooks. Looks like I'll be able to lighten your load."

"Good. Saves me a trip to Peterborough."

"You talking to Tammy Crawford tonight?"

"All set up for an hour from now. I'm gonna meet Dunne on the way back."

"Watch out she doesn't try to jump your old bones."

"Very funny."

"If you see Fitz, give him my regards," Marshall said, as the flight attendant returned, her frown replaced with a glower.

"Will do." He laughed, thinking of Marshall's former partner from his days in Toronto. "Listen, I gotta go. We're leaving."

"Good luck."

He closed the phone with an apologetic smile as the attendant returned.

"Can I get you a newspaper?" Apparently, she didn't hold a grudge.

"Sure," he said, reopening the phone after she had gone. He had noticed a new text from Valerie. He read it quickly then shut down the device and tucked it into the seat back pocket.

"Well, that's over," he muttered to himself, eliciting a puzzled look from the young man across the aisle. As the engines started up, the flight attendant returned with the newspaper. He scanned the front page and quickly lost interest, tossing the paper onto the empty seat and stretching out his legs.

As the plane backed up and headed out to the runway, he turned his mind to the case, and the possibility that Dmitri Kurtisov might turn into a legitimate suspect. He had a breakfast meeting with Brooks at nine, after which he would spend the day with the task force, and hopefully interview Kurtisov personally, if they had managed to set it up. His mind drifted as they taxied into take-off position, but as the engines revved up and his heart began to flutter with pre-flight anxiety, he had only one thing on his mind, and she had nothing to do with the case.

❋　❋　❋

Smith sat in the hotel restaurant with Dan Brooks, sipping his coffee as Brooks finished off what had begun as an enormous platter of bacon, eggs, hash browns, and toast. Brooks himself was large in scale, as was the amiable laugh that emerged between bites, as he told stories about his years covering the Peterborough junior team.

"The best one was when the cops hauled over the team bus just outside London, after a Saturday night win. Turned out one of the players had called in a tip that one of the trainers was involved in a robbery earlier that night. A couple of us press guys were around when the coach found out — boy did he hit the roof. I think they traded the poor prankster a few weeks later. Can't remember his name. I wonder if he ever made it to the show." Brooks wiped his mouth with his napkin and took a sip of coffee before leaning back in his chair. "But listen to me going on with my tall tales. That's not what you wanted to talk to me about, is it?"

"Actually, it is, in a way," Smith said. "I didn't realize you travelled so closely with the team."

"Well, we don't anymore, but in the old days we'd sometimes end up on the team bus. Now, things are different, what with all this email and tweets and shit. You can't blame them for not wanting us anywhere near them, for fear their every word will end up floating around the planet thirty seconds later."

Smith laughed. He liked Brooks's old-school manner and could sense he was part of a dying breed, as Brooks himself seemed to recognize. "What can you tell me about Curtis Ritchie?"

"Best natural goal scorer I ever saw. And I've seen some beauties in my day, I'll tell you. He didn't hit much, and backchecking wasn't part of his repertoire, but get him the puck anywhere inside the blue line and he was lights out."

"Quick release, huh?"

Brooks nodded. "Like greased lightning, and he got all of it — I mean *all*. The goalies all said the same thing — they just never saw it until it was too late. He was a good playmaker too — he had most assists last season, but it was nothing compared to his scoring ability. It really is a damn shame."

"What about Curtis the person. How did he get along with his team, and you guys in the press, the fans?"

Brooks frowned. "He was an eighteen-year-old with the world at his feet, and he knew it. At the start of the season last year, the only question was who was going to take him, not whether he'd go first. And everyone knew eventually he'd get huge money."

"I've heard he could be cocky."

"Sure. Wouldn't you be?"

"Probably." Smith chuckled.

"He never gave me any trouble personally, though some of my colleagues complained about his availability, and his attitude. I think he was pretty good with the fans. He sure signed his fair share of programs, sticks, and hats. That much I saw first-hand."

"And the other players?"

Brooks sighed and sipped his coffee. "There were rumblings about some squabbling — some verbal sparring in the room or on the bus, maybe after a loss or whatever."

"What about over women?"

Brooks nodded. "There were rumours about that too, yeah. I guess you heard about the Ridgeway girl, with the paternity suit?"

"Yeah, we talked to her. I was more interested in conflict with his teammates, over girls."

Brooks finished his coffee and nodded as the waitress pointed to his plate. He waited for her to clear the table before speaking. "Apparently Ritchie and Quesnel — that's Paul Quesnel, a defenceman — had a scrap at the beginning of the year over a girl. Quesnel was traded a couple of weeks later. Not that he was any good — I think he was a minus five when they dealt him — but the timing was odd."

"So, if you played with Ritchie, your girlfriend was fair game?"

"As if that's not the reality anyway. Most of these girls know what they're getting themselves into, and what they're after. Who can blame them for wanting to get their hooks into a young stud who's gonna be pulling down a few mil a year in the very near future?"

"Puck Bunnies," Smith said, thinking of Melissa McAdam's comment, and scribbling Quesnel's name into his notebook. "What about Tom Saunders?"

"The stepdad?" Brooks's eyes widened a bit.

"You know him, then?"

"Kinda hard not to notice him, he was a permanent fixture, a few rows up behind the bench, screaming his head off every game like a good ole bleacher creature."

"Screaming at who?"

"The refs, the other team, his own team, the coaches … you name it. He'd lay into Curtis every once in a while, too, just to be even-handed with it, I guess."

"That must have made him popular."

Brooks gave a grim chuckle. "The coach couldn't stand him, and I can't blame him. I guess he was part of the package you got with Curtis."

"Apparently, Curtis didn't think so," Smith said, watching Brooks's reaction.

"What do you mean?"

"I understand Saunders expected to be Ritchie's agent, and wasn't too happy when Curtis cut him loose last winter."

Brooks shrugged his shoulders. "I'm sure he got over it. You should see the house Curtis was building for him and Ellen in Peterborough." Brooks whistled. "I'm sure that smoothed out any ruffled feathers. Besides, it's not like he wasn't gonna be taken care of, as Ellen Ritchie's boyfriend, or whatever."

Smith thought of the remainder of the signing bonus, as well as the insurance payout that would go to Ellen Ritchie. He couldn't help thinking it seemed like small change compared to even a tiny percentage of a fifty-million-dollar contract.

"I can't say I blame Curtis, though," Brooks continued. "He spent five years listening to Saunders in the stands, and his old man was just the same, even back in pee wee."

"Ritchie's father, you mean?"

"Adoptive father. Yeah."

"Right, he was adopted."

"Bob Ritchie made Saunders look like a pussy cat by comparison. That guy was something else."

"You knew him?"

"I went to high school with him." Brooks patted his stomach and leaned back in his chair. "He played for Peterborough himself — he was pretty good, but he didn't have Curtis's scoring touch. He spent a couple of seasons in the Toronto farm system, but he never made the big team."

"What did you mean by Saunders being a pussy cat compared to him?"

"He was the ultimate extreme hockey parent. He coached for a few years, but he got thrown out of so many games, for screaming at the kids or the refs, the minor hockey association gave him the boot. They had no choice, really. It got so bad, Bob's teams couldn't find a tournament he wasn't banned from."

Smith could imagine how it had played out. The minor leaguer who never made it sees his adopted son as his chance to make things right. It was a common theme in a lot of sports, but especially hockey, where it seemed to take on a particularly ominous character.

"What did he die of?"

"Heart attack. All that screaming must have got to him."

"And Curtis ends up with Saunders as a substitute a couple of years later. Now I know why he went out and got his own agent."

As the waitress delivered the bills to the table, Brooks looked at his watch. "Well, is there anything else I can do for you? I've got a few things to do before I head to the rink."

"When's the game?"

"It's a two o'clock start. Then back to Peterborough for another afternoon game tomorrow."

"Well, I really appreciate your time. I'm glad we were able to meet — it was good luck that we ended up at the same hotel."

"If there's anything else I can do, let me know." Brooks handed over his card.

Smith thanked him again and watched as he lumbered off toward the lobby. He was reaching for his phone to confirm his meeting with his task force contact when the ringer went off. He didn't recognize the number, but answered the call anyway.

"It's Melissa ... McAdam."

"Oh, hi Melissa."

"I was calling to see if you still wanted to meet with Matt Jones. I understand you're in Toronto?"

Smith assumed she had talked to Marshall already. It also occurred to him that the first game of the Raftsmen's road trip was tonight in Toronto. "Yes. I do want to talk to him."

"Well, tonight's game would be a good opportunity. Jones made the trip but he's not in the lineup tonight. If you want to swing by the arena, I'll leave your name at the gate. He'll be there from about four on."

"That should work. I'm not sure how my day's going to turn out, but I should be available this evening for sure. Thanks."

"My pleasure."

He hung up the phone and checked his watch again as he headed out into the lobby. He noticed a couple with two young kids, obviously weekend tourists. The kids were playing tug of war with a teddy bear while the parents looked at a map, no doubt planning out the most efficient way to get to the CN Tower, the ROM, or wherever they were headed for a day of sightseeing. He envied their obvious happiness and smiled as the little boy won the battle for the bear and ran off across the lobby toward him, his sister in hot pursuit. He found himself instinctively checking his phone for text messages, and finding none, he set out for the taxi stand.

CHAPTER 17

Smith sat at the table in the little boardroom, poring over the mountain of documents the organized crime task force had compiled on Dmitri Kurtisov in the past two years, since he had come to their attention as a person of interest in the murder of an importer. He had been given the material after a thorough briefing from Dean McGregor — Beaudoin's contact, and one of the investigators on the OC task force — a briefing that had left his head spinning. If even half of what Kurtisov was suspected of being involved in were ever proven, he would be facing the rest of his life behind bars; and that only covered his activities in Canada over the past two years. Smith could only imagine what he was up to in Russia. He had come across one report from Interpol in the file already, and there were bound to be more. Since returning from a quick lunch with McGregor, he had spent over two hours combing through the documents, and was still only halfway through. He heard footsteps out in the hall and then the door opened to reveal McGregor's stocky frame.

"He's here."

Smith tucked his notebook into his jacket pocket and got up from the table. Kurtisov had agreed to the interview on condition that his lawyer came along, despite the fact that McGregor had been explicit about it being an informal chat. Then again, Smith thought, as he followed McGregor down the hall, he could see why Kurtisov might be wary of contact with the police, given what he knew about the Russian's activities so far.

"Interesting reading, huh?"

"I don't understand why we keep letting him in the country," Smith remarked, though he knew the answer — Kurtisov hadn't been convicted of anything, yet.

"That makes two of us, but we're making progress. It's just a matter of time. My biggest fear is that he'll slip back to Russia before we can prosecute him here. And that'll be that."

Smith nodded, guessing the chance of successful extradition from Russia wasn't good.

"I assume you'll want to ask the questions," McGregor said, as they rounded a corner and walked toward an open interview room, where Smith could see two men in suits standing by a table.

"You bet, but feel free to jump in."

McGregor led the way into the room and introduced himself, though in his case it was unnecessary. He had met both Kurtisov and his lawyer on several occasions. "And this is Jack Smith, an investigator with the Ottawa Police."

Though he had heard of the name in the past, Smith had never seen Kurtisov's picture, but the man who offered his hand was exactly what he expected. His Slavic eyes and cheekbones, framed by dark hair, tinged with grey and combed back immaculately, gave him the hardened look of someone familiar with the sharp end of business, despite a bespoke pinstripe suit and a broad smile.

"A pleasure to meet you, Detective Smith," he said, his thick accent underlying every word. "I hope you won't mind my bringing my lawyer along."

The other man seemed to share Kurtisov's ethnic background, though not his smile. He was younger, and his tie brighter, and when he spoke, Smith detected no hint of an accent.

"Perhaps you might enlighten us as to why we're here," he said, as he released Smith's hand and slipped him a card.

"We'll get to that, Mister ..."

"Bilak."

"Right. Have a seat, gentlemen."

The lawyer's features darkened, but a nod toward the chairs from Kurtisov was enough to get him in his seat.

"Yes, while I am always happy to co-operate with the authorities," Kurtisov said, settling in his chair, "I must say I'm on a tight schedule today."

"Well, we appreciate you coming in, and I promise we won't keep you for long." Smith paused and glanced at Bilak, who was eyeing him suspiciously. "Let me cut to the chase. I wanted to ask you about Curtis Ritchie."

"I heard about that," Kurtisov said, shaking his head. "What a tragedy, a young man of his age, with the future that lay ahead for him."

"What, specifically, are you asking?"

Smith ignored the lawyer and directed the question at his client. "I understand you had some discussions with Ritchie about the possibility of him spending a year in Russia with your team."

"I did," Kurtisov said, putting a thick hand on his lawyer's forearm. "Though they were confidential discussions … not that anyone respects confidentiality these days, right, Mr. Smith?"

"Well, given that the other party to the discussions is dead, and the subject of a murder investigation, I think confidentiality is the least of our concerns."

"My client has the right —"

"Relax, Alex." Kurtisov let out a sigh. "I have nothing to hide. Yes, we had some informal discussions, but they never came to fruition."

"Did you offer him a one-year contract?"

Kurtisov laughed. "If I were going to sign him, it would have been for more than one year. Of that, I can assure you. But I think you have been misinformed."

"Really, how?"

"There was never any offer of any kind. The discussions were extremely … preliminary. It was clear to me that Curtis's dreams lay here."

"So there was never any written offer from you, or anyone in your … organization?" Smith said, glancing at Bilak as he emphasized the last word.

Kurtisov looked at him for a moment, perhaps to see if he was bluffing, then gave a little grin. "No, there was not."

"When did these preliminary discussions take place?"

Kurtisov stroked his upper lip with a finger. "February, possibly early March."

"So, what happened?"

"Nothing happened, Detective," he said with a smile, as his lawyer fidgeted in his chair. "That was the problem. We discussed the possibility and he clearly wasn't interested, so … end of discussion."

"But you met with Ritchie on several occasions — you or one of your representatives." Smith made a show of flipping through his notes and stopping at one page in particular as Kurtisov looked on.

"I met him once, in Toronto. There was some follow-up with my associates over the next few weeks."

"Which associates would they be?"

"I don't recall."

"It would good to know," Smith said, looking at Kurtisov, then his lawyer.

"We can provide you with that information," Bilak said, making a note on his yellow pad with an ornate fountain pen.

"I'm curious, Mr. Kurtisov," Smith continued. "If Ritchie was uninterested in your offer, why the multiple meetings?"

"Simple courtesy, Detective. Besides, you never know. Just because a player is uninterested now does not mean he will always feel that way. I always take the time to lay out the details, so people can make an informed decision, whether it's now or later."

Smith watched Kurtisov as he delivered his answer with the smoothness of silk, and knew he was lying. The only question was whether he was lying to conceal his involvement in Ritchie's murder, or some other illicit activity. Having spent the day acquainting himself with Kurtisov's less-than-savoury activities, the range of possible crimes to conceal was broad, indeed.

❄   ❄   ❄

Smith came up out of the subway station and was instantly lured off course by the aroma of ground coffee. Spotting the source of the glorious smell, his stomach rumbled and he realized that he hadn't eaten anything in hours. With no set time for his meeting with Matt Jones, he decided he had time for a detour. Entering the coffee shop, he noticed the clientele and realized a muffin and a coffee in this place was probably going to cost triple what he was used to, but he didn't care. He was in line to place his order when his phone went off.

"Jack, it's Dean McGregor." Smith's first thought was that he had left something behind at the task force office and instinctively checked his jacket pocket for his wallet.

"Hi, Dean. What's up?"

"I just got a little intel I thought you might be interested in."

"Shoot," he said, putting his hand over the tiny mouthpiece as he ordered a coffee and pointed to a sticky bun in the glass case in front of him.

"You remember that associate we were talking about?"

"Yeah?" Smith felt a rush of adrenalin, knowing he was referring to Anton Kurtz, a man linked to Kurtisov's various businesses, and the person they suspected of doing the dirtiest work, including the two murders they suspected Kurtisov had ordered. After the interview, McGregor had mentioned that they had been successful in obtaining a wiretap on Kurtz's phone, and would look into whether they could place him in the Ottawa area on the morning of Curtis Ritchie's death.

"Well, we know he was in Montreal on Saturday night, and that he drove back to Toronto on Sunday."

Smith processed the timeline as he handed over a ten-dollar bill. Ottawa was less than a two-hour drive on the way back from Montreal. Kurtz could easily have left Montreal, stopped off to kill Ritchie, and been back in Toronto by early afternoon, after another four hours on the road. "Nothing in between Montreal and Toronto though?" he asked, hopefully.

"He didn't use the phone, so no. We might get lucky some other way, but not if he was trying to conceal his itinerary."

"You mean a visa receipt or something?" Smith said, instantly realizing how unlikely such a break would be, given the fact that people like Kurtz usually dealt exclusively in cash.

"Yeah, but like I said, chances aren't great."

"No, but it's good to know."

"We can flesh it out tomorrow, but I thought I'd let you know now."

"Yeah, I appreciate it," Smith said, taking the couple of coins of change from his ten and putting them in his pocket. "You sure I'm not wrecking your Sunday morning?"

"It's already shot. My kid's got a 6:00 a.m. practice.

"Smith laughed. "In that case I don't feel so bad about our nine-thirty meeting. I'll see you then."

Smith took his overpriced purchase over to a seat by the window and took a bite of the bun, thinking about the news as looked out the window toward the massive concrete structure of Toronto's home rink, adorned in the blue and white of Ottawa's archrival. There was something about Kurtisov, for sure, but he didn't seem patient enough to wait six months to unleash Kurtz if he wanted Ritchie dead. Smith picked up his phone and dialed Marshall's number. His partner answered on the fourth ring, and sounded as though he was still chewing.

"Interrupt your burger?" Smith imagined him sitting at his desk, leaning over a ketchup-splattered square of wax paper that had once surrounded a double bacon burger.

"Celery sticks, if you can believe it. Connie's idea."

"I figured it wasn't yours. How's it going?"

"I was just gonna check in, actually. I've had an interesting day."

"Me too," Smith said, leaning back in his chair and taking a sip of his coffee. "You go first."

"I talked to Peter Dunne."

"And?"

"Seems he left out a few things when we talked to him out at the arena the other night."

"Like what?" Smith's curiosity was instantly piqued.

"Like Ritchie kept hinting about something big that was going to happen. When Dunne asked what he was talking about, Ritchie would clam up, only to drop another hint later."

"What kind of hints?"

"Nothing concrete, but Dunne had the impression that whatever it was, it was big. He assumed it had something to do with Curtis's contract, or his role on the team."

"Nothing more specific than that?" Smith was intrigued and disappointed, all at once. As he drank his coffee, he noticed an attractive woman at a nearby table peering over her laptop in his direction and smiling. He smiled back.

"But that's not all," Marshall continued, still munching on celery. "He also said he was at Hearst's party, and he overheard the run-in between Ritchie and Hearst. According to Dunne, Hearst was pissed off because Ritchie was making moves on *his* wife, not O'Neill's girlfriend."

"Is he sure? Could he have confused the two?"

"He said he overheard Hearst telling him to 'stay the fuck away from Mandy' — that's his wife's name. I checked."

"Don't tell me you've been using Google again, Marsh. You're getting all high-tech on me. But why didn't he tell us any of this the other night?"

"He was afraid of breaking the code."

"I forgot — the hockey mafia."

"What goes on the road stays on the road. I guess it applies at home as well. He's a rookie fighting for a spot on the team. The last thing he needs is to make enemies, especially if it's the captain."

Smith nodded, remembering that Dunne hadn't even made the road trip, which meant his position was even more precarious — just a phone call away from scrapping it out on the farm team.

"I guess he figured it was safer to talk to you after the team hit the road. What about the interview with O'Neill's girlfriend?"

Marshall whistled. "You should have seen this gal."

"I knew we should have traded."

"She looked like she just slid down a pole. I can definitely see her as a major tease. And I'm pretty sure there was a bruise on her face, though I wasn't sure with all the makeup."

"You think O'Neill might have slapped her around?"

"It's possible. Her version of events is slightly different, though. She says it was all a big misunderstanding. She was just being friendly with Ritchie. And according to her, Ritchie was more interested in Mandy Hearst anyway."

"So Dunne was telling the truth."

"And Hearst was lying. Which means we're going to have to have another word with him for sure. The wife, too."

"I'm talking to Matt Jones in a bit. You want me to try to talk to Hearst as well?"

"What do you think?"

Smith considered it for a moment. "I'm thinking we should hold off. See what Jones says, then we can compare notes before we sit down with Hearst again — a little more formally this time."

"Sounds good," Marshall said. "So, how's it going over there, anyway?"

"Good. I've got some news as well. Seems our Russian friend is into all kinds of stuff, and having met him, I can honestly say I don't believe half of what he told me. He's a slick one."

"You think we should be taking a hard look at him?"

"I'm still only halfway through the task force material on him, but I just found out the guy who supposedly does his dirty work was in Montreal on Friday night, then back in Toronto on Sunday afternoon."

"Fits our timeline, except for the same lag issue as with Saunders, and everyone else."

"That's the part that's missing," Smith said, sketching out a timeline from February to mid-September, with points on the way representing Kurtisov's meeting, Saunders' blowout, and Hearst's party. He added one for the tussle with John Ridgeway in Peterborough for good measure, but it didn't change the large gap between Ritchie's interactions with either Kurtisov or Saunders and the murder. "There's got to be something we're missing. Something must have happened over the summer."

"Hmm…. Oh, by the way, how was your reporter?"

"He was more useful than I thought," Smith said, setting his pen down and abandoning his timeline. "He said Saunders was a bleacher creature."

"A what?"

"He spent his time screaming at everyone in the stands; a real pain in the ass. Says he can see why Ritchie dumped him as his agent. He also said Ritchie's adoptive father was just the same. Crazy hockey parent — the kind who picks fights with the other team's parents."

There was a pause in Marshall's crunching at the other end of the line. "That's interesting."

"Yeah, except it's not very helpful, unless we're going to exhume him and ask him where he was last weekend."

"I meant Ellen Ritchie's choice of men. Or maybe it was something in Ritchie himself that brought out the worst in people."

"He obviously brought out the worst in someone last Saturday morning." Smith sighed. "I don't know about you, Marsh, but I feel like we're just weaving this big spiderweb that keeps getting bigger and leading us further away from the centre."

"We'll get there. We just need to catch a break. It's still early."

"I'd better go if I want to talk to Jones."

"Good luck. When are you back tomorrow?"

"Flight's at six."

"You want to grab a beer when you get in?"

"Sure. I'll be in touch before then anyway."

Smith ended the call and ate the last of the bun. The woman with the laptop was looking over again. He finished his coffee and stood, glancing in her direction. She really was attractive, with wavy blonde hair up in a yellow headband bearing a familiar logo. He smiled back, then headed for the door. The things he did for work.

Smith crossed the street and went to the main entrance of the giant arena, spotting a security guard as soon as he stepped into the foyer.

"I have a meeting with someone in the Raftsmen's management," he said, pulling his notebook out to find the contact name Melissa McAdam had given him. The guard waved over a ticket attendant and looked at Smith.

"Name?"

"Jack Smith."

"You got a Jack Smith on the list, Marjorie?"

"Yup. Follow me."

Smith followed her through a side door, then down a circular hallway that led to another locked door, which she opened by entering a code. As they continued on down the wide concrete hallway toward a group of young men playing soccer, he realized he was looking at half of the Raftsmen's starting lineup. The coach was standing beyond the soccer game, talking to a woman whose back was turned to Smith. When she turned around, he saw it was Melissa McAdam. She spotted him and came over.

"Hi, Jack," she said, offering her hand. She was dressed in a navy pantsuit and heels that put her eyes almost level with his. He remembered her distinctive perfume from their last meeting.

"I didn't realize you were in Toronto."

"I decided to make the trip at the last minute. He's fine," she added, looking at the attendant, who nodded and turned to leave.

"Come with me," she said, leading him away from the assembled players. As Smith followed the click of her heels on the concrete, Dennis Hearst emerged from the dressing room and he saw the flash of recognition in the captain's eyes.

"Oh, hi," he said, seemingly unsure whether to stop, as he glanced between Smith and McAdam, who kept walking. He winked at Smith and whispered, "Watch out for her. She's a tiger."

Smith looked ahead as McAdam reached a junction with another hallway and turned toward him, waiting.

"I thought it would be better if you talked to Matt discreetly," she said, when he caught up. "I want you to have full access, but we do want to minimize distractions given they're playing in a couple of hours."

"I wouldn't want to mess with the karma, especially not right before the battle of Ontario."

The sparkle in her green eyes matched her bright smile. He also noticed the elegant pearl choker at the base of her neck and the lightly tanned skin exposed in the neckline of her crisp, white blouse. He had thought her attractive before, but up close she seemed to exude a sexuality that was hard to resist.

"So are you here for other … meetings, or did you just come for Matt?" she asked.

"No, I've been in meetings all day. More tomorrow."

"Well, if you don't have any tonight, you can be my guest at the game."

"Well, I do need to discuss some follow-up interviews with a couple of the players … and Toronto versus Ottawa's usually a pretty good game," he added, grinning. A growing rivalry over the years usually translated into gritty play when the two teams met, interspersed by a fight or two. "I'm surprised Jones isn't in the lineup."

"We've got a new prospect Dad wants to try out. Just called him up last night," she said, as they passed the door to a gym with a mix of free weights and stationary training bikes.

"A secret weapon, huh?"

"You could say that, yeah. We'll still have O'Neill out there, of course," she added, pulling up at the door to a room just past the gym, its door marked THERAPY. She watched him read the sign. "As in physical, not mental. Jonesy has a hamstring injury, but that's top secret."

"Got it."

He followed her into the room to a massage table at the far end, where Matt Jones lay face down, a physiotherapist working the muscles of his left leg.

"How's the leg, Matt?"

"Better. I could still play tonight, you know."

"I know, but take the chance to rest it. This is the detective I was telling you about."

Smith shook Jones's hand as the latter waved the therapist off and sat on the edge of the bed.

"I'll leave you guys to it. Come and see me when you're done," she said, laying her hand on Smith's shoulder. He enjoyed the sensation as her touch lingered a split second more than was necessary, and then she was gone.

"She's somethin', huh?" Jones said, breaking the silence that had fallen over them both as they watched her leave, the click of her heels disappearing in the hallway.

"What? Yeah, she's very ... nice," Smith said awkwardly, collecting his thoughts. "Do you want to talk here, or ...?"

"Let's grab a seat out in the stands. There's plenty of room and we won't be disturbed."

Smith followed Jones along the hall and out into

the arena's bowl, taking a seat a few rows up behind the visitor's bench. No one was on the ice, and the only people in the stands were stadium staff and a smattering of reporters on the far side. It was an odd sensation to be sitting in such a large space — where chaotic noise was the norm — and to hear the sound of their voices deadened by the still air.

"So, what did you want to talk to me about?"

Smith was familiar with Jones's edgy style of play — in fact he was one of Smith's favourite Raftsmen. But the sense of power he carried with him onto the ice, matched by the powerful build under the tight-fitting T-shirt, was missing from his demeanour. He seemed nervous.

"I assume Ms. McAdam told you I'm investigating Curtis Ritchie's death?"

Jones nodded.

"Did you know him well?"

"Not really. I met him at camp for the first time."

Smith asked him the same list of questions he had asked the other players, about Ritchie's manner and integration with the rest of the team. The answers from Jones painted the same general picture; that Ritchie was your typical rookie in most ways, though he did have a bit more arrogance than most, due to his skill and the big trades the Raftsmen had made to bring him to Ottawa. Smith gave him several opportunities to volunteer the details of the party at Hearst's house, but Jones didn't take them.

"We heard there was a team party at the start of camp, at Hearst's house," he finally prompted.

Jones nodded. "He does it every year, for the past few seasons anyway."

"You were there?"

Jones nodded and looked at his hands, as though he found them suddenly interesting.

"Anything unusual happen?"

"No, not really." He shook his head as Smith began to grow impatient.

"Look, Matt. I know about the player's code, but this is a murder investigation and I'd appreciate straight answers."

Jones looked shocked. "What do you mean? I don't —"

"I know there was an altercation between Hearst and Ritchie." He paused, seeing defeat in Jones's eyes just before he looked away. "I'm not interested in smearing anyone's reputation, or interfering with team chemistry, but a young man is dead, and I need to get to the bottom of it. Did you witness a scuffle between Hearst and Ritchie?" Smith hoped he wouldn't have to reveal the fact that someone else had seen him do just that. He had a feeling Dunne would be in for a rough ride on his return to the dressing room if he did.

Jones nodded. "Yeah. They were having a bit of a chat."

"A chat?" Smith raised his eyebrows.

"Okay, they were shoving each other. I was on my way to the bathroom when I noticed them. I went over to see what was going on."

"And what was going on?"

"They were arguing. Hearst was telling Ritchie to back off."

Smith waited for more, but Jones was looking at his hands again.

"Did it have to do with Ritchie's behaviour toward some of the other players' girlfriends, or wives?"

Jones kept his eyes down, but nodded his head.

"Who, in particular, Matt? Did Hearst tell him to stay away from his wife?"

"Yeah."

"What did Ritchie say?"

"He said he didn't know what he was talking about. He was just trying to be friendly."

"Did you hear Hearst mention Tanner O'Neill's girlfriend?"

Jones looked puzzled. "What do you mean?"

"Was Hearst telling him to stay away from her, as well?"

Jones shook his head. "No. I never heard him say that."

"So it was just over Mandy Hearst?"

"As far as I know, yeah."

Smith moved quickly to another question, but he was already more interested in the answers Hearst would give when he and Marshall talked to him again.

CHAPTER 18

Smith stood in the hallway outside the visitors' dressing room, looking at his watch and wondering what had happened to Melissa McAdam. She had said to meet him here to discuss follow-up interviews with some of the players, but it was getting late, and they had already gone out for their pre-game skate. He was debating whether he would stick around for a period or just head out and get something to eat.

"I'm sorry," McAdam said, appearing around the corner. "Something came up, and … well, anyway, I'm glad I caught you."

"No problem," he said, as another man in a suit came up behind McAdam and tapped her on the shoulder.

"Excuse me for a second," she said, turning to talk to the other man, who looked like an agent. A few minutes later, Smith was really getting tired of standing around when McAdam extricated herself from her conversation.

"I'm so sorry," she said, seeming to recognize someone else coming down the hallway. "Do you want to go get a drink? I'll never get a free minute around here."

Smith shrugged his shoulders. He could certainly use a beer. "Sure."

"Follow me," she said, leading them off down the hall toward an emergency exit that led into an outer corridor, then a loading area, and finally outside.

"You seem to know your way around the building."

"I can do better than that. I know there's a pretty decent bar and grill over there," she said, pointing across the street. He followed her as she darted through the gridlocked traffic and up to the entrance. Inside, a large bar dominated to the right, whereas the left side of the floor plan was devoted to a smaller dining room. From the crisp linens and sparkling glassware, Smith thought it looked a cut above his usual fare. But this was downtown Toronto, after all.

"You okay with sitting at the bar? Oh wait, there's a table coming open there," she said, heading off toward a corner table where a trio were standing. A waiter appeared and started to wave at her, but she brushed him off and continued to the table. "That was lucky. This place is always jammed," she said, as they settled into their chairs and the waiter cleared the remaining glasses, a frown on his face. Another server appeared to take their orders a moment later.

"One of your martinis, please."

"Draft for me," Smith said, as the waitress scribbled the orders and left.

"So, how was your talk with Jones? He tell you what you needed to know?"

"In a manner of speaking, yes."

"Sounds mysterious. Can you tell me if you've

made any progress, or would you have to kill me then?" She smiled and then put her hand over her mouth. "I'm sorry. That was in really bad taste. What with Curtis …" She put her hand to her forehead. "What a thing to say."

"It's okay. I'm used to dark humour."

"I guess it comes with the territory, huh?"

"Yeah. The truth is, there isn't much to tell you about the investigation anyway."

"Is that unusual? I mean, not to have a suspect after a week?"

"I didn't say we didn't have any suspects."

"Oh. Well, I guess that's good news, then. I think the sooner the case is closed, the better."

"You mean for the team?"

"I was thinking of Ellen Ritchie, actually," she said, as their drinks arrived.

"Of course." Smith nodded. "I didn't mean to suggest you didn't care about her. Just that it must be quite a distraction for the players."

"Good save." She winked and raised her martini glass. He did the same with his beer glass, and couldn't resist a smile.

"So tell me, Detec —"

"Call me Jack, please."

"Okay, Jack. Tell me, how did you get into homicide investigation?"

"The normal progression, I guess."

"Really? You seem pretty young to be in charge of the biggest murder investigation in Ottawa's history — at least, I'm assuming it is."

Smith shook his head. "First of all, I'm not in charge of the investigation, I'm just part of a team."

"Don't be modest," she said, sipping her drink. "It doesn't suit you. You're ten years younger than the average homicide detective. You must be good."

"I never said I wasn't good."

She smiled, skewered the green olive, and popped it in her mouth. "That's better."

"What about you — what made you leave Bay Street?"

She laughed. "How long have you got?"

"I didn't think it was a trick question. I thought you'd just say you loved hockey, or you wanted to work with your dad."

"Liar." She was smiling as she said it.

"Okay, I don't really see hockey management as your area of interest."

"Why not?" Her back straightened visibly.

"Well, you don't seem to like hockey that much, for starters."

"Is it that obvious?" Her face broke into a devious grin.

"Not at all," he said, straight-faced. She waited a second and then laughed.

"Fair enough. But you don't have to be a fan to be good at management, just like you don't need to be a good driver to run a car company. And yes, my dad's a big part in all of this. Bad enough he had to have a daughter, but then to have her run off to Bay Street."

"You're an only child?"

She nodded. "My mother couldn't have any kids after me, so I guess we both ruined Dad's hopes of having a son to play hockey with."

"He seems very proud of you." Smith said, as she finished her drink. His beer was almost gone too. He assumed the fancy little glasses were to blame.

"You want to get some dinner?"

Smith looked at his watch. "Don't you have to be back for the game?"

She laughed. "Like you said, I'm not really that big a fan. I don't usually watch the games."

"In that case, yeah, I'm starving."

❄ ❄ ❄

"So, what *can* you tell me about the investigation?" McAdam asked as they sipped their post-dinner cappuccinos.

Smith sighed. "You really are relentless, aren't you?"

"I've got the team to think about."

"You mean the team that's playing across the street? Aren't you even interested in the score?"

"You sound like my father. I'll get the score after it's over, don't worry."

He smiled. "Honestly, there's not much to say. There are some people of interest that we're looking into. I'm sure we'll catch a break soon."

McAdam pouted. "That's not telling me much."

"Maybe you have a theory?"

"From what I've heard of Curtis, it was probably a jilted husband."

"I understand he was quite a player." Smith turned the little cup around on its saucer, adding: "In the non-hockey sense of the word."

239

"I think he got around," she said, sipping her coffee and leaning her chin in her hand, the movement of her wrist triggering the release of a trace of her familiar perfume. Her suit jacket lay over the back of the chair, and the neckline of blouse plunged seductively with the forward motion. "How about you, Jack," she asked, pointing to his hand. "No ring?"

He shook his head. "You?"

"I don't think I'm cut out for marriage. Besides, it seems to end in misery so often, I wonder why anyone bothers."

"You're awfully young to be so cynical."

"You know a lot of happily married people?"

Smith smiled. He knew Marshall's marriage was solid, but she had a point. A couple of his best friends' marriages had imploded before the five-year mark, with disastrous results, and of the ones that hadn't, he wasn't sure happiness figured prominently in the equation.

"Some," he said.

"I don't think either of our careers are particularly conducive, either. I can't imagine your hours are normal."

Smith shrugged. "People manage. They make it work."

"Maybe, but I'm still not convinced by the overall concept. My parents are a case in point. When they were married … an unhappier pair I've never known."

"How about now?"

"They get along like old friends; which is what they were, once upon a time. Your parents still married?"

"Yeah."

"That's nice, and it explains your optimism. Ever been close?"

"Not really," he lied. He had no intention of letting that elephant enter the room.

"Well," she said, looking at her watch. "I guess I should be getting back to my hotel."

"You really aren't heading back to the rink?"

"I told you, I usually don't even go on the road. I plan to get up early and hit Yorkville tomorrow. I need my beauty sleep," she said, waving to the waiter for the cheque.

He pulled out his wallet. "I'll walk you back, if you like."

"A gentleman, how nice." She smiled as she slipped into her jacket. "But put your wallet away. I have very strong opinions about protocol, and I invited you, remember?"

He resisted until she made it clear she was serious. "Well, at least let me buy you a nightcap," he said, as the waiter took her card.

"Why not?"

❄ ❄ ❄

Smith awoke with a start around eight. He had been dreaming about Curtis Ritchie again. This time he had been in hot pursuit of the killer, along the canal path, when he had awoken. He took a look around and did a double take. The room looked different from the night before, which was understandable, since it wasn't his. His clothes were in a heap on the floor, and an open bottle of champagne sat on a little table next to two half-empty glasses.

"Good morning." He felt a hand slide around his waist and the warmth of naked skin on his back as Melissa McAdam's familiar perfume wafted up from the pillow. "What time's your meeting?"

He glanced at the clock before turning to face her. There was a thin ray of light through the drapes that let him see her — as beautiful now as she had looked the night before. He knew he shouldn't be here, but he knew he didn't care.

"We've got time."

CHAPTER 19

Smith sat opposite Marshall in the corner of their favourite pub, listening as he described his interview with Tanner O'Neill's girlfriend, particularly the low-cut top she had chosen for the occasion, and the surgical enhancements it revealed.

"And what about Dunne?"

"Like I said, the biggest surprise was what he had to say about Hearst. The stuff about Ritchie referring to some kind of storm brewing was interesting, too, but I'm not really sure what to make of that. How about your Russian?"

"You mean Kurtisov?"

"No, the other guy. What was his name?"

"Kurtz," Smith said. "Anton Kurtz. McGregor said he's going to track him down for a chat, but he doesn't expect a confession, if you know what I mean."

Marshall crossed his arms and frowned. "All this is interesting stuff, but I'm not sure where it leaves us."

Smith noticed an incoming text and resisted the urge to check it, tucking the phone into his pocket instead. "You think we should focus on Saunders?"

"Unless we get something concrete on this Kurtz guy, or Kurtisov, yeah."

"All right, let's put him under the microscope and see what we find," he said, stifling a yawn.

"Keeping you up?"

"Long day."

"Did you track down one of your Newfie buddies last night and hit the bars?"

"Naw. I didn't do much," he lied. He knew Marshall would rib him mercilessly if he found out he had slept with Melissa McAdam. Smith had debated the ethics of it as well, but he decided he had done nothing seriously wrong. She wasn't material to the investigation — other than arranging meetings with the players and giving them details of Ritchie's contract, which they could have gotten from Ritchie's agent, as well. He figured he was guilty of minor indiscretion, at worst. Certainly not a hanging offence.

"What do you say we spend an hour or so going over what we've got on Saunders."

"What time's he coming in tomorrow?"

"Ten-thirty."

"Sounds good," Smith said, as they finished their beers and got up to leave. He put some money on the table. "My round."

"If you insist." Marshall led the way out, as Smith peeked at his texts and saw one from Melissa. He knew she had come back on an earlier flight, rather than follow the team to the next game. "Gotta go to Chicago tomorrow for a couple of days. Hoping we could pick up where we left off." He looked at his watch, then texted her back: "C u around 11."

"What are you smirking about?" Marshall said, holding the door open for him as he hit send.

"Nothing." Smith looked up, thinking it was going to be hard to concentrate for the next hour.

"And watch where you're going, will you? You people drive me crazy, wandering around staring at your little screens."

"Okay, gramps."

❊ ❊ ❊

Smith watched as McAdam got up from the bed and strode across the bedroom floor, apparently unconcerned by her nudity. She had no reason to be, Smith reflected, as her graceful form disappeared through the door. He heard the clinking of glass in the fridge and she returned a few seconds later, a disappointed look on her face as she slid back onto the bed next to him.

"I think a trip to the grocery store is in order," she said, running a hand down his chest.

"What were you looking for?"

"Something to drink, actually. What kind of bachelor are you — you don't have a beer lying around in the back of the fridge?"

He laughed and looked at the clock radio on his night table. "There's a pub around the corner that's still open. I'll buy you a drink."

"You're on," she said. "But I'm not done with you yet, she added, as they stood to get dressed.

"It's just a refreshment break," he said, as he slid on his jeans and a shirt and waited for her to finish dressing. Her hair was mussed, but with a couple of strokes of her fingers she was ready to go. *Low maintenance*, he thought.

They arrived at the pub with half an hour to go before last call and as they turned from the bar, drinks in hand, Smith barely avoided a collision with a passing patron.

"Jack?"

He looked up from the sloshing liquid to find himself face to face with Lisa White and a man he didn't recognize.

"Oh, hi," he said, as she looked from him to McAdam and back.

"I guess I shouldn't be surprised to see you in this neck of the woods." She looked at McAdam again and Smith could see there was no avoiding an introduction.

"This is an old friend," he said, pointing to White as McAdam looked on. "Lisa, meet Melissa."

The two women shook hands, their bright smiles concealing a cold mutual appraisal. Smith was wondering whether it was obvious that they had crawled out of bed to come here. Lisa didn't miss much.

"Melissa McAdam. Nice to meet you."

The other guy looked on with interest. If he was annoyed that his date seemed oblivious to his existence, he wasn't saying anything, but Smith found Lisa's demeanour curious.

"Oh, this is Brad," she finally said, seeming embarrassed at having forgotten him completely. The two men exchanged wary nods as Melissa gestured to a nearby table.

246

"You're welcome to join us if you like," she said, and Smith detected a distinctively mischievous undertone in her invitation.

"We were just leaving," Lisa replied, a little too quickly. "Enjoy your evening." Her smile had faded by the time she turned to leave.

"Old flame?" Melissa asked, as they sat at the table.

"That obvious?"

"That she's still into you? Yeah." Melissa tapped her glass off his and they drank. "Didn't you see how she ignored the guy she was with? Poor Brad. What's the story, Jack? Did you break her heart?"

"We dated a few years back. It's ancient history," he said, finding Melissa's assessment ironic. Oddly though, he had no desire to follow Lisa out the door. For once, he was quite content to stay exactly where he was.

❄ ❄ ❄

Smith was sitting at his desk, reviewing his notes from the last interview with Tom Saunders, when Marshall appeared behind him.

"I think we might have caught a break. You remember we were waiting to hear back from that security guard at Ritchie's condo building?"

"Not really…. I thought someone had talked to the building security guards."

"Most of them, yeah. But one of them went on holiday the night before Ritchie was murdered. Apparently we tracked him down and, get this, he says he saw Saunders on Friday night, just before he knocked off work."

Smith flipped through his notebook and reread his notes. "Didn't Saunders tell us he hadn't been in contact with Ritchie since Wednesday?"

"Yup. And you remember he told us Curtis was scheduled to do a promotional photo shoot the week after he was killed?"

"Yeah, I talked to the receptionist at the studio. She confirmed the appointment for the Thursday."

"I just got off the phone with the photographer. *He* says Saunders called Friday afternoon to say that the shoot was cancelled. He also said Saunders sounded pissed off."

"You thinking what I'm thinking?"

"That we might have found our trigger — the spark that lit the fuse."

"Solves the timing problem, doesn't it?" Smith was nodding.

"He's pissed off in March, but he gets over it, figuring he'll cash in on Ritchie another way — as a front man for this clothing line. Except maybe Ritchie had other ideas about that as well."

"What was the name of this stuff again?" Smith turned to his computer.

"The clothing line? Coolwear, Cool ice …"

"Coolite, that's it," Smith said, typing the name in and waiting as the search results popped up onscreen. He scrolled through the results and clicked on a link. He recognized the site from the brief search he had done a few days ago to confirm the existence of the business. Viewing it the second time, it occurred to him that the site looked homemade, and the clothing itself looked pretty cheesy, despite the claims about the fabric being lightweight and having space-age, moisture-wicking characteristics.

"I don't blame Ritchie for not wanting to front this crap," Marshall said, looking over his partner's shoulder. "I think we really might be onto something. And Saunders has certainly got some explaining to do."

"He'll be here in half an hour. We'll ask him then."

❄ ❄ ❄

Tom Saunders had appeared irritated the first time he had come in for an interview. He looked decidedly pissed off by the time Smith and Marshall entered the small interview room, where they had let him stew for twenty minutes while they discussed the approach they would take to the questioning.

"About time," he said, apparently unconcerned with concealing his distaste.

"You in a hurry to get somewhere?" Marshall's smile was overdone, but Saunders didn't get the sarcasm.

"Now that you mention it ..."

"Well, let's both try not to waste any more of each other's time, how about that?"

"What's that supposed to mean?"

"Relax, Tom. We just want to ask you some questions, but before we do, I want to caution you again." Marshall glanced toward the camera on the wall.

"I know, this interview is being recorded, and all that," Saunders said, the irritation obvious in his voice. "I know my rights, okay?"

"I forgot, you were a paralegal," Marshall said. "But

we have to go through the motions anyway, as I'm sure you understand."

Saunders frowned as Marshall cautioned him formally.

"Let's get on with it," he said, as Marshall finished reading.

"Do you know anyone who lives at the Residences, on Sussex?"

"That's Curtis's building."

"Apart from Curtis, that is."

Saunders shook his head.

"And when was it, again, that you last saw Curtis?" Marshall tapped a finger on his top lip.

"I told you … Wednesday."

"Well, that's really strange, because one of the security guards at the Residences says you were there on Friday night."

Saunders looked back and forth between Smith and Marshall. "He must be mistaken."

"No." Marshall shook his head. "He seemed pretty sure. We asked twice, believe me. We asked twice because we know you told us the last time you saw Curtis was Wednesday, not Friday. Do you want to tell us what you were doing at Curtis's building on Friday?"

Saunders looked down at his hands, then sighed and leaned back in the chair. "I went to see him, but he wasn't there. It's not like I lied to you or anything."

"But you didn't exactly tell us the truth, did you?"

"You asked when I saw him last, and I told you."

"All right, fair enough. Why'd you go to see him on Friday?"

"I was in the neighbourhood and I thought I'd see if he wanted to grab a bite, that's all. He was out."

"Do you know where he was?"

"No."

"So you called him?" Smith asked. They had already established from Ritchie's phone records that his cell had received a call from Saunders at around six p.m., then again twenty minutes later.

"That's right. I already told you I called him Friday night."

"Yeah, but you didn't mention that you were calling from the lobby of his building. Why not?"

"You didn't ask."

"Pretty weak, Tom. But let's move on for now. Tell us more about your clothing line. What's it called again?"

"Coolite."

"Right. You said Curtis was your partner?"

Saunders nodded.

"That's not what Dan Avery told us."

"Like you can believe anything that guy says," Saunders snorted in disgust.

"He seems to have a better batting average than you right now," Smith remarked. He was getting tired of the attitude, but more and more curious with each answer, and the increasing discomfort Saunders exhibited as the interview progressed.

"Avery denies that Curtis was your partner in that venture, or in any other, as far as he knew."

"We just didn't have anything in writing. Didn't need it. And like I said, Avery's just a mouthpiece who

251

thinks he knows everything — he doesn't, so it doesn't surprise me he hadn't heard about it."

"I didn't say he hadn't heard about it," Marshall corrected him. "Actually, he said Curtis had mentioned it a few weeks ago, as something you were asking him to get involved with and that he wanted no part of. Avery says that was the only time it ever came up."

"That's bullshit. Curtis loved the idea."

"He told Avery the clothes were crap and he wasn't going to be associated with it. Did he tell you that too?"

Smith watched as Saunders' features darkened. "I told you, Curtis liked the concept, and he was excited about the business."

"Must have been a bit of a distraction for him, no? What, with training camp and a new team, Curtis's plate must have been pretty full. Still ..." Marshall stood for a stretch. "I can see why he might have felt obligated to you, after the draft. That would explain why he told you he'd go along with endorsing it, don't you think?"

"How many times have I got to tell you?" Saunders was leaning forward, arms on the table. "It's not like I was forcing him to do it. He was behind it, one hundred and ten percent."

"Why'd he cancel the photo shoot then?" Smith asked, seeing the slight delay in Saunders' response.

"Just a scheduling conflict."

"When did you guys reschedule for?"

"In a ... we were gonna do it after the road trip."

"Well, I've got to tell you, Tom." Marshall regained his seat. "I talked to the photographer this morning, and he says it wasn't rescheduled. He said it was cancelled, and he also said you were furious about it."

"That's not true. I told —"

"You'd better start telling the truth, Tom, because right now you're not looking so good. We've got two different witnesses who say you were very angry with Curtis on Friday night — one of whom saw you at his building — and we've got Dan Avery, who tells us Curtis never had any intention of endorsing your shitty clothing line." Marshall paused to see if Saunders would take the bait, but he just sat there stewing. "And then there's you, telling us your version is the only right one, despite the fact that it doesn't fit with the evidence. You've already admitted to failing to give us all of the relevant facts."

"I didn't kill him," Saunders said, shaking his head.

"But you were at his building on Friday night?"

"Yes, but I didn't see him."

"But you were pissed off at him for backing out of his endorsement, right?"

Saunders nodded. "He could be a selfish little prick sometimes ..." He stopped and looked at the two detectives. "You don't honestly think I had something to do with his death, do you?"

Smith looked at Marshall. *Could Saunders really be this naive?*

"I mean, I'd have to be pretty fucking stupid to do that, wouldn't I?"

"I don't know, Tom. You've got a reputation for having a bit of a temper, wouldn't you say?"

"What are you talking about?"

"All the times you took him to hockey practice. All those early mornings at the rink, and this is the way he pays you back? Pretty damned selfish …"

"I know what you're trying to do," Saunders blurted out. "But I'm telling you, I had nothing to do with this. I told you, I was staying at my sister's. Ask her."

"We did. She and her husband both say you were there when they went to bed Friday night and when they got up on Saturday morning. But they didn't get up until almost ten, which leaves plenty of time for you to have gotten down to the canal and back."

Saunders stared at Marshall, and something seemed to click. He sat back in his chair and crossed his arms.

"Not another word."

"What's that, Tom?"

"I'm not saying another word without my lawyer. And I'm gonna sue your asses off, both of you. This is total bullshit."

"You want to clam up, that's your call, Tom. You can call your lawyer, but it's not going to change anything. Sooner or later, we'll get the truth, whether you get the chance to tell your side of the story or not."

Saunders just stared at the table in front of him as Marshall looked at Smith. They both knew the interview was over.

CHAPTER 20

Smith sat at his desk mid-afternoon, poring over the murder book. After the interview with Saunders, he and Marshall had debriefed Beaudoin and let him know they were going to take a hard look at Saunders, while still following up on Kurtisov, just in case. He was reviewing the inventory of evidence from the crime scene when his phone went off. He looked down at the display and saw Lisa White's number. He paused before answering, then decided he might as well take it.

"Lisa?"

"Hi, Jack. How are things?"

"Not bad, you?"

"Same. I know you're busy, but I'm in your neck of the woods and I thought I could buy you a quick coffee."

"Where are you?"

"The Java Post," she said, referring to Smith's favourite coffee shop, just down the street from the Elgin Street station.

"I'm kind of busy."

"You can't spare fifteen minutes?"

"What's this all about, Lisa? I thought you didn't think coffee was a good idea?"

There was a slight pause at the other end of the line. "How difficult does this have to be, Jack?"

He looked at his watch and was about to refuse, but for some reason he couldn't quite. "Order me a cappuccino. I'll be there in five."

"Since when do you drink ... whatever."

Smith grabbed his jacket and headed out into the street. The air had turned much cooler overnight, and summer suddenly seemed a long way away. Arriving at the busy coffee shop, he spotted Lisa at a corner table and headed over.

"Cappuccino, huh? I'm impressed."

He grinned. "A guy can't expand his horizons?"

"So, how's the case coming along?"

"It's coming."

"And you're meeting new and interesting people?" she added, as he took his seat.

"She's in the Raftsmen's front office. A lawyer, actually."

"All the more reason to watch yourself. As if her being the GM's daughter wasn't enough. What have you got yourself tangled up in, Jack?"

"What are you talking about? I had a drink with her, so what?"

She gave him an appraising look from over her cup. "Really? It seemed like you two had shared more than that."

Smith could feel his cheeks colouring. "And so what if we did? It's not like she's ... maybe this was a bad idea." He started to stand.

"Take it easy. I'm just pulling your chain," she said, waving him back to his seat. "Jeez, what happened to your sense of humour?" When he didn't respond, she set her mug down. "Have you talked to Valerie lately?"

Smith scoffed. "Not since you warned her off me, no. Thanks a lot, by the way."

"I didn't warn her off you."

"Bullshit. She told me, Lisa."

"Valerie makes her own choices," she said. "But she deserves to know if you've moved on."

"Are you kidding? She's the one who decided to call it off, after she talked to you, of course."

She shook her head. "That's not what I heard. Anyway, I'm not here to tell you what to do."

"Really? I could have sworn that was exactly why you were here. And since we're being all moral, does Brad know you're here?"

"What's that got to do with anything?" Her confidence seemed to turn to outrage before his eyes, as she became agitated. Smith had seen her like this before, but not often. Taking advantage of a rare shift in power, he went for the kill.

"I think your first instincts were right, Lisa. We probably should keep out of each other's lives. I'll admit Valerie was a mistake, but that's over now. From here on in, let's agree to wish each other the best and move on."

She nodded, trying her best to conceal her discomfort.

"Thanks for the coffee, but I really am busy."

"Watch yourself with her," she added, as he turned to leave. "I hear she's a man-eater."

"I can take care of myself, Lisa. Have a nice day."

❋ ❋ ❋

Smith was staring at crime scene photos, but his mind was still in the coffee shop, annoyed at Lisa for interfering again. His irritation was tempered by curiosity though, as he recalled her reaction: *Could it have been jealousy?* He tried to focus on the inventory again and came across an item that gave him a thought. A cigarette butt had been inventoried, and according to the grid coordinates for the site, it had been near the entrance to the other side of the pedestrian bridge. He looked up Dean McGregor's number and gave him a call.

"Dean, it's Jack Smith. Got a quick question for you, if you've got a minute."

"Shoot."

"Any idea if Anton Kurtz is a smoker?"

There was a chuckle at the other end of the line. "Is the Pope catholic? These guys are all chronics. I guess it doesn't help that one of their business lines is cigarette smuggling. Anyway, I know Kurtz smokes for sure, those stinky American ones."

"Don't know the brand off hand, do you?"

"No, but I could probably find out if it's important. We've had him under surveillance off and on for the past year. I'm sure someone recorded it somewhere, along with what time he takes his first dump every morning."

"That I don't want to know," Smith replied. "But the crime scene guys inventoried a cigarette butt in the area I'm guessing the killer would have waited for Ritchie. It's a couple of hundred feet from the kill spot, but it's the best vantage point."

"Let me talk to some of my guys and get back to you."

"Thanks, Dean."

Smith rubbed his temples as Marshall put down his own phone.

"Turns out we'll get to talk to Hearst sooner than we thought. He took a slap shot in the foot last night. Hairline fracture. They sent him home from Chicago this morning."

"Bad news for him, good for us. I'll call Melissa and see if I can set something up for tonight?"

"Melissa, is it?" Marshall smiled.

Smith gave a loud sigh as he composed a text to Melissa. He still hadn't mentioned that he had met with her in Toronto — much less that he'd slept with her there, and at his place the next night. He didn't like keeping things from Marshall, but he knew it was for the best.

"What a fucking mess," Marshall muttered, flipping through the pages of the murder book, and examining the pictures of the wound to Ritchie's chest up close.

"We can get DNA off a cigarette butt, can't we?" Smith asked, after he had sent off his text.

"Hmm," Marshall looked up from the photos. "Depends, I think. Prints are a long shot, but with DNA it comes down to how long it's been out in the elements, how much saliva was there to begin with, stuff like that. Saunders doesn't smoke, though, does he?"

"I was thinking of Kurtisov's goon, Anton Kurtz. I just noticed there was this Marlboro butt in the inventory and wondered if it might be something. You can get them in a few places around town, but they're not that common."

"And he's a smoker?"

"Yeah, according to MacGregor, he smokes American cigarettes. He's gonna get back to me on the brand. If it's a match, we could maybe run a few tests on the butt."

"Yeah, sure. Look at this." Marshall was pointing to one of the close-ups of the gash in Ritchie's chest."

"What?"

"This marking, on the left side of the wound. You see that?"

"Not really. You mean the red part."

"Yeah, it runs the full length of the cut."

Smith flipped to the post-mortem report. "Did Lake mention it?"

"I don't think so," Marshall said, as Smith's cell started ringing.

"Let's make a note to ask him," he said, answering the phone. "Smith here."

"It's Melissa. How's eight o'clock tonight? For Hearst, I mean. At his house out in Kanata."

Smith put his hand over the mouthpiece. "Eight tonight out at Hearst's house okay?"

Marshall nodded.

"Yeah, eight's fine."

"Your partner there with you?"

"Uh-huh."

"Were you disappointed?"

"What do you mean?"

"That I wasn't talking about meeting me instead?"

Smith pretended to be still listening to conversation as the silence ticked away before she spoke again.

"Good news. I'm flying back in a couple of hours — some stuff I've gotta do in Ottawa tomorrow. How's eleven? Let's make it my place this time: 330 Laurier West, Apartment 1503. I know you can't talk, so 'thanks a lot' means I'll see you there."

"Thanks a lot."

"See you later. Look forward to it."

She rang off as Marshall looked on. If he noticed anything in Smith's reaction to the last part of the call, he wasn't showing it.

❊ ❊ ❊

Smith and Marshall were both surprised when Hearst's front door opened just after eight. Instead of a wounded six-foot winger, they were met by the even taller and much more attractive Mandy Hearst. Smith had seen her picture in the sports pages once or twice, but they obviously hadn't done her justice. Dressed simply in jeans and a long-sleeved T-shirt, her dark hair tied back in a ponytail, she possessed that rare, effortless beauty that transcended fashion or makeup.

"Mrs. Hearst? I'm David Marshall, and this is Jack Smith. We're with the Ottawa Police."

"Come in. Dennis is expecting you. Don't bother with your shoes," she added, as she led them across the double-height foyer, past a winding staircase that led up to the second floor and toward a large sitting room to the right. Dennis Hearst was sitting on a leather couch, his right leg resting on a matching ottoman, the foot encased in a cast. He flicked off the big-screen TV over the fireplace and started to get up.

"Don't —" Marshall put out his hand to stop him, but he stood anyway.

"It's not as bad as it looks." Hearst grinned as they shook hands.

"Can I get you something to drink? Coffee? Tea?" Mandy Hearst asked, standing inside the doorway. They declined politely as they arranged themselves, Smith on the couch and Marshall in a chair facing Hearst.

"Well, I'll leave you to it," she said, and disappeared.

"Great place," Marshall said, as he glanced around the room, his eyes ending up on the foot cast. "How long are you out?"

"Officially, six weeks, but I'm thinking it will be a lot less. It's only a hairline fracture."

"What happened?"

"Friendly fire. Shot from the point got deflected and caught me off guard. It was a bullet, too — lucky it didn't do more damage."

"Well, thanks for seeing us again."

"My pleasure. What can I do for you, anyway?"

Marshall nodded. "We wanted to follow up on our last interview. You said the altercation between you and Curtis was about him flirting with Tammy Crawford."

Hearst nodded and adjusted his foot on the ottoman. "That's right."

"Was there any other reason why you needed to talk to Curtis that night?"

"Not sure I know what you're getting at."

"Let's just say we've talked to a number of people who were there that night, and while we were initially met with a lot of unwillingness to say much, those people were convinced to tell us what they saw and heard, given the importance of the investigation."

"I'm still not following you."

"Was your wife at the party, Mr. Hearst?" Smith asked, as Hearst turned to look at him.

"Of course she was there. We were hosting it."

They let him consider a response for a few awkward moments of silence and were about to ask him point blank when he shook his head and sighed.

"All right. Mandy told me Curtis was acting ... inappropriately."

"You mean he was coming on to her?"

Hearst nodded.

"That's in pretty bad taste," Marshall said, "given she's the host ... and the wife of the team captain."

"No kidding. Mandy was really pissed. She wanted me to throw him out on his ass, but I decided to talk to him instead. Then I saw him and Tammy going at it and I had to put a stop to it right away."

"Why didn't you tell us this last time?"

"Come on, guys, you can understand why. Besides, I didn't think it made any difference."

"What did you say to him, about Mandy?"

"I told him ... I don't know ... stay the fuck away or something like that, I guess."

"Did you threaten him?"

"Probably. Wouldn't you?"

"So it's fair to say you were more concerned about Mandy than Tammy Crawford?"

"I was more pissed off at him disrespecting Mandy, and me, yes. But I was more concerned that things might escalate with Tammy, if you know what I mean?"

Smith hadn't met Tammy, but from what Marshall, and even O'Neill himself had told him, Hearst's comment made sense. Also, although he had only met Mandy Hearst for about thirty seconds, he already had difficulty thinking she was the type to jump into bed with some eighteen-year-old flavour of the month. From what he had read about Dennis and Mandy Hearst, apart from their numerous Ottawa charities, they kept a very low profile. They had three kids and seemed the perfect couple. She had come from money herself, and Hearst had done pretty well over the years.

"Curtis was pretty reckless, then, wasn't he?" Smith said, as Hearst adjusted his foot again.

"He was young and stupid. He needed some direction, that's all. We would have given it to him."

"But he seemed to have an almost destructive streak, when it came to women, in particular, wouldn't you say?"

Hearst gave a grim smile. "He made some bad choices, yeah."

"Like what, Dennis?" Smith leaned forward.

"I think you know."

"Like the waitress in Peterborough?"

Hearst grinned. "There were probably a few like her. No, I'm talking about really ill-advised stuff, like fishing off the company wharf."

Smith looked to Marshall, and it was clear neither knew what he was talking about. Hearst sighed.

"Come on, Detective Smith. I warned you about her the other night, in Toronto."

Marshall looked on, perplexed, as Smith tried to maintain his composure despite a shock that hit him like a punch in the gut. "You mean Melissa McAdam?"

"I'm pretty sure, yeah."

"How so?"

"You can usually tell, can't you? I mean, you're the detectives."

"So you think Curtis was sleeping with Melissa McAdam?" Marshall asked, as Smith's mind swam in murky waters.

"I got the sense it was over, like maybe they had a fling over the summer. They would have met shortly after the draft, and over the contract. Listen, I'm telling you this because you already think I held out on you, but I don't want this getting back to Quinn, okay?"

"He didn't know?"

Hearst shook his head and let out a loud whistle. "Fuck, no."

"Why are you so sure?"

Hearst was about to say something, then seemed to reconsider. He looked at his hands, then back at Marshall. "You just know, that's all."

❄ ❄ ❄

Marshall pulled into the lot at the station and put the car in park.

"Drink?"

Smith looked at his watch. "Sure, a quick one."

"You got a hot date?"

"Maybe." Smith grinned, concealing the discomfort he felt inside. He was still shocked by Hearst's revelation, even if he was unconvinced of its truth. They crossed the street and walked to a bar and grill just down the street from the Elgin Street station.

"So, what did you think?" Marshall said, after they had taken a seat at the bar and ordered a couple of beers.

Smith shook his head. "I can't see Hearst being our guy."

"Me neither. We should follow it through, though. He did have a run-in with Ritchie a few days before the murder, and he acknowledged knowing Ritchie's running route before."

"Agreed. We're probably not going to be able to cross him off our list altogether. It's tough for anyone to have an iron-clad alibi for six-thirty on a Saturday morning." They had spoken to Mandy Hearst before they left, and she had confirmed her husband's location on the morning in question: at home until nine-thirty, when he had left for the rink.

"She really is something else, isn't she?" Marshall whistled.

"She's beautiful, all right, and it isn't difficult to believe that he'd rather be lying in bed with her than out jogging at the crack of dawn."

"What'd you make of what he said about McAdam's daughter?"

"I suppose he's got no reason to lie," Smith said, sipping his beer.

Marshall nodded, took a sip of his own beer, and looked back at his partner. "No. I'm just wondering whether Quinn knew. I'm not sure he would have been all that happy."

"Except, out of everyone, he probably has the most to lose from Ritchie's death. His team's got a gaping hole and the trades he made to get the future of the team now look like shit. Did you see the sports page this morning?"

Marshall shook his head.

"I guess the period of mourning is over," Smith said. "Now they're calling for McAdam's head on a block. The odds are about ten to one against him making it to Thanksgiving."

"Yeah, I certainly wouldn't want to be in his shoes." Marshall picked at the label on his bottle. "I didn't know the daughter was in Toronto. I thought she said she wasn't making the trip."

"Yeah, that's what I thought, too." Smith was debating how much of his evening with her he was going to disclose when his phone went off. He had a brief conversation and then closed the phone.

"News?" Marshall looked on.

"That was Dean McGregor. Turns out Anton Kurtz smokes Marlboros like a chimney.

"I guess we'd better talk to forensics in the morning about that cigarette butt, then."

Smith nodded, taking a long pull of his beer. "We've got Ellen Ritchie at ten, right?"

"Uh-huh. By the way, she confirmed that she's law-yered up for the interview."

"Which means Saunders has told her we're looking at him. Should be an interesting meeting." Smith looked at his watch. "I'm bagged."

"Me too. You want me to drop you off?"

"Sure."

They chatted on the ride over to Smith's apartment, and Marshall was his jovial self, but they were both aware of a silent wedge between them. Smith knew he was going to have to tell him about Melissa sooner or later. But he needed to find out a few things for himself first.

CHAPTER 21

"Here, try this," she said, handing him a glass of red wine as he sat on her sofa. Melissa had answered her door in a red silk kimono, and by the way it moved it was clear she had nothing on underneath. She curled up on the couch next to him and adjusted the silky fabric over her knees. "It's from a wine-tasting tour I went on this summer, up in Niagara. It won some awards, I think."

"It's great," he said, after taking a sip. He wasn't much of a connoisseur, but he could tell it was better than the house red he was used to, on the rare occasions he drank wine. "So why are you back, anyway? I thought you'd be on the road for a few days."

"I missed you," she said, running a hand over his chest as she pressed herself against him, the soft flesh of her breast against his arm. "That," she added, sitting back to take a sip of wine, "combined with Dad wanting me to do some research back here."

"Research?"

"Contractual ramifications of possible trades — I'm afraid I'd have to kill you if I told you," she said, with a mischievous grin.

"I guess it's all pretty sensitive information. You must have to be really careful about potential leaks."

"That's why you won't get anything out of me, Jack, no matter what you do to me." She slid her thigh over his, the silk slipping over the wool of his pants. Smith tried to maintain his focus.

"Speaking of sensitive information," he said. "Your dad told me about Kurtisov — about him leaving that coffin in Curtis's hotel room."

"Pretty creepy, huh?"

"You knew, then."

"I knew there was RHL interest in Curtis, but I didn't know about specific talks," she said, sipping her wine. "Dad didn't mention the coffin incident, or the fact that Kurtisov had threatened him as well, until the other day."

Smith nodded and took a sip of the full-bodied wine.

"I'm sure he didn't want to worry me," she continued. "Or, God forbid, get me involved in any way with those Russian gangsters. I'm sure you've heard all about what they do to their own players when they try to leave to play over here."

"You mean threatening their family members back home?"

"I think they do more than just threaten, and from what I've heard of this Kurtisov character, he's one of the worst. But I'm sure you know that already."

Smith felt suddenly dizzy, whether from the heavy red wine or fatigue he didn't know, but he leaned forward to set the glass on the table. He should really go home and get a good sleep before tomorrow's interview with Ellen Ritchie. But when he turned back toward

Melissa, she had undone the belt of her kimono and was reaching for him.

"That's enough talk for now," she said, crushing her lips against his as they fell back onto the sofa.

❄ ❄ ❄

Smith stood over the kitchen sink, drinking the cold water in the grey-blue light of Melissa's ultra-modern kitchen. The blue light of the range clock read three-fifteen. He should have left earlier, he knew, as he downed the rest of the water. Now, he would have to wake her so she could lock up after him. He tiptoed back to the bedroom and peeked around the door to find her sleeping soundly, unmoved from when he had gotten up. The soft light from the doorway fell across the foot of the bed, while her bare shoulders, layered with wisps of her blonde hair, were visible in the half-light of the room. He stood watching her sleep for a moment, envying her slumber as he headed back out into the hallway in search of food.

He was on his way back to the kitchen when he passed by a small room that had been set up as an office. He went in and sat at the desk. The motion triggered the blue light of her screen saver — a background of azure water around a school of vibrantly coloured fish. To the left was a bookshelf that held various legal texts, dictionaries, and a few fiction titles. On the desk, to the left of the monitor, was an unruly pile of paper. He slid open a desk drawer to reveal an assortment of pens, paperclips, and Post-it Notes of all different shapes, sizes, and colours. Sliding it back in silently, he opened the deeper, lower drawer and saw a series of colour-coordinated folders in a hanging file system. He pulled one out and read the label: 2012 Contracts — General. He dropped it back and plucked the next one: HR Matters. He looked over his shoulder and paused, waiting for any sign that Melissa was awake, but there was utter silence. He shouldn't even be here, he thought, let alone rifling through her work files. He wondered what Marshall would think if he knew where Smith was now, or what he was doing. Beaudoin would have a shit-fit, he knew for a fact. He turned back around and was about to slide the lower drawer shut when another label caught his eye: Ritchie — Misc.

He plucked the folder out and set it on the desktop. The first document was a copy of Ritchie's contract with the Raftsmen, which Smith had already seen. Next was a series of letters between James Cormier and Ritchie's agent, Dan Avery, and a law firm in Toronto that Smith recognized from reviewing Avery's file. The other papers were an assortment of articles on Ritchie from the major hockey publications, about the draft and his signing with Ottawa. Smith recognized Steve Hunter's one-by-one black and white photo from the sports page of the Ottawa paper, and even remembered reading parts of the article, which had been written in early August and predicted a banner year for the Raftsmen as a result of their new acquisition. He flipped through some notes and stopped at a sheet of yellow paper with a date in the top right-hand corner of the page: August 25, 2012. Ritchie's name was written in the middle of the page and was circled, with a line connecting the circle to two more, above and to the left that contained two more names — Bob Ritchie and Joan Ritchie. Smith puzzled at the name in the fourth circle, above that of Ritchie's adoptive parents, unable to make it out clearly. The surname looked like Riggs, but the first was scribbled to the point of being illegible. He guessed at Michelle. The only other writing on the page was set apart, further down, just inside the left margin, it appeared to read "Speelay."

Smith started at the sound of the bed creaking in the next room and he quickly slid the papers back into the file, put it back in the hanging folder, and slid the drawer shut quietly. He got up, adjusted the swivel chair back to the way he had found it, and padded back to the bedroom. Melissa was still asleep, having turned over onto her back. Her hair obscured the left side of her face and one arm was curled up above her head. He slid under the covers next to her as she rolled over and draped her free arm over his chest, her soft breathing sounding in his ear as he tried to go back to sleep.

❄ ❄ ❄

"You almost ready? They're here," Marshall said, as Smith drank the last of his coffee.

"Be there in a sec," he said, sliding the printout into a file folder before Marshall could spot it. He had been staring at Ritchie's cellphone records from late July and early August, and noticed a cluster of calls from the same number. He had gotten the confirmation five minutes earlier that the number belonged to a phone registered to Melissa McAdam — a different number than the one she was currently using. The coffee swirled in his stomach and caused a gurgle as he gathered his notes for Ellen Ritchie's interview. There would have been all sorts of reasons for Melissa and Ritchie to be in regular phone contact in the days and weeks following his signing. Melissa's job, after all, was to look after legal issues for the front office, including contracts. He assured himself of this as he made his way to the interview room, unconvinced that it really explained the late-night, even early-morning calls, or why she had later changed her cell number. Suddenly, despite Melissa's apparent aversion to the concept of puck bunnies, he had no choice but to consider Hearst's allegation of something more than just business between her and Ritchie.

Beaudoin was standing next to Marshall outside the interview room.

"Just thought I'd let you know," Beaudoin whispered. "She's already planning to sue." He grunted as he gestured through the open door to where Ellen Ritchie sat, accompanied by a grey-haired man in a charcoal grey suit.

"Who's the mouthpiece?" Marshall asked.

"Don't recognize him." Beaudoin shook his head. "Must be from out of town."

"So, are you saying take it easy on her?"

"Fuck, no. You ask what you gotta ask. Just be aware of the consequences," he said, before loosening his tie and heading back to his office.

"Well, that was helpful," Smith remarked, as Marshall started toward the door.

Ellen Ritchie's expression was a mix of annoyance and contempt. Her lawyer stood to greet them, then laid out the ground rules for the interview, after which they all took their seats and Marshall got started.

"Perhaps we could talk about Mr. Saunders' business dealings with Curtis, Ms. Ritchie."

She shrugged her shoulders. "That was between him and Curtis, for the most part."

"You were aware of Mister. ... can I refer to him as Tom?"

She nodded.

"You were aware of Tom's line of clothing? I believe it was ... it *is* ... called Coolite?"

"Yes. Tom's very excited about it."

"Must be a tough market to get your foot in the door," Marshall said. "I've got a kid in minor hockey, and every year the team orders hats and coats and warm-up suits, and there seems to be a different supplier every year."

"No different than any other business, I suppose," Ritchie said. "It all boils down to the quality of the product."

"And you think Tom's got a winner?" Smith was amazed that Marshall could deliver the line with a straight face. They had both seen Saunders' bush-league website, and the clothing hadn't looked much better. Fifty bucks for a grey hoodie with a cheesy logo, when you could get a brand name one on sale at the mall for half the price.

"He worked really hard to find the right supplier, I know that much. He was even on the phone to China at one point a couple of weeks ago. He's been going on about price points and distribution lines and all that."

Marshall nodded. "Sounds like he was really into the idea. He must have invested some money into it as well. I'm thinking calls to China can't be cheap."

Ritchie's gaze was stone cold in response to Marshall's jovial smile. "Not really. A couple of thousand in seed money, he made a couple of trips to trade shows in Toronto over the summer."

"Did Curtis go on any of these trips?"

She shook her head. "God no, he seemed to be so busy over the summer."

"Did Curtis ever talk to you about Coolite?"

"Like I said, that was mostly between the two of them, but he did seem supportive."

"How so? You mentioned he didn't go along to any of the trade shows. We know from Curtis's agent and business manager that they didn't have anything in writing. Did he actually tell you he liked the product, or was it just your sense?"

Ellen Ritchie crossed her arms, glanced off to the side, and then looked at Marshall, letting out a small sigh. "Curtis was over for dinner once, and Tom was showing him the material he had chosen for the warm-up suits. He seemed interested."

Smith pretended to take some notes in the silence that followed her account of Curtis Ritchie's less-than-enthusiastic response to Saunders' efforts.

"All right. Let's go back a bit," Marshall said, changing tack. "You and Tom have been together for how many years now?"

"About five."

"So Curtis was in his early teens when Tom came onto the scene."

"Yeah."

"And I understand he was quite involved in Curtis's hockey — driving him to practices and games, I mean."

Ritchie laughed. "I sure as hell wasn't getting up at six a.m. on a Sunday morning to stand in a freezing rink."

"What about road trips and such? There must have been a lot of them, at Curtis's level."

"He was on the ice every day, and there was an out-of-town tournament at least every second weekend. Then there was spring hockey, and summer hockey camp. It was year-round, basically."

"Must have been a big commitment, both in time and money. My son's in-house league and even his fees are expensive. I can only imagine."

"It's gotten crazy in the last few years," Ritchie said. "But even five years ago, it was significant. Luckily, I had the house paid off when Bob died, and I had some insurance as well. Plus, Tom was his own boss, so he could make his own hours. We were lucky, I guess."

"So Tom was pretty involved in Curtis's hockey ... career, I guess we'd call it ... even at that age."

"I guess so." She shrugged her shoulders. "He went to all the practices, and the games as well, of course."

"Did you go to the games with him?"

"I went to all the home games, yes. I didn't usually go on the road though, unless it was a big game, or Tom and I made a trip to the city out of it, you know?"

"Sure. Tom was a pretty big hockey fan, then, obviously?"

"Yeah, he liked the game."

"Got really into the games, did he?"

Ritchie's lawyer raised a grey eyebrow, which Marshall ignored.

"Sure."

"Did he ever yell at the referees, during a game?"

"If it was a lousy call, sure."

"What about Curtis's coach, like maybe if he wasn't getting enough ice time?"

"I don't know, maybe."

"How about Curtis? Did he ever yell at —"

"Can I ask where this is headed, Detective?" The lawyer was sitting up straight, and had set his pen down on the yellow pad in front of him.

"We're told Mr. Saunders had a bit of a reputation for being a hothead at the rink," Marshall said, ignoring the lawyer and addressing Mrs. Ritchie instead. "We just want to know if you ever saw him get angry at a game."

"That's hardly a crime, is it?" the lawyer interjected, refusing to be ignored. "If it was, you'd have to arrest most of the junior hockey fans in the country," he added, chuckling at his own joke.

"Did he?" Again, Marshall looked to Ritchie for an answer.

"He would yell, from time to time, yeah," she replied. "At the ref, or the coach, even Curtis sometimes."

"What about after the game? Maybe at the dinner table?"

"It was hard to avoid talking hockey in our house, but Tom wasn't riding Curtis, if that's what you mean."

"Like criticizing his play, saying he should have skated harder, passed, shot ... whatever," Marshall prompted.

"No. Well, no more than any parent trying to give advice."

"What about Curtis's coach? What was Tom's relationship with him like?"

"Relationship?" Ellen Ritchie raised an eyebrow and glanced at her lawyer.

"Well, you said he was at every game and practice, on the road for every tournament. They must have got to know each other over the season."

Ritchie sighed. "I really don't know. Look, I followed Curtis's hockey, but it's not like I was chatting with the coaches after every game."

"Not like Tom, then?"

"Tom was more involved, yes."

"Do you know if Tom ever got in arguments with Curtis's coach — either ..." Marshall looked down at his notes for the name of the Peterborough coach for the two years Ritchie played there "... Steven Grace, or any of his minor hockey coaches?"

"No ... I don't know. I'm sure they had disagreements."

"Are you sure about that?" Marshall made a show of reading his notes and pulling out a statement from Grace, in which he referred to several shouting matches with Saunders, including one in particular that had turned into a scuffle.

279

"I believe my client has answered your question," Ritchie's lawyer interrupted.

"That would be a no, then…." Marshall nodded, ignoring the lawyer's glare. "Would you say Tom had a temper, Mrs. Ritchie?"

"Everyone has a breaking point."

"What happens when Tom reaches his breaking point, as you put it?"

"He has never laid a hand on me, if that's what you're asking. His bark is much worse than his bite."

"But you acknowledge he has a temper?"

"He can yell with the best of them, but not at me. He knows I can give it right back."

Marshall smiled, flipped through his notes, and then stood. "Don't mind me — sore back," he said, starting to pace the length of the table. "Tom can't have been happy when Curtis hired Dan Avery right before the draft."

"Is there a question in there, Detective?"

"I was getting to it, if you give me a chance. What was Tom's reaction, when he found out that Curtis had hired Avery?"

"He wasn't happy about it, but it wasn't that big of a deal."

"Really? I would have thought he would have been pretty upset. I know I would have been, in his —"

"I said he wasn't happy."

"What did you think of Curtis's decision?"

"I didn't agree," she said, looking to her lawyer, then back at Marshall. "But I can understand why he did it."

"Why do you say that, Mrs. Ritchie?"

"Curtis was reaching a turning point in his life. Turning eighteen, gaining his independence. I think he just wanted to make his own way in the world. Maybe it had something to do with his being adopted, I don't know. He didn't do it to hurt Tom."

"But it did hurt him, didn't it?"

She sighed. "Of course."

"All those early mornings at the rink, as you put it earlier," Marshall said, with an understanding nod. "The time, the money he invested over the years." He stopped before the lawyer had put his pen down again. "Did Tom tell you about his run-in with Curtis in March?"

She nodded. "He was drinking, and he got carried away, that's all. Whatever he said, he didn't mean it."

"What did he say?"

"My client wasn't a witness to the incident in question, as you well know…."

Ellen Ritchie ignored the protest from beside her. "Curtis told me what he said. Tom said he was going to kill him, but Curtis knew he didn't mean it. He pretty much laughed it off."

"Doesn't sound like a laughing matter to us. It must have caused a bit of a rift between them, didn't it?"

She shook her head. "Tom apologized when Curtis got back from the road trip, and that was that."

"Just like that?" Marshall made a show of looking incredulous.

"Yes, just like that. I know what you're trying to do, but you don't know Tom at all. He wouldn't hurt a fly."

"Are you aware he was arrested twice for assault?"

Ritchie paused, seemingly stunned. "I know there was an incident at a game. Some loudmouth fan got in Tom's face and they got into a bit of a scrap. That was about a year ago. The other guy tried to press charges, but it didn't go anywhere. That's all I know about."

"The other incident was before you met him, about eight years ago, in Toronto. A bar fight."

"I don't know anything about that."

"Was there a conviction?" the lawyer asked.

Marshall shook his head. "He was charged with uttering threats and assault, but the charges were dropped. There's a bit of a pattern there though."

"Surely you're joking, Detective." The lawyer scoffed and waved his hands dramatically. "Two unrelated incidents over the course of eight years, neither of which resulted in conviction. That's hardly a pattern."

"Don't get bent out of shape, counsellor. Besides, who are you representing here, Mrs. Ritchie, or Tom Saunders?"

"I'll be representing them both — in a wrongful prosecution and harassment case, if this keeps up."

Marshall suppressed the urge to respond, and instead maintained an even smile as he continued. "All right, Mrs. Ritchie. You've said that Tom was never violent to you, and we believe you. Let's talk about Tom's latest business venture. Coolite."

Mrs. Ritchie sighed and put her arms on the table. "I thought we already did."

"How is business, do you know?"

"He's just getting started. It's too early to tell. But I'm sure he'll do well. Tom's always been a very good businessman."

"Yes, he had his own paralegal firm, right?" Marshall made a point of consulting his notes.

She nodded.

"When did he sell that, again?"

"Last winter."

"So, just before the draft, then."

"I think he sold it in January. The draft was in May or June, but whatever."

"Fair enough. We understand he didn't get a lot of money for it." Marshall pulled out his notes.

"I think he got around a hundred thousand."

"That's not much, for his life's work."

"He was happy with it."

"And this Coolite business, the start-up costs you referred to earlier, where did they come from?"

"Tom ... well, both of us."

"You have a joint account?"

"Yes we do, not that it's anyone else's business."

"Did Tom tell you that Curtis had cancelled his photo shoot last Friday?"

"No," she said after a moment's pause. Smith thought he detected a slight twitch in Ritchie's so-far unflappable lawyer.

"Did you know Tom had been to see Curtis at his condo the night before his death? Friday night. And that he seemed upset?"

This news clearly took Ritchie by surprise. She paused and tucked a piece of hair behind her ear, while her lawyer started scribbling on his yellow pad. "No."

"Why do you think he might have been upset ...?" He stopped, catching sight of her lawyer's disapproving look and abandoning the question. "How old is Tom?"

"He's fifty-one."

"So he's got a few years to go before he retires, right? A hundred grand isn't going to get him there, not these days. We understand he doesn't have much else in the way of investments. Then he starts sinking money into his new enterprise. If it doesn't work out ..."

"I think we'll do fine."

"He will now, sure."

"What's that supposed to mean?" There was fire in Ellen Ritchie's eyes.

"I mean that there are significant payouts under Curtis's contract with the Raftsmen — their insurer, actually. Those payments go to you, of course, as Curtis's designated beneficiary, but, as you said, you have a joint account."

"This is disgusting," Ritchie said. "I don't have to listen to this."

"Please, Mrs. Ritchie. I know these questions are difficult, but isn't it a possibility you should be considering?"

"What?"

"Let me give you our perspective. Tom drags Curtis to every game, practice, and tournament from Peterborough to the GTA to New York State and beyond, all at great expense in time, money, and business equity, for the past five years. He's advising Curtis all along, and Curtis isn't exactly objecting, until a few months before the draft — then Tom is unceremoniously dumped."

"That's not how it happened at all."

"Isn't it? We know Tom has a temper, even if he never let it loose on you, and we know he basically attacked and threatened to kill Curtis shortly after he was cast aside in favour of Dan Avery."

"That's not …"

"Those are facts, Mrs. Ritchie. But that's not all. Not only was he discarded like an old shoe as Curtis's agent, he discovers exactly one day before the murder that Curtis has no intention of endorsing his new line of clothing either."

"He just postponed the shoot, that's all."

Marshall shook his head. "We spoke to the photographer. The shoot was cancelled, not postponed, and Tom was furious — 'incensed' is how he was described. And maybe he had reason to be." Marshall pressed on despite the lawyer's brewing objection. "After all he had done, suddenly his paralegal business is gone, his agent's commission has evaporated, and his Coolite plans are up in smoke, as well."

Ritchie was staring down at her hands as Marshall paused to take a breath.

"This is all speculation, at best," her lawyer said.

"We know he was in Ottawa the morning of Curtis's death. We know you weren't with him, and that he had ample opportunity to slip out of his sister's place unnoticed. We know he was at Curtis's condo the night before, angry and demanding to know where he was. With all of that, Mrs. Ritchie, can you honestly say the thought would never have crossed your mind?"

There was silence in the room as Ritchie continued to stare at her hands, then raised her head slowly, a tear running down her cheek as she fixed Marshall with a stare from her red-rimmed eyes.

"You're wrong."

❄ ❄ ❄

Smith and Marshall stood outside the interview room, looking in as Ritchie and her lawyer talked in hushed tones and she wiped her eyes with a tissue.

"Don't I feel like shit." Marshall sighed.

"You did what you had to in there, and you did it well," Smith whispered.

"Well, I don't think it helped us any. She's obviously convinced he had nothing to do with it."

"You think she wants it to be Saunders? Look, she needed to hear it officially, and now she has. Maybe it'll make her think twice, shake something loose. You know better than I do how these things can go."

"I gotta take a wicked leak," Marshall said. "Then we'll wrap it up and let her go home."

Smith waited until he had left before going back into the interview room.

"My partner will be right back. Before we wrap this up, I was wondering if I could run a name by you."

Ritchie shrugged her shoulders.

"Michelle Riggs. Do you know who that is?"

"Never heard of her."

"You're sure?"

"Yes, why?"

"Just a name that came up, that's all," Smith said as Marshall returned.

After a few final questions, they were ready to let Ritchie go.

"Thank you for coming in, Mrs. Ritchie," Smith said. "We hope you know our only objective is to find Curtis's killer."

Ritchie waited until she was at the door before responding, glaring first at Smith, then at Marshall. "Well, you'd better keep looking."

CHAPTER 22

Smith and Marshall sat in front of Staff Sergeant Beaudoin's desk as the burly head of the Major Crimes Unit clasped his thick fingers together behind his head and leaned back in his chair. Marshall had laid out the case against Saunders, from his drunken altercation with Ritchie back in March — along with Jordan Connolly's statement that he had heard Saunders threaten Ritchie's life — to Ritchie's cancellation of the Coolite photo shoot the day before the murder. He ran through the statements of the two witnesses, the photographer and the security guard at Ritchie's building, who each described Saunders' state as angry and agitated on the eve of Ritchie's murder. There was the grainy video image from the camera at the corner of Somerset and the Driveway, which depicted a man of Saunders' general physical characteristics leaving the scene around the estimated time of death. Then there were the financial consequences of Ritchie's death, including a payout of five hundred thousand dollars to Ellen Ritchie from the Raftsmen's insurance company, in addition to what was left of Ritchie's signing bonus, and there was the fact that Ellen Ritchie and Tom Saunders had a joint account.

Beaudoin let out a sigh and rubbed his eyes. "It's all circumstantial. Don't we have anything from the crime scene?"

Marshall shook his head. "Not much. We think the perp was wearing gloves, and the surface of the path is concrete, dry at the time, so no luck with a footprint either. Ident pulled a couple of hair samples from Ritchie's clothing, but that's it."

"And from what I saw of the video, it's not worth shit. It could be my mother-in-law in the frame, for Christ's sake." Beaudoin shifted forward in his chair and ran a finger over his lips. "What about the other leads — this Russian hockey guy, in particular?"

"He's pretty shady," Smith jumped in. "And Ritchie appears to have made an enemy of him last winter, so we can't rule him out. The guy suspected of doing his wet work could have been in the Ottawa area at the right time, but that's really all we've got. I was hoping to catch a break on a cigarette butt we found at the scene — a Marlboro, which is what this Kurtz guy smokes — but we got nothing. Forensics thinks it had been at the scene for a week or more before the murder, and they couldn't get anything usable from it, due to exposure to rain."

"Plus," Marshall said, "it doesn't really fit with the theory that the killer was posing as a jogger while he waited for Ritchie."

Beaudoin grunted. "Not too many runners puffin' on a butt while they're stretching, I guess."

"We also looked into some altercations with team-mates over wives and girlfriends," Marshall said. "Ritchie was a bit of a player, and maybe a little indiscriminate as to *whom* he was screwing around *with*...."

"Like Tanner O'Neill's girlfriend." Beaudoin leaned his elbows on the desktop.

"Right, but he might have made some moves on Mandy Hearst, as well."

Beaudoin shook his head. "Jesus."

"There was an on-ice incident with O'Neill at training camp, and Hearst had some words with him at a team party, but we don't really like either of them for the murder."

"Why not? I would have thought Ritchie's life took a dramatic drop in value the minute he crossed O'Neill."

"O'Neill's got no history of violence — off the ice, I mean," Smith said, "though both men could have known Ritchie's running route and schedule."

"Alibis?"

"Yeah, but as leaky as everyone else's — that's the problem with a crime at 6:30 a.m — everyone's asleep, so it's hard to confirm with any certainty." Marshall shrugged his shoulders.

Beaudoin let out an irritated sigh. "And what about the guy in Peterborough? The brother?"

"John Ridgeway." Marshall shook his head. "We don't think he's our guy. Apart from anything else, he's a little on the bulky side to fit the image on video."

"I don't like that we've got nothing in the way of physical evidence," Beaudoin said, leaning back and crossing his arms across his chest. "Then again, there's an awful lot pointing to Saunders. Let's bring him in. Maybe we can shake something loose."

Marshall and Smith nodded and got up to leave.

"But for God's sake, try and do it quietly."

❄ ❄ ❄

Saunders answered the door at his sister's house, and Smith could hear the sounds of a meal being prepared in the background.

"We'd like you to come with us, Mr. Saunders, to give us a formal statement, in connection with the investigation into the murder of Curtis Ritchie."

The blood drained from Saunders' face as he braced himself against the doorframe.

"Do you…? Can I get my…? I have to talk to Ellen."

"We're not here to arrest you, Tom, but if you don't come, we will get a warrant. Right now, we just want to talk, and we don't want to make a big scene on your sister's front porch."

"What's going on?" Ellen Ritchie appeared behind him at the door, took one look at Saunders, and seemed to know exactly what was going on. "It's all right, Tom. You go ahead. I'll call the lawyer and we'll meet you at the station. By the time he's done with these two, they'll be sweeping cells." She patted him on the shoulder as Smith took him by the arm and led him down the steps.

✳ ✳ ✳

"Whaddya mean he won't talk?" Beaudoin said in a hoarse whisper, as he stood next to Marshall and Smith outside the interview room. Saunders was sitting at the interview table, arms folded across his chest, staring at the wall.

"Fucking lawyer was waiting for him when we brought him in," Marshall said. "I guess he told him he's got more to gain from keeping his yap shut than trying to co-operate."

"Fuck," Beaudoin growled.

"We'll keep him for twenty-four hours. Maybe he'll change his mind after a night in the cells."

Beaudoin shook his head. "Get a DNA sample, then cut him loose."

"But Sarge, we could …"

"I said cut him loose, and not out the front either. Did you see the fucking press vultures gathered out there? I don't know how they found out, but they seem to know we're holding Saunders. I swear this place is leakier than a Russian trawler, and if I ever find out who's responsible, I'll have their nuts in a vice." Beaudoin took a deep breath before continuing, registering the surprised look on the faces of his detectives. "Talk to the Crown first thing tomorrow, and see if there's enough to arrest him. I want a full debrief."

"Sure," Marshall said, as Beaudoin stormed off.

"He really is worried about a wrongful prosecution beef," Smith said.

Marshall shook his head. "I don't know, but someone sure got to him."

❄ ❄ ❄

Smith was walking through the door of his apartment when his phone rang.

"Jack? You not answering your texts these days?"

He kicked off his shoes and collapsed onto the couch. "It's been one of those days. I haven't checked messages in a while." He was curious as to why Lisa White was getting in touch with him for the second time in as many days.

"How are you doing?"

"I'm kind of beat, actually. What can I do for you?"

"I wanted to talk … I guess I'm kind of worried about you."

Smith sighed, apparently loud enough for her to hear on the other end of the line.

"There's no need to get huffy."

"I really don't get you, Lisa. First we end up in bed —"

"That was a mistake," she interrupted.

"As you pointed out. Then you fuck up whatever I had going with Valerie."

She laughed. "We both know that wasn't going anywhere. Come on, Jack."

"You can't have it both ways, Lisa," he said, his irritation growing. "You decided we're not good together, and you know what? I'm fine with that. But you need to let go." He enjoyed saying the words, knowing the sting they would deliver. Lisa was nothing if not proud, and was likely fighting her urge to hang up and never speak to him again.

"Melissa McAdam is bad news, Jack. I'm telling you that as a friend."

"I'm sure you are," he replied, the sarcasm dripping from his voice. "You don't even know her. How could you possibly —"

"I know *of* her, from a colleague who worked with her in Toronto. You don't even want to know —"

"I'm not listening to this crap. First you smear me to Valerie, now you're trying to do the same thing to Melissa. It's pathetic, and I'm done with it."

"She's a psycho, Jack. Her last boyfriend had to get a restraining order against her. If you don't believe me, check it out for your —"

"Goodbye."

He hung up and stared at the phone, the blood pounding in his ears. He hated how easily she got to him. He was about to toss the phone onto the couch when he noticed the string of text messages, all from Melissa, the first from thirty minutes ago. The most recent was only five minutes old: "I'm in a cab. You'd better be there."

He was still reading her message when he the doorbell rang. He walked to the door and opened it, standing back as it swung open to reveal Melissa McAdam standing there in a long trench coat. Her hair looked different, as though she had come from a wind tunnel, or off the stage of a heavy metal concert. Her eyes were darkened with eyeliner, and her lips adorned in a vibrant red lipstick that was in stark contrast to her fair skin. He stood speechless as she locked eyes with him, then slowly undid the belt of the coat and let it fall open, confirming a suspicion that had formed as soon as he noticed the coat — that it was her only clothing, other than the three-inch heels that put her at eye level.

"You gonna ask me in, or what? It's cold out here."

He reached for her and pushed the door shut as she shed the coat, threw one arm around his neck, and wrapped her legs around his hips, clawing at his pants with her free hand as he carried her toward the bedroom.

❄ ❄ ❄

Smith rolled off her and fell back onto a pillow, his heart beating through his chest and his entire body glistening with sweat. He gulped in the musty scent of sex as he tried to catch his breath.

"I hope your neighbours are heavy sleepers," she whispered, between pants.

"What got into you?" he said, as her forearm flopped lazily across his thigh.

"I don't know. I must have a cop fetish or something," she said, propping herself on one arm and letting her head rest on his stomach as it rose and fell in time with his breathing. "And when you didn't answer my texts, I thought maybe you weren't here. It made me …"

"What?"

"It made me want you even more."

Smith laughed. "Well, I'll have to remember to ignore your texts more often."

She gave him a playful slap on the stomach. "What were you doing, anyway?"

"I was working. I was only home five minutes before this sex bomb showed up at my door."

"Did you like the outfit?"

"What do you think?"

"Hmmm. I think it turned you on, too."

They lay in silence for a while, as she rested her head back on his stomach and ran her hand up and down his thigh. His eyes were getting heavy as his breathing and heart rate returned to normal and a warm numbness spread through his body. He barely heard her when she broke the silence, her voice a lazy whisper.

"You're not seeing anyone else, are you?"

"Hmmm?"

"You heard me, Smith. Or should I say Smitty. Isn't that what your partner calls you?"

"No, I'm not seeing anyone," he muttered, his head lolling to the side as she continued to caress his leg. "You?"

"You think I'm some kind of whore?"

He looked down at her, to see if she was joking. Her expression was serious, and he was about to respond when she broke into a wide grin.

"Just kidding. Still, I wouldn't want you to think I show up at people's doors dressed like that on a regular basis."

"You weren't dressed at all, as I remember."

She grinned. "How's the case going, anyway?"

He let his head fall back on the pillow.

"Anything come of the Kurtisov connection?"

"I meant to ask you when I might be able to talk to Tanner O'Neill again," he said, avoiding the question. "The team's back in a couple of days, right?"

"Don't be coy, Jack. Everyone knows Kurtisov's a gangster."

"Come on, Melissa, you know I can't discuss the case with you."

"All right. I'm just saying …"

They were quiet again for a moment, then Smith rolled onto his side and slid down to face her. "How come you're not dating some hotshot lawyer, or a millionaire hockey player? What are you doing with a lowly cop?"

"I've dated enough lawyers already. As for players," she said, lifting herself onto one arm and reaching over him for the glass of water on the side table, "I don't fuck the help."

"You must get hit on all the time though, or are they all afraid of your dad?"

"I can look out for myself."

He chuckled. "I believe that."

"You don't seem afraid of my father," she said, taking a sip of water before setting the glass back on the night table.

"You're a grown woman, Melissa. I assume you can make your own choices." He hadn't really thought much about what Quinn McAdam would make of his relationship with his daughter, probably because he was more concerned about Marshall, or Beaudoin. He didn't exactly relish the idea of being confronted by the Raftsmen's GM, though.

"What are you thinking?"

He brushed a strand of hair from in front of her eye, then ran a finger down her cheek to the nape of her neck, over the swell of a breast and down. He stopped at the silky smooth skin on the inside of her thigh.

"Oh," she said, as she rolled onto her back and pulled him to her.

❅ ❅ ❅

Smith heard the sound and knew something was wrong. He opened his eyes and looked at the clock — it was too early. He reached over Melissa's sleeping form for his cellphone, then realized he had left it in the living room. There it was again — the sound of the doorbell.

Disorientation giving way to annoyance, he muttered a curse and dragged himself up from the warm cocoon of the bed, replacing the covers over Melissa's naked skin as she stirred, rolled over, and resumed her deep sleep. He slipped into his jeans and hurried out of the bedroom, throwing a T-shirt over his head as he reached the door, just in time to pre-empt another ring. The door swung open to reveal Marshall standing there, two coffee cups in his hand.

"Wake up, sleepyhead."

"What the fuck, Marsh, it's seven-thirty. I thought we said nine?"

"You don't answer your phone — you give me no choice. Here," he said, handing over a large double-double as he waited for Smith to step aside. "The hair sample's a match with Saunders's DNA."

Smith sighed, took the coffee, and stepped aside as Marshall walked past him and settled on the couch, noting the trench coat on the floor as Smith stooped to pick it up and drape it over the back of a chair.

"Company?"

"Just a sec." Smith held a finger to his lips as he walked down the hallway and peeked into the bedroom. Melissa hadn't moved and her breathing was still heavy as he quietly pulled the bedroom door shut and tiptoed back to the living room.

"Who's the treat of the week?"

"You know I don't kiss and tell. When did you find out about the hair?"

"I got a call half an hour ago from one of the techs at the lab — an early riser. She said we could swing by and get the report ourselves if we wanted. I figured it would be good to have when we talk to the Crown later."

Smith nodded and sipped his coffee. "Yeah, sure." He was thinking he would have no choice but to wake Melissa and tell her he was going. "Just give me a minute to jump in the shower."

Five minutes later, he stood over the bed, getting dressed and toweling his hair as Melissa opened her eyes.

"You're leaving?"

"I was just going to wake you. My partner dropped by ... unannounced."

She smiled and put a finger to her lips. "I'll wait until you're gone," she whispered.

He leaned down and kissed her, grateful that she understood the situation. "I'll catch up with you later."

"I'll arrange something with O'Neill for you."

"Thanks."

He came out to the living area, where Marshall was sitting, drinking his coffee and looking at the coat.

"Ready?"

Smith was putting on his shoes when the sound of a ringtone froze him momentarily. He looked toward the coat as the sound continued — a distinctive refrain from a well-known pop song that Smith couldn't place. But he had heard it before, and as he turned toward Marshall, he knew his partner had too — in Melissa McAdam's office, when they had first met her. Any hope that Marshall might have forgotten evaporated as their eyes met.

"I think Melissa's phone is ringing," he said, as he opened the door and waited for Smith to follow. "Better let her get it."

CHAPTER 23

They had walked down to the car in silence, and it wasn't until they pulled away from the curb and started down toward Rideau Street that Smith spoke.

"It's not what you think."

"No?"

"It's not like she's a material part of the investigation."

"Maybe not," Marshall said, as he pulled up to a red light and looked across at him. "But Beaudoin'll want your head on a platter if he finds out, I can assure you of that."

Smith sighed. "It just kind of ... happened."

"It started in Toronto?"

"We went out for dinner after I interviewed Matt Jones, then one thing led to another."

The light turned green and they turned onto Rideau. "Of all the women in Ottawa, Smitty ... I don't know."

"Maybe I should put it on hold until after the investi —"

Marshall blew out a gust of air in exasperation. "Ya think?"

"Come on, Marsh. What's the big deal?"

"Are you fucking kidding? Obviously, you're letting your little head do the thinking, or you wouldn't be saying stuff like that. Whether you want to admit it yourself or not, it's inappropriate. You need to put it on ice, *now*."

Smith peered out the window.

"And I wouldn't want to be you if her dad finds out."

"It's not like she's fifteen or something. She's a grown woman," he heard himself say for the second time that morning, and realized how it sounded. "All right, I'll shut it down, for now anyway. But I really like her."

Marshall looked across at him deliberately.

"I mean it," he protested.

"Then you two lovebirds can pick up where you left off. Quietly, and after we've put Saunders behind bars."

They drove in silence as they headed up Elgin, past Marshall's favourite breakfast spot. "You wanna get something to eat?"

"I thought we were in a rush for the report?"

"It won't be ready for another hour."

Smith shook his head. "You sneaky fucker."

"Sorry, partner, I was just playing a hunch. What's McAdam doing slumming it with you anyway, you don't mind me asking?"

"I asked her the same thing myself."

"And?"

"She's got a thing for cops, I guess. She's had her fill of lawyers."

"What about jocks?"

"I asked her that, too. She said she doesn't fuck the help."

Marshall's eyebrows shot up, then he laughed. "She's a spirited gal, then."

"You could say that." Smith could still see her standing in front of him, her trench coat open wide, and feel her hot breath in his ear as they fell on the bed.

"You believe her, about not screwing around with the players?"

"Sure," he lied.

❄   ❄   ❄

They sat back in the booth, sipping coffee as the waitress cleared away their breakfast plates.

"I've got to get back to the gym," Smith said, patting his stomach. "Hanging out with you is gonna kill me."

"Nonsense. A good breakfast is the key to longevity, my friend."

"Depends on your definition of good, and I don't think that mound of grease qualifies."

They shared a laugh as Smith looked out the window at the brilliant fall morning. The forecast called for a high near twenty degrees but the morning air had the unmistakable crispness of fall, and the leaves were beginning to turn already. This time of year always reminded him of back to school, that mixture of excitement and anticipation over the changes ahead.

"Don't look so glum," Marshall said, misreading his expression. "We're one meeting away from solving this thing."

"You really think the Crown's gonna go for it?"

"Why not? Saunders had opportunity, and more importantly, motive — the house and the contract payout," Marshall said, ticking off the elements on his fingers. "Added to that, he's got a famous temper and a past history of violence."

Smith raised an eyebrow.

"He's got two arrests for assault," Marshall said.

"And no convictions, but don't let me stop your roll."

"There's circumstantial evidence up the ying-yang, and he's got an alibi we could drive a truck through...."

"I thought you were gonna use Beaudoin's Russian trawler analogy — I kind of liked that."

Marshall laughed. "And now, we've got his hair at the crime scene."

"We think."

"Well, we'll know for sure pretty soon." Marshall looked at his watch. "And now that we can rule out the Russian connection, there's really no one else."

Smith nodded. He had received an email from Dean McGregor to say that one of Anton Kurtz's associates had been picked up in a Toronto drug bust and Kurtz's name had come up in the course of questioning — more particularly that the dealer had spent the Friday night before Curtis Ritchie's murder on a bender with Anton Kurtz. They had been at a late-night strip club until five a.m., then gone to a diner for a lazy breakfast. One of McGregor's people had followed up with the diner staff and one of the waitresses had confirmed Kurtz's presence around six on the Saturday morning. They already knew Kurtisov himself had an alibi, which essentially crossed both of them off the list of potential suspects for the Ritchie murder.

Smith nodded. "When you put it like that, it does sound pretty convincing, and he fits the general physical specs of the guy in the video."

"So what's your problem?"

"Nothing. I just find it a little ... I don't know ... anticlimactic, I guess."

"That's a big word for a cop. You and Melissa been hitting the thesaurus together?"

"Keep laughing," he said, as they got up from the table. "But you don't know what I'm giving up for the good of the investigation."

"She's worth the flowers, I'll give you that. But I'm sure she can wait a little while."

Smith waved at the waitress for their bill. "I hope so."

❄ ❄ ❄

"Not so cocky now, is he?" Beaudoin said, as Saunders was led off to be fingerprinted and processed. The confirmation of the matching hair sample, along with everything else, was enough to convince the Crown to start the formal process of charging Saunders by laying an information. The warrant had been issued and executed in a matter of hours. "Good work, guys," he said, hustling off to coordinate a press release.

"I'm gonna take a run home for a couple of hours. You sticking around?" Marshall asked.

Smith looked at his watch. "Yeah, I'm gonna finish up some paperwork. I'll catch up with you later."

Smith decided to fuel up on caffeine before returning to his desk and, preferring the joe from any of the nearby coffee shops to the crap in the station, he decided to step out. His phone went off just as he stepped outside. He recognized Melissa's number and considered letting it go to voicemail. Then he remembered the night before and answered it.

"Hi, Melissa."

"Hey, Jack. Wondering if I could buy you dinner."

"You think I can't pick up the tab myself?" he said, guessing her response.

"Oh, you'll pay all right, but in other ways. I think you know what kind of compensation I'm after, Jack."

"Yeah, I know," he said. "Listen, where are you?"

"I'm in my car, just came off the Queensway."

"I can't do dinner, but let's have a coffee instead. Pick me up outside the convenience store at Elgin and Gladstone."

"See you in a sec."

A minute later, a midnight blue 5-series BMW turned onto Gladstone and pulled over. Recognizing her behind the wheel, Smith jumped in the passenger side. She leaned over and pecked him on the cheek, her hand sliding up his leg.

"Let's find somewhere quiet where we won't be disturbed," she whispered, biting his earlobe.

"I can't. I've gotta get back."

"Come on," she purred, her grip on his crotch tightening. He pushed her hand away.

"I'm serious. I really can't."

"I see what you're doing. You want me to show up at your doorstep again."

"Look, Melissa. I wanted to talk to you about this.

I think we should take it easy for a bit."

She recoiled as though she had been slapped.

"What are you talking about?"

"It's just that while this investigation is going on, it's not really appropriate for either of us to be … involved like this."

"That's funny, you didn't mention that last night."

"Look, I don't like it either, but …"

"You're serious, aren't you?" She was glaring at him, her eyes narrowed to slits. "Un-fucking believable."

"I'm just saying we should take it easy for a bit, that's all."

"You piece of shit. I thought you were different. I thought we had something special."

He could see the emotion in her face. "Let's just hold off until Saunders goes to trial."

"You arrested Saunders?" Her demeanour seemed to change instantly.

Smith immediately regretted the slip. He assumed she would already have heard, somehow. "That's not important."

"Of course it's important. It could be months before he goes to trial, couldn't it?"

"I'm not saying we have to wait until then. Maybe we could just keep a lower profile."

"Or maybe we don't," she said, with a coldness he hadn't anticipated. The mix of surprise, hurt, and anger she had displayed just moments ago had vanished. "Get out," she said, looking straight ahead and smoothing the sleeve of her jacket as she put her hand on the gear shifter.

"Melissa, it doesn't have to be like this."

She stared ahead in silence as he tried to think of something to say.

"Are you going to get out or should I call 911?" she said in a bored tone.

"You think this is what I want?" he said, reaching for the door handle. She didn't respond, just revved up the engine and rammed it into first as he stood to get out. His feet were barely on the sidewalk when she popped the clutch and the car peeled away from the curb, the door slamming shut and leaving him standing there by the side of the road as the sleek blue car roared off down Gladstone.

CHAPTER 24

Smith stared at the file folder in front of him and felt his stomach contract. He had ordered the CPIC search the day before and when the results had come in he had ordered copies of the related documents. With Marshall at home in the east end, enjoying a couple of hours with his family, Smith sat at his desk and opened the file. Lisa was right. There had been two separate peace bonds filed against Melissa McAdam in the past five years, both by men who had accused her of various types of erratic, even violent, behaviour. He had only received one of the supporting files so far, but it sounded like the bond in that case had been sought following the breakup of a relationship — to which Melissa had reacted badly, apparently. The affidavit filed by the complainant alleged that Melissa had threatened to kill him, and she had also allegedly threatened the complainant's new girlfriend — presumably the woman she had been dumped for. He noted the name of the Toronto constable who had appeared as a witness at the bond hearing and looked him up on the police contact database. He picked up the phone and dialed the number, and was in the process of formulating his voice message when he was surprised by a live voice.

"Weber."

"Constable Darren Weber?"

"Yeah."

"Hi. This is Jack Smith, from the Ottawa Police. I wasn't expecting to get you live."

"Guess it's your lucky day."

"Have you got a minute?"

"Sure."

"I wanted to ask you about a peace bond application a couple of years ago that you testified at. The complainant was," he rifled through the paperwork for the name. "Don Tavener, and the respondent was ..."

"Melissa McAdam."

"You remember?"

"How could I forget? She was a total whack-job. A real bunny boiler." Smith was surprised by the gravelly voice at the other end of the line. He had expected someone younger, but the unmistakable reference to *Fatal Attraction* confirmed his suspicion that Weber was more veteran than rookie. "She get dumped again? Whoever the guy is, you should put him in protective custody."

Smith swallowed hard. "No, her name came up in relation to an ongoing investigation. She's not a suspect or anything. It's more out of curiosity, really."

"What do you want to know?"

"It says here that you witnessed a domestic dispute?"

"Yeah, the neighbours called it in. It was one of those fancy condos down on Front Street, you know the kind that cost too much and have paper walls? They called 911 over the racket coming from Tavener's apartment. They said they thought someone was gonna get killed if we didn't break it up. So we roll up, knock on the door, and this hot young thing shows up at the door, all sweet as pie."

"McAdam?"

"Yeah. I don't know if you've seen this gal, but she's pretty easy on the eyes, if you get my drift."

"Right."

"So we ask her what's going on, and she says nothing. There's no sign of anyone else, so we ask if she's alone and she says no, her boyfriend's in the bathroom, and I get this weird feeling — you know, my Spidey sense start tingling. So I say we want to talk to him. She makes a fuss but we insist, and she eventually lets us in and says she'll go get him. So my partner and I are standing there for five minutes, wondering what the fuck is going on, when this guy comes out, white as a sheet. I don't think I've ever seen anyone that scared in my life. He's got a cut over his eye that's been taped shut, and he's walking with a limp."

"What happened?"

"The little minx had kicked the shit out of him, that's what happened, and this guy was too terrified to come out of the bathroom and tell us in front of her. We took him back to the station and he spilled the beans. We're talking multiple assaults — the cut was from her clubbing him with a hairdryer, and she booted him in the nuts as well, for good measure. There was a pretty good case for unlawful confinement as well, not to mention threatening all sorts of heinous shit, killing him being the least of his worries. She threatened to cut off his balls and feed 'em to him, that kind of thing. Girl's a real psycho."

"But she was never charged with anything, was she?"

"No, this guy — some hotshot corporate lawyer — was too much of a pussy. He didn't want anything to do with an assault charge, but she scared him enough that he wanted the bond. He was embarrassed as hell at being bitch-slapped, but he was more afraid that she was gonna do something *really* crazy."

"Did he go into detail?"

"Not really. We gave her a look anyway, found out she had a juvie file, but we never got around to getting it unsealed. What's the point, right?"

"Sure." Smith's mind was swimming. "One last thing. Did Tavener tell you what set her off?"

"He started seeing someone else at the office, so he broke it off with McAdam. Big mistake."

"Right."

"Whatever you do, don't date this chick."

"Thanks for your help," Smith said, as he hung up the phone and stared at his computer screen. He flipped through his notepad, to the names he had scribbled from his furtive search of Melissa's home office. He entered both Michelle Riggs and Speelay into his search engine and scrolled through the top ten hits for each, but saw nothing of any relevance. He tried again and followed a few links before abandoning his search and, in response to a rumble from his stomach, decided to go grab some dinner.

❄ ❄ ❄

Smith sat at a window table, chewing the last bite of his burger and swearing to himself that he would refrain from eating all of the fries. He couldn't pin this one on Marshall, but the effect on him was the same. He was going to have to get back to better eating habits sooner or later. He plucked his cellphone from his jacket pocket and stared at the display. Lisa White's last message had been a plea to meet, but that was before yesterday's call, when he had told her to get on with her life. Would she even answer his call now? He dialed it and held his breath. She picked up on the third ring.

"I'm surprised to get a call from you."

"Yeah, well … look, I wanted to apologize about yesterday."

"Where are you?"

"I'm at Tony's"

"Marshall with you?"

"No."

"I thought you didn't eat that crap anymore, unless you had no choice…. Anyway, it doesn't matter. I'm around the corner. You gonna be there for awhile?"

"Yeah."

"I'll see you shortly."

Smith looked up a few minutes later to see her coming through the door. She was clad in workout gear, with a fleece vest on top and a yoga mat slung over her shoulder, her hair tied up in a ponytail. It always amazed him that whatever she wore, or whatever she had been doing for the past hour, she always looked fresh.

"I hope I didn't interrupt your workout."

"You caught me coming out of the shower," she said, sitting opposite him as he inhaled a warm breeze of citrus body wash and tried, almost successfully, to skip over the mental image she had just planted in his mind. Was it on purpose? He never knew with Lisa, but it certainly wasn't beyond her.

"Listen, I really am sorry about yesterday."

She waved a hand. "Don't worry about it. As long as you know, I was only calling out of concern."

"Yeah, I know," he said, as the waitress came over and took her order for sparkling water. "So, what exactly did you hear about Melissa that's of such concern?"

"You really want to know? I thought you didn't want …"

Smith gave her a frown. "Come on, Lisa. I know you're dying to tell me."

"It's not that, I assure you," she said, though she had to look away for a moment. "She really is bad news, from what I'm told."

"By who?"

"Several people, actually. One of the clerks at the office worked with her in Toronto — said she was a bitch from hell."

"This clerk a he or a she?"

"Definitely a he. He said McAdam harassed him, got him booted out of the firm. The managing partner's a friend of her father's."

"Sounds like sour grapes to me. You lawyers are a prickly bunch at the best of times. Throw in job jockeying and some sexual tension and things are bound to get nasty."

"Glad to see you have such a high opinion of us, Jack," she said, though she seemed to acknowledge some truth in what he had said. "But that's not what worries me, anyway. She tried to run over an ex-boyfriend."

"Come on."

"I'm serious, Jack. She's a real psycho. Did you check her record?"

"I couldn't tell you if I did," he said, lowering his voice. "And I couldn't tell you if I had checked and found no record of any such incident on her file."

"I have it on pretty good authority."

"You mean some other cut-throat articling student who lost out in a head to head with her at the office?" He shook his head. "I don't buy it, Lisa."

"I know she's attractive, but I'm just saying be careful."

"You mean real beauty's not skin deep? What's your excuse, then?"

"I'm trying to be serious, here. If you want to be immature about it …"

"All right, all right." He looked at his watch. "I should probably be getting back. Thanks for dropping by. You look good, by the way."

"Thanks," she said, slipping into her fleece vest. "Still trying to lose those extra couple of pounds."

"Hmm," he said as they got up. She had been saying the same thing for years, but if she was carrying any extra weight, he didn't know where she was hiding it. "By the way, have you ever heard of the name Speelay?"

She slung her yoga mat over her shoulder. "Sounds vaguely familiar. I think it might be a case, can't remember off hand what it's about, though."

"I hadn't thought of that," he said, as they stepped out onto Elgin. "I'll look it up."

She snapped her fingers. "Contracts, that's it. It's a famous case on contract law — capacity, I think. I don't remember the facts."

"Pretty impressive."

She grinned. "How many times do I have to tell you, Jack? I'm not just a pretty face." They stood on the sidewalk in an awkward moment of silence. "Well, take care of yourself, okay?"

"I will." He leaned in and kissed her on the cheek, and she half-hugged him. She watched him make his way back up Elgin while she crossed over and headed off down Cooper, oblivious to the midnight blue BMW parked facing her as she walked by.

CHAPTER 25

Smith was staring at his monitor, scrolling down through the first page of the Speelay case, a decision of the Ontario Court of Appeal, and wondering how he had ever imagined attending law school. The head note alone was five pages, the case itself was almost a hundred, and he had no intention of reading it in full. Lisa was right — it was a contracts case, and he skipped to the end of the head note and arrived at the result. The appeal court had reversed the trial judge, who had held that a contract was enforceable, despite the plaintiff's less than obvious mental capacity to enter into and understand all of the terms. He pondered the case for a moment, as an uneasy feeling settled in the pit of his stomach, as he wondered why Melissa might have made a note of this particular case. There were any number of reasons, he assured himself. After all, she presumably came across all sorts of legal issues with the numerous Raftsmen player contracts, not to mention the ones covering the coaching staff, suppliers, concessions, and media rights. He sat staring at the screen for a while, considering the daunting task of reading all ninety-five pages. Then he activated the search function and typed a word into the box and hit enter. The cursor stopped in the middle of the screen, in front of the word he had selected, surrounded in blue highlight and shining at him like a beacon. He drew a deep breath and read the surrounding text.

"Fuck," he muttered, oblivious to his surroundings as the implications of what he was reading sank in. He racked his brain to find some confirmation of the hunch that had been growing at the back of his mind over the past few days. Suddenly, it occurred to him there was one area he hadn't fully explored, and he headed over to a small filing room at the rear of the Major Crimes Unit, where the evidence from the Ritchie investigation was being stored. He read the labels on the banker's boxes on the shelves, skipping over the personal effects from Ritchie's condo, then spotted the Ashcroft files at the far end of the top shelf. He dragged down the first box and set it on a small table by the door.

Removing the cover of the box, he flipped through the various file folders, recognizing some of the names from the time he had spent in Ashcroft's DC offices. There hadn't been time then for an exhaustive review, and someone else had taken over the in-depth review of the files. He retrieved the second box and flipped off its cover, and was about to go through the same process, when he noticed a typed index of files taped to the inside of the lid. He noticed Nancy and John Ridgeway's names among the list, next to Stephen Gravelle, but it wasn't until he reached the second-last name that his heart skipped a beat — Micheline Riggs. He fingered through the folders until he identified the one dedicated to Riggs and pulled it free. It was thin, compared to the others, and as he flipped it open, he could see it contained only a half-dozen pages of paper — a mix of handwritten notes and a typed report. The last item on file was a cheque stub, for ten thousand dollars, dated August 7. The stub was stapled to a one-page, typed internal memo on Ashcroft letterhead. Smith read the report, the gist of which was that the client had insisted on the payment, against advice from the account manager — it was signed by Chad McCleod.

Smith was standing there, staring at the file, when he sensed someone in the small room behind him. He got a start when he spun around and almost bumped into Beaudoin.

"Jeez, Sarge, you scared the shit out of me."

Beaudoin didn't smile, or even bother with his trademark grimace. Instead he just stared at Smith, the tension evident from the narrowing around the eyes, and the vein over his left temple that bulged visibly. He seemed a shade pinker than usual, as well.

"Everything okay, Sarge?"

"You tell me."

"What do you mean?"

"You want to tell me anything about Melissa McAdam?"

Smith froze at the sound of her name, and he could tell from Beaudoin's reaction that he had done a poor job of concealing his shock.

"Well?" Beaudoin crossed his massive forearms in front of his chest and waited, his eyes boring into Smith for an answer.

"Look, Sarge. It's not what —"

"Jesus Christ, Smith. I haven't got enough to worry about, between wondering whether we've got enough on Saunders to stick, or whether Ellen Ritchie's lawyer's going to succeed in his threat to dismantle the entire force over this arrest, you have to fuck a potential witness!"

"She's not —"

"Not another fucking word! I don't want to hear it. You're on leave, effective immediately. You're not to set foot in here again until this is cleared up, do you understand?"

"But Sarge —"

Beaudoin held up a hand to cut him off, then glared at him one last time. "Out, *now*. I mean it." He was almost through the door when he turned and looked back at Smith. "And I'd advise you to steer clear of Melissa McAdam, if you ever plan on coming back to Major Crimes."

❊ ❊ ❊

Smith sat on a bench built into the retaining wall that formed one side of the canal jogging path, looking out past the iron railings at the murky water beyond, still, except for the occasional ripple caused by a falling leaf. A couple of months from now, the water would be drained down to a few feet in depth and the air would be filled with the sound of steel crunching ice, from the thousands of skaters who would flock to the canal for Winterlude. Sitting here now, with the late afternoon sun blocked by the still-thick canopy of overhanging leaves, Smith felt a chill as he glanced at the exact spot where Curtis Ritchie had died just a couple of weeks earlier. It wasn't the murder itself — he had been in the job long enough to have developed a certain familiarity with death — or even his banishment from Elgin Street that really bothered him, though it would make it difficult for him to get to the bottom of what had been bothering him for the past few days. He took a deep breath and broke down in his mind what he knew, once again.

First, he had a bad feeling that Dennis Hearst was right about Melissa and Ritchie, and her evasion when he had raised the topic had only heightened his suspicion. That meant that she had lied to him, or at least omitted material information. Then again, he didn't think he had ever asked her directly whether she had slept with Ritchie and, anyway, there were plenty of reasons why she might not want to reveal the fling. He had only to look to his own encounter in the evidence room a few hours earlier with Beaudoin — a direct result of blurring the lines between work and intimacy. Strange how he had been unable to see the train wreck coming until it was too late. Maybe it had been the same for her with Ritchie: her judgment blinded by a moment of weakness that she immediately regretted and wanted nothing more to do with. The motives for obscuring the relationship in that sense were certainly not difficult to understand. But he knew she had concealed much more than her fling with Ritchie, and the outline of an alternate scenario was slowly but steadily forming in his mind. But he needed to be sure — now more than ever, thanks to his forced leave, which saddled him with a considerable handicap in filling in the missing pieces of the puzzle. He leaned forward, resting his forearms on his knees and watching a pair of ducks paddling their way toward him, the copper spires of the Château Laurier rising in the distance behind them. He wondered how Beaudoin had found out. Not that it mattered.

In fact, he decided, as he stood and started walking down the path toward the Somerset Bridge, the only thing that mattered now was finding the answers he needed, and quickly. There were really only two possibilities lurking in the back of his mind. Either there was a perfectly reasonable explanation for everything, one that he hadn't considered, or he had made an error in judgment so grave that it could cost him everything.

CHAPTER 26

Smith knew from the familiar rap on the door who it was before he opened up.

"Not disturbing anything, am I?"

"You like to save that for early mornings," Smith said, stepping aside to let Marshall in. They both headed to the living area and sat on opposite ends of the couch.

"I guess you heard?"

Marshall nodded. "It's just leave, right?"

"For now, yeah."

"Listen, I didn't …"

"You don't have to say a thing, Marsh." Smith held up his hand. "I fucked up, pure and simple. I should have known better."

"Maybe so, but I didn't rat you out, in case you were wondering."

"I wasn't," Smith said, feeling a wave of relief.

"Word is, Beaudoin got an anonymous tip about you and Melissa. He came to see me, and … well, I guess my poker face needs some work."

Smith shook his head. "I'm the one should be apologizing. I just hope I haven't dragged you into the shit with me."

"Beaudoin'll get over it. Just stay out of his face for a while. He's just a bit rattled over Ellen Ritchie's threats."

"You mean suing for wrongful prosecution?" Smith shrugged his shoulders. "Like nobody's ever threatened us with that before."

"I don't know why, but Beaudoin's taking it seriously this time. Maybe he thinks the case is weak."

They sat in silence for a long time before Smith spoke. "What do you think?"

"The lawsuit? It's bullshit."

"No, I meant the case."

Marshall looked at him, trying to read his thoughts. "Why, are you having doubts now, too?"

Smith smiled, then shook his head. "No. Besides, it wouldn't matter if I was, right? I'm the last person in the world Beaudoin's gonna listen to at this point."

"So what are you gonna do?"

"I'm going to Toronto for a few days. Take that trip I was planning before all this shit happened."

Marshall nodded. "Let off a bit of steam. That's good. I wish I was going with you, but it turns out I'm taking a few days' leave to paint the rec room."

"Again?"

"Again. Apparently, it's too dark," Marshall said with a sigh, as he stood. "Well, I'll leave you to it."

"Thanks for dropping by. I appreciate it," Smith added, patting him on the shoulder as they reached the door.

"Enjoy some time off, and let this blow over. This time next week, everything'll be back to normal, you'll see."

Smith smiled as the door closed. Somehow, he didn't share his partner's optimism, though.

❄ ❄ ❄

Smith rolled down the window to clear out the funky mix of coffee and bad breath that had accumulated over the past four hours. He had gotten up relatively early, showered, and swung by a drive-through before hitting the road. It was cloudy when he started south, but by the time he hit Kingston, the sun had broken through and stayed with him as he made his way west along the 401. It was mid-afternoon as he drove past the entrance to York University — its concrete clusters visible beyond the treed expanse of green at its perimeter. He followed the map he had printed off this morning, and five minutes later he was at Jane and Finch — an area he wouldn't want to venture into after dark. Even in the brilliant fall sunshine, there was something sinister about the succession of grubby high-rises — an overwhelming desperation that the odd chain-link-ringed playground did little to counter. He looked for numbers on the buildings, and pulled into a parking lot as he spotted the one he was looking for. A group of teenage boys, clad in baggy jeans and hoodies, eyed him as he got out of the car and locked the door. Ignoring their taunts, he headed over to the entrance to one of the high-rises and wasn't surprised to see the front door lock disabled, allowing him to enter the lobby without having to call ahead. By the state of the battered directory, the call button probably didn't work anyway. Thankfully, he was only going up five floors and didn't encounter anyone in his brief ascent, coming out of the stairwell on the fifth, and entering a hallway that stank of a mixture of sweat and urine. He stopped in front of apartment 502 and rapped lightly. He heard some rustling and footsteps on the other side of the door, and then it opened a crack and part of a woman's face appeared behind the security chain.

"Micheline Riggs?"

The eyes narrowed, then blinked. "Who are you?"

"I just wanted to talk…. Are you Ms. Riggs?"

"She's not here." The door began to shut.

"Wait," he put his hand on the door. "I'm with the Ottawa Police." He took out his identification and held it up to the crack in the doorway. The woman looked at it, then back at Smith.

"I told you, she's not here."

"Do you know where I can find her?"

The door slammed shut, and for a moment he thought she had just closed it to remove the chain, but then he heard footsteps walking away.

"You looking for Micheline?"

Smith turned to see a woman in her forties standing in a doorway across the hall.

"Yes, do you know where she is?"

"She's dead."

❋ ❋ ❋

Smith sat on the cracked vinyl-covered chair in the eating area while Angie Dupree poured coffee in the cramped galley kitchen. Apart from the dinette set for two, the apartment featured a tattered couch and chair, an old TV on an overturned milk carton, and not much else. She brought two cups and set one in front of him and sat at the little table.

"Mind?" she said, putting a cigarette between her lips.

"Go ahead."

"So how did you know Micheline again?" she said, after she had lit up and taken her first greedy drag of nicotine.

"I didn't," he said, sipping his coffee. He didn't want to mention the murder investigation, partly because he didn't want to scare her off, and partly because he knew he shouldn't be here at all, and if Beaudoin found out.... He tried a different approach. "Did Micheline tell you she had a son?"

Dupree blew out a stream of smoke and nodded her head. "Do you know him?"

Smith saw the hope in her eyes and decided to skirt the truth. "That's how I got Micheline's name. I know they met a month or so ago."

Dupree smiled through a cloud of smoke. "She was so excited. I never knew she had a son — she gave him up for adoption, like, twenty years ago. Somehow, she found out where he was and contacted him."

"Did she tell you his name, or anything else?" Smith said, as Dupree took another drag of her cigarette.

"She said his name was Curtis. I talked to her the day before they met, and she was going on about how her life was gonna change. She was gonna straighten herself out, for him. Make up for all the lost time, you know?"

Smith nodded, and let her carry on. She tapped her cigarette in the ashtray before continuing. "I bumped into her in the hall the day after they met and she was out of it. She was using again — I could tell. Said her heart was broken."

"Micheline had a drug problem?"

Dupree nodded. "She was always trying to kick something. Heroin, crack, pills — you name it. She was a good person but she was always losing the battle, you know what I mean?"

"I think so."

"When she was clean, she was the nicest person you could ever meet. So thoughtful and caring, but then her demons would drag her down, and she'd turn into … someone else."

"How did she die?"

"She overdosed a week or so after she met with … Curtis."

"Around mid-August, then?"

"Yes, about then, I guess."

They both paused at the sound of a high-pitched scream out in the hall, followed by the sound of breaking glass and someone running down the hall shouting obscenities.

"That'd be the couple that took over Micheline's apartment. Not a day goes by they don't get in a fight over something." Dupree shook her head. "I sure miss her."

"You said she was using again the day after she met Curtis. Had she been clean for a while?"

"Not really. She'd usually stay clean for a few days, then fall off the wagon, and start the cycle all over."

"How did she pay for the drugs?"

"She had her monthly cheque, but I really don't know what she did to feed her habit. We never talked about it, but I know she was friendly with a lot of the dealers and she was a good-looking woman, you know?" Dupree glanced down and tapped her cigarette on the edge of the ashtray. "She sure seemed to have a steady supply the last couple of weeks, though. I hardly saw her leave the apartment, and didn't notice anyone else coming or going."

"Who found her?"

"Super. He came to get the rent or something. Poor woman was lying dead on the floor of her living room."

"When did you last see her?"

"A couple of days before she died. I dropped by to see if she wanted anything at the grocery store. She looked awful, and I knew she wasn't eating properly. She secmed like she was in a trance. I asked her what had happened with her son, and at first she wouldn't say. But we chatted for a while and she eventually said he didn't believe her. Said she was just out to hustle him, like everyone else."

"Did she say he gave her some money?"

"No, she didn't mention it. All she said was he told her he never wanted to see her again, and he called her some names — hurtful names, you know?" Dupree stood and walked over to one of the kitchen cabinets and pulled out a shoebox. She retrieved something from it and returned to the table, holding out what looked like a plastic bracelet.

"She said she tried to give this to Curtis, but he wouldn't take it, and he got really angry with her. She told me to hold onto it for her, and to make sure he got it if anything ever happened to her."

Smith took the bracelet, bearing the name of a Toronto hospital, and that of a baby boy named Curtis Riggs.

"Can you make sure he gets it?"

Smith barely heard her as he reread the date of birth.

"Can you?"

He registered her question and her pleading eyes, before looking away. "I'll do what I can, Ms. Dupree."

CHAPTER 27

Smith was walking out of a gas station in Napanee when his phone went off and he recognized Don Brooks's number.

"Jack Smith."

"It's Don Brooks, returning your call."

"Thanks for getting back to me. I wanted to ask you a question about Bob Ritchie."

"I heard you guys arrested the stepdad."

"Yeah, this is just a loose end I'm tying up. It's actually Bob's wife I wanted to ask you about. Did you know her?"

"Joan? Yeah, sure, I knew her."

"How did she and Bob get together?"

"We were all at the same high school, but they never really hit it off until a couple of years later. She was a hockey fanatic, just like Bob. She watched all his games."

"What did she do?"

"You mean apart from follow Bob around from rink to rink?" Brooks chuckled. "She worked for the provincial government, I think."

Smith scribbled a note, then reviewed his sketched timeline. "And she would have died when Curtis was about five?"

"I'm not sure, but that sounds about right. Breast cancer. Bob was a mess at the funeral. He really loved her. They were like two peas in a pod. After he hung up the skates himself, they still went to all the Peterborough home games together."

"And they never had kids of their own?"

"They couldn't. That's why they adopted."

"Right," Smith said, pulling the baby bracelet from his pocket and looking at it again. "You're a reporter, Don. How would I find out which department Joan Ritchie worked for?"

There was a pause at the other end of the line. "Well, you could go down to Queen's Park, I suppose, but if that's all you want to know, I can find out for you."

"How's that?"

"One of Joan's best friends works at the paper. I'm sure she'd remember. I could give her a call if you like?"

"If you wouldn't mind, that would be great."

"I'll call you right back."

Smith ended the call and checked his watch. He still had a couple of hours on the road back to Ottawa, but he'd have daylight, or at least dusk, for most of it. He decided to get himself another coffee. As he was adding cream, Brooks's number appeared and his phone went off.

"That was quick."

"Yeah, I caught her at home. She said Joan worked at the land registry in Peterborough."

"Oh," Smith said, disappointed.

"She transferred there when she moved up from Toronto. She was with Vital Statistics there."

Smith stopped stirring his coffee.

"Does that tie up your loose end?"

"What?" he said, remembering Brooks. "Yes, yes, it does. That's really helpful. I want to thank you for your time."

"Pleasure. And congratulations on getting your guy. I hope he gets what he deserves."

"Thanks," Smith said, hanging up. "Me too," he muttered, as he put the lid on his coffee and hurried out to his car.

❋ ❋ ❋

Smith was mentally exhausted by the time he parked in front of his apartment building. He had debated what to do during the last two hours of the drive home, as he fitted the pieces of the puzzle together in his mind, still stumbling over one missing piece. He could feel the fatigue from the long drive in his legs as he walked up the two flights to his floor. He was reaching in his pocket for his keys when his senses went on high alert. The hallway beyond his door was dark — the bulb having burned out several days before — but he knew she was there somewhere, by the familiar smell of her perfume. As his eyes adjusted to the light, he watched as a form emerged from the shadows and his body tensed, unsure what to expect.

"Melissa?"

"Why are you doing this?" she asked, coming toward him, an anguished look on her face.

"What are you doing here?"

"I want to know why."

His feet seemed glued to the floor as she approached him, one hand in the pocket of her raincoat. He tensed as he watched her pull out her hand, but saw that it was empty, as she ran it through her hair. "What have I done to deserve this?" she said.

"Look, do we have to go through this again? You know …"

"I don't know shit," she hissed, her voice wavering. He noticed her eyes were red-rimmed.

"Calm down, okay?"

"You're ditching me because you found out I slept with Ritchie, and you're surprised that I didn't tell you. Don't you see a contradiction there?"

"I didn't ditch you. I just said we should hold off for a while. And as for Ritchie, you should have told me. I was investigating his murder, for Christ's sake."

"What's my ill-advised fling got to do with that? It's not like I kill …" She stopped, and her eyes widened noticeably, as the rest of features seemed to freeze. "So," she said, seeming to have difficulty getting the words out. "Now you think I *killed* Ritchie. Are you fucking kidding me?"

"I'm saying I think we both know it's not appropriate for us to be involved right now. I wish you could understand that."

She shook her head. "I can't believe this. I can't believe you would …" Her face hardened as she held her head upright and started buttoning up her coat. "At least have the balls to say what you think, and don't use the investigation to hide what's really going on."

Smith stepped back as she walked past him toward the stairs, keeping a close eye on her hands. "What are you talking about?"

"That bitch you're screwing on the side — the one we bumped into at the bar the other night. Don't look so shocked. I know all about her, and your history. And she's not the only one who can dig up dirt, believe me."

He stood speechless as she disappeared through the door to the stairwell and he heard the echo of her heels as she descended. It wasn't until he heard the door slam at the bottom that he exhaled and hurriedly unlocked the door to his apartment. He pulled out his phone and dialed Lisa's cell, getting voicemail.

"Fuck," he muttered, fumbling through a drawer for her card and office number. He tried her there, then sent her both text and email messages telling her to contact him urgently. He looked at his watch — it was almost 8:00 p.m. and she could be anywhere. He looked out the living room window over the parking lot. Nothing. He ran to the kitchen and looked out the patio door, just in time to a see a sleek, dark sedan pull away from a side street and tear off toward Rideau Street. He felt his chest tighten as his phone went off in his hand and he recognized Lisa's number.

"What's the matter?"

"I need to talk to you, right away. Can we meet somewhere?"

"Well, I was just … I guess you could drop by here if you want, What's going on?"

"I'll be there in five."

❋   ❋   ❋

She was at the door before he could knock, and for a moment it occurred to him that she might not be alone. But the sweatshirt and yoga pants told him he was probably only interrupting a good book or a movie. Her glasses, which she rarely wore in public, were the clincher. He hadn't seen her like this himself in years — in her natural state.

"Sorry to drop in on you like this."

"What the hell's going on? You've got me all freaked out."

"I need your help, Lisa. I think you may have been right about Melissa, more than you know."

"What do you mean?" She stood aside. "You might as well come in."

He took a deep breath before stepping through the doorway. He knew the address, and had even driven by a few times, but he had never set foot inside. Doing so now felt odd somehow. "Nice place by the way," he said, taking in the high ceilings, the gleaming hardwood, and the overstuffed couches accented by a carefully arranged colour scheme picked up in the cushions, the rug, and even the paintings on the wall. It was the place she had always said she wanted when they had lived together.

"Thanks. Now what's going on?"

He sat on the sofa next to her and took a deep breath.

"I have a question for you, on contract law. I think I know the answer but I have to hear it from a lawyer."

"Okay, what is it?"

"The age of majority in Ontario is eighteen, so someone under eighteen can't be bound by a contract, right?"

Lisa frowned. "Generally, no. Is this to do with that case we were talking about — Speelay?"

"Yeah. But let's imagine, for a second, that we're talking about a professional services contract — like for a hockey player."

"Would you just cut the shit and tell me what's going on?"

"I'm talking about Curtis Ritchie. What happens to his contract with the Raftsmen if he was underage when he signed it?"

Lisa looked puzzled for a moment, then seemed to focus on the question. "Well, it's unenforceable, for starters."

"And what does that mean, for the Raftsmen?"

"It means there is no contract."

"So, they don't have to pay him?"

"No."

"And on the flipside?"

"He doesn't have to … play for them." She stopped after speaking the words, and looked at Smith. "Is this for real?"

"What happens to all the trades the Raftsmen made to get Ritchie?"

"If you mean trades between teams with the rights to draft Ritchie, they're perfectly enforceable."

"In other words, they couldn't ask for the players back?"

"Look, I'm not a sports lawyer, Jack, but I can't see how. I mean, they would be valid contracts with third parties — namely, the other teams or players. Are you saying Curtis Ritchie was underage when the Raftsmen signed him?"

Smith got up and started pacing the floor in front of the couch. "I think he's underage now, and will be until he turns eighteen in April."

"But surely the Raftsmen must have checked all this out before they signed him, as part of their due diligence."

"By doing what? Asking for a birth certificate?"

She nodded.

"And what if it had been doctored?"

"You can't just add a year to your age without someone noticing."

"What if it was done a long time ago? Look, Curtis was five when his adoptive mother died of breast cancer. His adoptive father remarried Ellen Ritchie a couple of years later, so she wouldn't have known if —."

"I'm not sure I follow, Jack."

"Bob Ritchie was the ultimate extreme hockey parent. He coached Curtis until the league kicked him out for screaming at the kids and the refs. He was obsessed with Curtis making it to the pros, something he never did himself, despite years in the minors, on the verge of being called up." He paused, noticing Lisa's confused expression. "I'm saying he would have done anything to get Curtis an edge, so why not an extra year?"

"You mean being a year younger than anyone else he's playing against? How would that help?"

"That's a huge advantage for a developing player. Curtis was a pretty big kid, so there would have been no real physical disadvantage," Smith said, leaning forward on the sofa. "And it would have been outweighed by having access to higher level players and coaches a year early. If he's got some natural talent to start with, his development would be all the more accelerated. Pretty soon he's making the select teams every year — the ones with the best coaches, and who play against higher-calibre opponents — he's getting invited to the select summer camps, and so on."

Lisa was shaking her head. "I hate to sound negative, Jack, but this all sounds pretty theoretical."

He held up his hand. "I'm getting to that. What if I told you Joan Ritchie, Curtis's adoptive mother — also a hockey nut — worked in the vital statistics office in Toronto, before she moved to Peterborough, and that I found her name, alongside a reference to that Speelay case, on a sheet of paper on Melissa McAdam's desk?"

Smith sat back on the sofa as Lisa processed the information. "Melissa would have been responsible for due diligence, I guess, so if something was missed in the contract, it would probably fall at her feet."

Lisa was frowning again. "But if Curtis knew, then it was fraud. And what about the mother — I mean, Ellen Ritchie?"

Smith shook his head. "Remember, Joan Ritchie died when Curtis was five, so if she did alter the birth records before then, Curtis would never have known.

It would have been before he started school. Who's gonna question a five-year-old's age, anyway? Ellen Ritchie probably had no idea either — why would she? Bob died a couple of years after their marriage, then Tom Saunders shows up a few years later — he sure as hell wouldn't have known, if Ellen didn't."

"So Ritchie himself never even knew," Lisa said, more to herself.

"Who knows what Bob's long-term plan was, or whether he ever planned on telling Curtis."

"And now both Bob and his wife are dead, so I guess we'll never find out." Lisa shrugged.

"But what if Curtis found out," Smith said. "Recently …"

"You mean after he signed on with the Raftsmen?" White looked excited. "Technically, he could set aside the contract. If I'm Melissa McAdam and it falls at my feet, I've got to be really worried. It's only the biggest deal in the Raftsmen's history, and she blows it, puts her dad's job on the line to boot." She stopped and frowned. "But why would he want to void it? It was going to pay him millions, wasn't it?"

"Rookie contracts are capped, so the big money was still a few years away, but I agree he would have to have a good reason to want out from under it."

They both sat in silence for a moment, as they considered the possibilities.

"My God," Lisa finally said. "Do do you really think …"

"I don't know what to think, Lisa."

"But you and Melissa … Christ, Jack."

"We're over, believe me. But Beaudoin found out and put me on forced leave. That's why I'm here, instead of at the station with Marshall. If it turns out I've been sleeping with Curtis Ritchie's killer, I'm done. Beaudoin'll have my head. Saunders and Ellen Ritchie are already threatening a wrongful prosecution suit — can you imagine if they're right and they find out …" He shook his head. "But I don't give a shit about any of that."

"But Jack, you've got to tell them what you know."

Smith got up from the couch. "I gotta go."

"Where are you going?"

He stopped and took hold of her upper arms. "Look, Lisa. If what I'm thinking is true, you may be in danger."

"Me? Why?"

"I saw her tonight … Melissa. She mentioned your name…. I don't know. You said yourself she was a psycho."

"Don't you think you're being a little melodramatic?"

"There were a couple of peace bonds taken out against her — I did check, and I spoke to one of the cops involved, who said she was pretty unstable. This could be for real, and if it is … is there somewhere you can go, just for a while?"

"What have you got me into?" Lisa shook her head. "I'll go stay at Val's."

Smith nodded, but she saw the reluctance in his eyes.

"Don't worry, I'll make something up — say's it's man trouble. Shouldn't be hard."

"All right. Go right away. And keep in touch." He paused. "I'm sorry, Lisa."

"What about you? What are you going to do?" she said, following him down the hall. He stopped in the doorway.

"I really don't know."

"Be careful," she said, as he set off down the front steps and into the night.

CHAPTER 28

Smith took the stairs up to the second floor of the Elgin Street station and made his way quietly down the hall to the Major Crimes Unit. The lights were on, but as he peered through the glass, he didn't see anyone inside, so he opened the door and stepped in, listening for the rustling of paper or the click of a keyboard — anything that would alert him to the presence of a colleague who might ask him what he was doing there against Beaudoin's orders. But the area was deserted, so he closed the door behind him and went straight to the filing room, and the boxes of evidence compiled over the past couple of weeks. He sifted through the folders containing reports and interview transcripts, before focusing on a file on Ritchie's personal effects. He flipped through photos of his condo — shots of his bedroom, kitchen, and living room, and one from his enormous walk-in closet, showing the contents as of the day of his death. There was a picture of his shiny new Porsche, still sitting in the impound yard somewhere, and an attached piece of paper with some typed text. He scanned the text and saw it was a printout of the various places Ritchie had gone in the week before his death, as recorded by the factory-installed GPS. There were lots of trips to the rink, and one to Saunders' sister's house on the Wednesday night before he was killed, presumably to drop Saunders off after their dinner.

From Wednesday on, the only place the car had been was back and forth between the rink and the condo, and he was about to abandon the sheet when he noticed the time of a Thursday morning visit to the arena — 2:00 a.m. He thought it odd that Ritchie would have gone out for a skate at that hour, but he supposed the Raftsmen players had any number of reasons to go to the rink, whether for a skate or to work out, or attend physio or other therapy sessions. But 2:00 a.m. still seemed strange. He noted an asterisk by the time, and a reference to a report number. Tossing the paper aside, he rifled through the rest of the folder until he found the report in question. There was a notation of Ritchie's travels during the week before his murder, and a remark by the investigator — Greg Wills — that the odd timing had prompted him to check with security at the rink for late Wednesday/ early Thursday. They had confirmed that Ritchie had spent just under an hour there. Of the other Raftsmen players or management, only Quinn McAdam was listed as being there at the same time.

Smith flipped through his notebook, to his record of their initial interview with McAdam, at which he had said the last contact he had with Ritchie had been on Tuesday. It was always possible the two hadn't encountered each other in the building at that hour, but it seemed unlikely. He froze as he heard the sound of a door opening out beyond the conference room, and flicked off the filing room light. He stayed where he was, listening as someone rummaged through a desk, made a phone call, and then seemingly left. After a few seconds of prolonged silence, Smith ventured out into the conference room and peeked into the main work area of the Major Crimes Unit. He had just opened the door to leave when he heard a voice behind him.

"Hey, Smitty."

He turned to see one of the senior investigators looking at him from his cubicle at the rear of the unit.

"Oh, hi, Dan. Didn't know anyone was here."

"Just doing some paperwork. Thought you were on leave for awhile?" It was more query than challenge, but Smith couldn't be sure. "I am. I just dropped in to pick something up. I was just leaving."

"Take it easy."

Smith nodded and slipped out the door, wondering how quickly Beaudoin would find out about his late-night visit. By the time he reached the end of the hall, it didn't matter. He had dialed Melissa's number and was waiting for an answer. It had rung four times and he was about to give up when he heard her voice on the line.

"What do you want?"

"Melissa, we need to talk."

"I don't think that's such a great idea ..."

"We need to talk right away, and I think you know why."

"What are you talking about?"

"Where are you?"

"I'm at the rink. What the hell's going on?"

"There's a sports bar called the Zone on Eagleson. I'll meet you there in twenty."

"Whatever it is, you can tell me over the phone. Don't you think you've caused enough trouble …?"

"Just be there in twenty. It's about your dad."

❄ ❄ ❄

Smith's call went to Marshall's voicemail for the third time as he made out the exit for Eagleson Road through the wall of rain on his windscreen that overwhelmed the determined sweep of the wipers. He decided to leave a message as he exited the Queensway and pulled up to a red light, just as the downpour turned to hail.

"Hey, Marsh, it's me. Listen, I'm back from Toronto and I need to talk to you about the case," he said, practically yelling over the staccato of hailstones pelting the roof of the car. "Something's come up and … just give me a call as soon as you get this. It's around nine-thirty."

A few minutes later, he was pulling into the parking lot outside the sports bar when he spotted Melissa's midnight-blue Bimmer at the far end of the lot. She was sitting at a table near the door when he walked in, shaking off the wet. The expression on her face told him he would have to get to the point quick.

"Thanks for coming. It's really getting bad out …"

She remained stone-faced as he took a seat. "You said something about my dad?"

He glanced around the room. The place was three-quarters full and the competing noise of rock music and two different pre-season hockey games on an array of big-screen TVs meant that they were unlikely to be overheard.

"I need you to tell me the truth about Curtis."

"What's my dad got to do with it?"

They were interrupted by a passing waitress, who took their order. After she had gone, Smith leaned forward and looked Melissa in the eye. "What happened at that late-night meeting at the rink?"

Melissa kept staring straight at him, though he knew he had detected a minute flinch at the question.

"I need the truth, Melissa."

"What meeting?"

"Your dad and Curtis met at two o'clock in the morning on the Thursday before he was killed. What were they meeting about?"

"I don't know about any meeting," she said, her eyes darting down to her hands. When she looked back up at him, he knew she was lying.

"It's not too late to tell me, Melissa. I can understand you wanting to protect him, and all you're guilty of so far is willful blindness. But I'm asking you a direct question, and I know you understand the consequences of lying to me now."

She looked away again for a moment, then fixed him with her steely blue eyes. "This sounds awfully official for someone who's off the Ritchie case."

"How do you know if I'm on the case or not? Because your dad told you?"

She seemed to trip over the question, so he continued.

"I know he called Beaudoin, so let's stop bullshitting each other. I'm going to ask you one more time — what happened at that meeting?"

"I don't have to be here, remember? So don't think you can interrogate me, or I'll walk out that door, and you know it."

"Bullshit. You want answers as bad as I do. I can see it in your eyes, Melissa."

There was an awkward pause as their drinks arrived.

"Let's try another question," he said, when they were alone again. "When did you find out Curtis was underage?"

Melissa seemed stung by the question, her glass still at her lips, her slightly widened eyes locked on his. She put the glass down deliberately as Smith continued.

"I know you were doing research on capacity and enforceability of contracts, so I know you found out. And I know you must have felt bad, since you would have been responsible for due diligence on Curtis's contract."

"How do you know —"

"What happened at that meeting?"

She was staring at her hands now.

"If you won't tell me, I'll have to fill in the blanks myself," Smith said, leaning across the table. "I'd say it went something like this: Curtis told your father he was underage, and could void the contract with the Raftsmen whenever he wanted. What the hell else was your dad gonna do, Melissa? He'd staked the team's entire future on Ritchie, not to mention his own career."

"No." She was shaking her head.

348

"No? Your father was already under scrutiny for the deals he made to get Curtis here. I can only imagine the shit that would hit the fan if it turned out that Curtis wasn't eligible, that he could walk away from the Raftsmen. It wouldn't just be his job in Ottawa on the line either; he'd be ruined. Everything he ever worked for, gone. You wouldn't come out looking too good, either."

"That's not true. We were going to petition the league to have our draft picks restored, get our players back. Everything would have been fine."

"Is that what he told you? And you believe that?" Smith shook his head, then looked out the window at the sheet of rain sliding down the windows. "All right, then. Suppose it was something else." He waited for her to look at him before he continued. "Like maybe he found out about you and Curt —"

"It had nothing to do with that," she said, but her eyes betrayed her.

"Your dad wouldn't have been too pleased to find out that Ritchie had treated his only daughter like one of his puck bunnies."

"Stop it! I told you, it wasn't that."

"Wake up, Melissa. He found out, and we both know he had to do something ..."

"Don't even say it ..."

"What, that he murdered Curtis?" he said, in a raw whisper. "You know it's true. He had no choice, for both of your sakes."

"That's not true!" she said, tears welling in her eyes as the people at a nearby table glanced over, only to meet Smith's glare and suddenly lose interest.

"Then tell me how it really was," he said, reaching across the table and touching her forearm. "What happened at that goddamned meeting?"

She was shaking her head, her eyes downcast.

"What did Curtis say to your father? Was it about the two of you? Was that the final straw?"

She looked away, wiping tears from her eyes.

"Curtis said he was going to Toronto. He was going to tell the media about his real age, walk away from his contract with the Raftsmen, and sign with Toronto when he became eligible in the spring."

Smith's head swam at the reaction Quinn McAdam must have had to hearing that the superstar he had dealt the future of his team to get was going to not only walk away, but go to their divisional archrivals down the 401. It was the ultimate slap in the face, and a death sentence for McAdam's career … or maybe for Ritchie himself, as it turned out.

"Jesus."

"Dad wouldn't hurt anyone. Not like that. It can't have been him."

"Where's your dad now?" Smith stood up and pulled out his phone.

"What? At home, I guess."

"Stay here. I've got to make a call."

Smith stepped out into the foyer and dialed Marshall's number again, getting voicemail. He hung up and tried his home number, hearing his wife's voice after a few rings.

"Connie, it's Jack. Sorry to bother you, but I'm trying to get a hold of Dave and he's not answering. You know where he is?"

"He's working."

"I thought he was taking a couple of days off?" Smith's senses instantly went on high alert.

"He said he had a loose end to tie up. He'd only be a couple of hours. What's going on, Jack?"

"Nothing. I just wanted to talk to him."

There was a pause at the other end of the line and Smith wondered whether Marshall had told her about his forced leave.

"Did he say where he was going?"

"He said he had to make a quick run out to Manotick."

Smith's heart skipped a beat. He knew Quinn McAdam's place was south of the city, on the Ottawa River. "When did you last talk to him?"

"About an hour ago. What's going on, Jack? You're starting to scare me."

"It's nothing, Connie. Don't worry. I'm sorry to bother you at home. I've gotta go."

He ended the call and went back into the bar. He was barely through the door when he noticed the table was empty. For a split second he thought Melissa had gone to the ladies' room, but his instinct sent him back outside and around to the side of the parking lot where he had seen her car when he came in. He had to shield his eyes from the driving rain, but he could see the spot was empty.

CHAPTER 29

Smith peered through the beam from his headlights and searched the gatepost for the number he was looking for, finding it in the sudden illumination of a lightning flash. He drove through the open gate as an earsplitting bang announced that the storm was directly overhead. As he followed the wandering driveway, he watched for falling trees as windswept branches slapped at the windshield and jammed the wiper blades. A few seconds later another bolt of lightning lit a clearing up ahead, where the outline of a large house burned itself into his mind before fading into the jet black that followed. His heart stuck in his throat as his headlights lit up Marshall's car in front of the house, next to Melissa's BMW. He stopped the car and shut off the ignition as he scanned the house for signs of life, checking his watch and realizing backup was still ten minutes away. He ignored the dire warnings Beaudoin had uttered on the phone when he had called in for help. He knew he couldn't wait and he was facing severe disciplinary measures anyway, his career being the least of his concerns right now. He still didn't know — and Beaudoin didn't either — why Marshall had decided to call on McAdam, but the midnight-blue BMW in the driveway could only mean that Quinn McAdam knew Smith was onto him, and now Marshall was in there with him.

Smith checked his Glock 10 and got out of the car, approaching the picture window at the front of the house from the side. He peered through the glass as an enormous fork of lightning lit the sky like a torch, and he saw clearly into the empty living room. The thunderclap was a second later this time, so loud as to shake the ground as Smith moved to the front door and tried the handle, finding it locked. He thought he heard a voice from inside, but the sound of the storm around him drowned out any remaining echo. As he strained to listen for confirmation, he moved around the side of the house to the patio. He tried the door and breathed a sigh of relief as it slid open. Stepping inside, his sidearm raised, he scanned the dimly lit kitchen and adjusted to the relative silence. He was about to move on when he heard a dull knocking from around the corner. He followed the sound to a hall-way at the other end of the kitchen that led toward the garage. But as he passed another door off the hallway, he froze at the sound of a muffled voice on the other side. He readied himself with the gun in one hand as he flipped off the latch on the door with the other and whipped it open. Slumped on the floor in the near corner of the wine cellar, with her hands behind her back, Melissa looked up at him, her eyes wide with fear and her mouth covered in duct tape.

"Melissa?" He ripped the tape off her mouth and put a hand on her shoulder as he bent down to look at her, noticing a small cut over her right eye. "Are you all right?"

She nodded. "It's Dad. He's …"

"He did this?"

"He … went crazy. I told him…. Oh my God!"

"Where's Marshall?"

"He's got him. He saw your car and he put me in here and … he said it was for my own good."

"Are they in the house?" Smith looked instinctively behind him, then pulled at the tape holding her hands together.

She shook her head as the tape ripped and her hands were freed. "I heard them go out the back. I think they're going to the boathouse. It's down at the river, a hundred metres."

"Look at me," he said, taking her by the hand. "Backup will be here any minute. I want you to go out front and wait for them."

"I want to go with —"

"No, you need to wait out front, and tell them where I've gone, and that your dad has Marshall. Are you clear?"

She swallowed hard, then looked up at him and nodded. "He's got a gun. I didn't even know he had one…. Be careful."

Smith helped her up and pointed her toward the front door, then slipped back out through the patio door into the yard.

❄ ❄ ❄

Smith ran through the driving rain, down the rolling lawn toward the water, finding the start of a crushed stone path in the glare of a bolt of lightning. He took the path and headed downriver for a couple of hundred feet, and as he neared the end of the path and made out a structure in the distance, he thought he heard the cough of a motor, muffled by a roll of thunder. He waited by a large tree for the next bolt of lightning, which lit the boathouse a few seconds later, fifty feet across a clearing in the trees. He waited and used the cover of thunder to drown out the sound of his footsteps on the gravel as he reached the rear door. He peered inside and saw McAdam standing at the controls of a large powerboat. Marshall was seated on the bench beside him with McAdam's gun trained on him.

McAdam turned to face the door, but kept the gun pointed at Marshall. "I guess we're not going anywhere, after all," he said, his voice echoing in the rafters of the boathouse, which seemed eerily quiet compared to out-side in the storm. "You can come on in, Detective Smith."

Smith stepped through the door with his weapon raised.

"Put the gun down, McAdam."

"So you can shoot me? I don't think so. You put yours down, or I'll put a hole in your partner."

"It's all over. Half the police force is on its way. You all right, Marsh?"

"I'm fine," Marshall called out, looking at Smith, then back at McAdam and the gun still trained on him. "Just take it easy, both of you."

355

"I didn't think he'd cleaned out the fuel lines yet." McAdam laughed, pointing to the open engine cover at the stern of the boat. "The neighbour's kid. I pay him to help out around the house. The one time he shows some initiative and does something on his own, and look where it gets me."

Smith took a few steps closer. "Let's talk about this, Quinn."

"Quinn now, is it?"

"We don't want to make matters worse here."

"Like they're not completely fucked up already? Why couldn't you just leave well enough alone? You had Saunders. Only reason he didn't do it himself was he didn't have the balls. How'd you find out, anyway?"

"The birth mother."

McAdam looked puzzled.

"But as you know by now, Curtis's adoptive parents fudged his birthday by a year, putting him in an unusual situation."

"Of walking out the fucking door," McAdam said. "He was gonna go to Toronto, can you fucking believe that? The little bastard was nothing but trouble."

"I'm sure you were under a lot of pressure," Smith said, as he thought he heard the distinctive crush of gravel under thick boots outside. He knew they were running out of time. "Mitigating factors that the Crown will take into account."

"I don't think so," McAdam said, adjusting his grip on the gun. Smith put a little more pressure on the trigger of his own weapon and tensed as he prepared to fire. McAdam glanced toward the house. "Tell Melissa I'm sorry."

Smith yelled out as McAdam raised the gun under his chin and a shot rang out. A second later, McAdam's considerable bulk pitched back and fell over the rail of the boat, into the water inside the boathouse. Smith ran to join Marshall as he looked over the rail, watching as McAdam's body floated up to the surface, the water around his head a darker shade than the rest.

"We're all clear," Smith said, turning to face the tactical team that had just entered the boathouse, weapons drawn. "The perp's down. We need a paramedic, and probably the coroner."

He turned back to Marshall and ripped the tape holding his partner's hands together. "You sure you're okay?"

He nodded. "Thanks, buddy."

"For what?" he said, looking down at McAdam's body being dragged out of the water onto the dock. "If it wasn't for me, McAdam would be in a cell right now." He patted Marshall on the back and jumped down onto the dock to begin the walk back up to the house, where he would have to tell Melissa her father was dead.

EPILOGUE

Smith sat at the bar, nursing the last of his beer and debating another. It's not like there was anyone waiting for him, he thought, as he spotted the passing waitress. He decided to let her make the call for him, and when she smiled his way and pointed to his glass, he nodded.

He glanced at the television over the bar and noticed the banner above two sports talking heads whose banter was drowned out by the music and noise inside the bar: "Raftsmen to Rebuild." Smith let out a grim chuckle at the suggestion that they had any choice in the matter. In the days following Quinn McAdam's death, Smith had found himself in the unusual situation of following media reports of what was going on, his forced leave preventing him access to frontline information. Marshall had kept in touch and given him the big ticket items, but as a private citizen he was puzzled and even amused by the wide range of conspiracy theories that had arisen as word got out that the Raftsmen's GM was dead. First it was a cop that had killed him, then a deranged fan. Smith eventually started tuning out conversations he overheard in bars or at the supermarket — reality was quite enough to deal with.

On that front, Beaudoin had resisted calls for Smith's immediate dismissal from the force, when the news of his affair with Melissa became more widely known. It still wasn't public, as far as he knew, but it was only a matter of time before a reporter found out. It was just too juicy to stay buried for long. With Tom Saunders still threatening a wrongful prosecution case, as well, Smith considered himself fortunate to be on paid leave while they figured out what to do with him. He had solved the case, after all, but there was the matter of his being instrumental in arresting the wrong man for the crime first, all while he was sleeping with the daughter of the murderer. Any way you sliced it, it wasn't good, but that's not what bothered Smith as he sat there waiting for a fresh beer. It was the look on Melissa's face when he had returned to her father's house on that rainy night and told her what she already knew. It was only then that he realized how badly his own judgment had failed him.

The last word from Marshall was that the Crown didn't want to proceed with obstruction charges against Melissa, and Smith hoped it stayed that way. She hadn't told him everything, it was true, but her failure paled next to his own. He imagined she would leave town and try to set herself up somewhere else, and he wished her well.

Lisa had offered to represent him in his upcoming hearing, and while he was grateful for her support, he knew she offered it only as a friend. He realized that any chance of there being more than friendship between them had passed and he was resigned to the fact, at least most days.

As he looked back at the television screen and an image of James Cormier, his thoughts turned to the owner's recent pledge to challenge the trades McAdam had made for Ritchie in the courts. Whether he would succeed or not was another thing, but the game would go on and the fans would still come out every winter. He thought of Bob and Joan Ritchie, and wondered if they ever would have imagined the series of events their little deception could have set in motion. Marshall had told him that a search of hospital and adoption records had confirmed that Curtis Ritchie had indeed been born Curtis Riggs, and that Joan Ritchie had done a good job of making the adjustment of his birth certificate virtually untraceable. In the end, it hadn't mattered. It was clear in piecing together the events of August and September that Curtis was on a collision course with just about everyone of importance in the Raftsmen organization, and he must have been as surprised as anyone to learn — unwittingly, via his birth mother — that his adoptive parents had given him an excuse to walk away. He could have worked it out with McAdam or Cormier, or even made a move to a team in another division. But his threat to go to Toronto seemed spiteful and, in the end, it had been too much for Quinn McAdam — even worse than Ritchie sleeping with his daughter. Now Ritchie was dead, along with McAdam and Riggs. It all seemed so pointless.

As for his own future, Smith sensed he was at a crossroads. He knew he could ride out whatever disciplinary storm was coming, but he wondered whether he had lost sight of what was important somewhere along the way. As the waitress arrived to deposit the beer, he smiled and took a sip, patting his jacket pocket again, feeling for the hastily scrawled resignation letter that had been there all day.

ACKNOWLEDGEMENTS

I would like to thank the team at Dundurn for their hard work and support, especially my editor, Allison Hirst, for improving the manuscript (and rescuing me from the slush pile), and Allister Thompson for championing the book. I am grateful to Ken Warren and Stuart Konyer for taking the time to read the manuscript and providing guidance and suggestions, whether on the ins and outs of rookie contracts and media relations (Ken) or the principles of criminal procedure (Stu). Any remaining errors are my own. Thanks also to Sergeant Dan Berrea of the Ottawa Police Service for showing me around the Elgin Street station and to Dr. Greg Brown for his help with all things medical. My friend and former colleague David Jacques also reviewed an early draft and provided comments and lots of encouragement along the way. Special thanks to Kate for her work on the website and all things technological (you rock!), and to Ben for making me laugh.

Most of all, thanks to Tanya — always my first reader and number one supporter in all the ways that matter.

Go Wildcats! Go Raiders!

Of Related Interest

Birds of a Feather
A Jack Taggart Mystery
Don Easton

Lily Rae is on holiday in El Paso, Texas, when she's kidnapped by a Mexican drug cartel. El Paso borders on one of the most dangerous places in the world — Ciudad Juarez, Mexico — a city caught in the grip of a violent war between cartels. Her disappearance is investigated by undercover Mountie Jack Taggart, who discovers a Canadian link to the cartel and penetrates the organization. Taggart is sent to El Paso, where he is partnered with special U.S. Customs agent John Adams. Neither Taggart nor Adams knows they have been paired together for a secret purpose.

Although Taggart has strict orders to stay out of Juarez, his gut instinct tells him otherwise. The investigation seems to be going smoothly — until the cartel discovers his true identity. Practically torn from the headlines, *Birds of a Feather* will keep you on the edge of your seat and leave you questioning right and wrong.

Twilight Is Not Good for Maidens
A Holly Martin Mystery
Lou Allin

Corporal Holly Martin's small RCMP detachment on Vancouver Island is rocked by a midnight attack on a woman camping alone at picturesque French Beach. Then Holly's constable, Chipper Knox Singh, is accused of sexually assaulting a girl during a routine traffic stop and is removed from active duty. At another beach a girl is killed. An assailant is operating unseen in these dark, forested locations. The case breaks open when a third young woman is raped in broad daylight and gives a precise description of her assailant. Public outrage and harsh criticism of local law enforcement augment tensions in the frightened community, but as a mere corporal, Holly is kept on the periphery. She must assemble her own clues.

Presto Variations
A Ray Tate and Djuna Brown
Mystery
Lee Lamothe

Detectives Ray Tate and Djuna Brown are back from a vacation in Paris — fraudulently funded by a stolen State Police credit card. While waiting to find out if they're going to be fired or jailed, the two are assigned to the Green Squad, a dead-end job shuffling paper and counting contraband money. But while interrogating a money smuggler, Tate and Brown uncover a massive currency stash they hope will keep them out of jail. Their target is drug trafficker Laszlo "Marko" Markowitz, who has millions in cocaine profits to be laundered and shipped into Canada.

As Tate and Brown try to penetrate the Markowitz organization, they uncover an underworld choking on its own profits and find a homicidal madman who has created the perfect blend of criminality and anarchy.